RANCID

P. A. Douglas

For if the dead do not rise, then Christ is not risen.

1 Corinthians 15:16

Author's Note

Although Clarksburg is a real place, I have taken some geographical liberties. So, if you live in or near this small town, don't bother looking for your favorite sandwich shop or street corner. It will not exist among the pages of this book, because the dead have taken over, leaving everything in shambles. The darkness can be a scary place, so don't go looking unless you intend to find what lays in wait.

Acknowledgements

To everyone at Severed Press, my lovely wife for an amazing job on the cover art, Dane Hatchell for being my friend and the extra set of eyes with this book's first few drafts, Barrett Bailey for providing the photograph on the back of the book, and to Corporate America for being ridiculous enough. Because of you, this story could come true.

ONE

Clarksburg, Virginia was smaller than small. So, when Jared heard that his favorite band was going to be playing in town, he just couldn't pass it up. This was a once in a lifetime opportunity. No one ever came to Clarksburg, and nothing exciting ever happened.

"Come on, Jared. You've got to be kidding me," Noel said. "Where did you put my keys?"

She smelled of an obnoxious amount of cheap hairspray. Her black hair was piled high on her head, reminding Jared of something from the old movie *Greased Lightning*. Except, one side of her head was shaved. She was like that. What some would call eccentric. Her lips were black and the eyeliner thick. He smiled while watching her frantic search. Her septum piercing jiggled back and forth, as she dug through the couch cushions. A crusty, stale potato chip came away in her hand.

"Nasty…" She dropped the chip to the floor, and wiped her palm against her skin-tight black jeans, her fingernail polish a perfect match.

Jared laughed.

"It's not funny, Jared. We're going to be late."

"Oh, come on," Jared insisted. "You know these things never start on time. Besides, I could care less about most of the bands on the bill tonight anyway."

"If you don't care for the bands, then why the hell are we going to the show?" Noel rested both fists on her hips.

The half dozen bracelets on her wrists rattled as she shot Jared a stern look.

Jared liked it when her faced crunched up like that. Her eyebrow piercing shifted slightly and her cheeks looked pudgy. It was a dead giveaway for irritation. He loved pushing her buttons. It was just so easy. He smiled.

"Why the hell wouldn't we be going to this show? Freaking August Burns Red is the headliner. Or did you miss that memo?"

"I don't get what you see in that band anyway…" Noel dropped to her knees, digging under the couch for her keys. "Metal is metal. You've heard one, you've heard them all!"

"Number one, Noel… August Burns Red isn't metal. They're hardcore." He stroked his brown beard. "And need I remind you that they're the freaking pioneers of the genre. They don't sound like everybody else. Everybody else sounds like them!"

Noel smirked with lack of interest. "Well then, are you going to help me find the keys or not?"

Jared snickered, lifting his girlfriend's keys out for her to see. He had them the entire time. They clinked in the air in front of his face, hiding his grin.

"Jared!" She said, snatching them from his grip.

Jared Garrison always played around like that, with everyone. He was a kidder. A prankster. The class clown back in his days at school. His relationship with Noel had only fueled the games and silly antics. He knew that it was his sense of humor that made him attractive to her.

In the two years they had been dating, he had learned every one of her quirks. He knew that seeing any living creature suffer made her sad, and had watched his fair share of vegan related animal documentaries with her. There was one spot just under her left knee that made her squirm like the cute little lady she was. He loved making her smile, something he could do with ease. Knowing that he was probably the only person she let see beyond the hardened gothic exterior made him proud to be her boyfriend.

Sadly, it would be this witty charm that would end up getting him in trouble, and possibly cost him his life.

"Always joking around like that is going to get you in big trouble one day," Noel insisted.

"Oh yeah, are you my mother now?" Jared pulled a switchblade from his back pocket. Pressing the button, a comb popped out, instead of a blade. "You are even starting to sound like my teachers from high school."

He proceeded to brush the green spikes on his head and started toward the door.

"Come on, let's go…"

"What happened to *I'm not in a hurry*?" Her inflection was high as she waved her hands in the air.

"Hell, if I am going to pay fifteen bucks just to get into this stupid venue, we might as well get our monies worth." He grinned, handing Noel her leather jacket, and respectfully opened the door.

He would do anything for Noel. Even kill someone if he had to. At least, that was what he had told himself when he purchased the engagement ring that sat tucked away in his front pocket. It took him six paychecks to get it too. He hoped it would be the right size. Not wanting to give any hints away about popping the big question, he had refrained from asking her. Even Kelly, Noel's best friend, didn't know about it. He didn't want that big mouth bozo giving it away. Tonight, after the show was to be the night he would hide the secret no longer.

Jared was nervous, but hid it well. After the show there was supposed to be a meteor shower and Kelly's boyfriend had promised it to be a good one. If any night would be the night to ask, why not make it as special as possible? It wasn't like this meteor shower crap happened all the time. Hell, he had never seen one. So it must be special, right?

It wasn't long before they were on their way to the show, but not before picking up that skank, Kelly, and her boyfriend, Trevor. He didn't mind her boyfriend too much. He could be a bit annoying at times with his know it all, badass mentality. Overall, he was a nice guy. Although he had just recently met Trevor, he didn't want to share the big surprise. Because if he knew, then so would Kelly. Now Kelly on the other hand... Jared couldn't stand. In his opinion, she was a tramp. Not staying with the same guy for more than a week and this Trevor dude was proof. She was the kind of girl that never quit smacking gum and twisting her hair with her finger. Super ditsy. When Jared approached this new boyfriend of hers about her getting around, the guy knew it and didn't care. She was hot and put out. That's all this new guy cared about. Jared didn't blame him. She did have good looks and a huge rack that made up for being a little chunky in the midsection. Noel had been friends with that girl since middle school, and because of that, Jared knew he wouldn't be getting rid of her any time soon.

The venue was a packed house and Jared was glad to have preordered tickets. They had pushed their way through the pit and to the front. The show was great and Jared couldn't have been any happier. Trevor seemed to have cared less. All he did was complain about a headache after the show. Jared insisted that headaches happen to losers that can't handle good music. He and Kelly were more into *prep*-pop, as Jared called it. Crap like Fallout Boy, Blink 182, Reliant K, and The Format.

Jared didn't mind. He could appreciate all kinds of music, except country. Now, there was a music choice that gave him a headache. He couldn't stand the nasally way male singers sang. Not to mention, most didn't even write their own music. Pathetic.

With the show over, and the party carrying itself into the car, Norma Jean blared over the speakers. Noel quietly powdered her nose using the visor mirror, occasionally giving Jared silly little seductive winks. They made his heart race. He was in love, and tonight she would be in for a treat. He bounced his head up and down, his green Mohawk barely grazing the ceiling of his beat-up VW bug. His fists pounded against the oversized steering wheel to the rhythm of Norma Jean's second record, *Bless the Martyr Kiss the Child*. Kelly and Trevor were cramped in the back seat and didn't seem to mind. Jared shook his head with disgust after seeing Kelly's hand go down Trevor's pants. Not wanting to see any of that, he took his eyes away from the rearview mirror and focused on the dark, narrow road ahead. If they were going to see this meteor shower that Trevor promised, he wanted to see it in the best way possible. In pitch-black darkness.

"Where the hell are you taking us?" Noel shouted over the music.

"What?"

"I said, where are you taking us?" She turned down the volume on the radio. "It feels like we have been driving forever."

She crossed her arms and gave him a pouty face. He knew why she was irritated. Jared had passed up on a big party that one of their friends was throwing. The guy's parents were out of town and some of the touring bands were crashing there. It was going to be off the hook. Oh well… She'd get over it soon enough. Once he busted out that rock that he had stashed away in his pocket all night, she would be putty in his arms.

He smiled.

"Yeah, man. If we don't stop soon, we are *totally* going to miss the shower!" Trevor said, and his California accent dug into Jared making him grit his teeth. "Like, we probably only got, like another thirty minutes left, bro."

Jared caught a glimpse in the rearview of Trevor eyeing his wristwatch.

"Uhh...," Noel hissed. "Don't tell me we skipped out on the party for some lame meteor shower!"

"Come on," Jared protested. "I thought you wanted to see it. I thought it would be cool. And besides, we always go to the after-show parties. I just figured it wouldn't hurt to do something different for a change. You know... have a little fun."

He winked, making her blush.

"That still doesn't tell me where you're taking us, bro." Trevor reached up from the back seat shoving Jared on the shoulder. "If we are going to like, catch this thing then we need to totally pick a spot, like soon, dude."

"Don't worry," Jared replied. "I know the perfect place. You said so yourself, Trevor. If we are going to get to see this thing, then it needs to be dark, right?"

Trevor nodded.

"Well then, I know just where to go."

"Oh, and were might that be?" Kelly said, with sarcasm in her voice and a finger twirling in her hair.

Jared grinned ear to ear, and stared at her wide eyed in the rearview mirror. "Stonewall Cemetery!"

"What in the world are you doing taking us out there for?" Kelly grumbled. "You know that place is haunted, right?" Bubblegum popped beneath her teeth.

"The cemetery, really? Come on now, dude. You totally got better class than that…"

"I guess not, *dude*!" Jared said, irritated.

Neither of them mattered. Kelly and her surfer-want-to-be boyfriend were merely flies that he could easily shoo away at any time. He knew that, because he had already paid Trevor to give him and Noel some space once they got to where they were going. In a way, Jared felt like he didn't even need to pay the guy. He had his tongue down Kelly's throat ever since they got in the car. It wasn't like they would need to be entertained. 'Better safe than sorry', his mother always said. Nothing was going to mess things up tonight.

He checked his pocket. It was still there.

"Awesome!" Noel was excited. "Stonewall Cemetery was where we had our first date. How romantic!"

Jared blushed, rubbing his hand through his spiky green Mohawk.

"Seriously… you two are freaking weirdoes."

"I'm not the one swapping bubblegum!" Jared insisted, and then started laughing at Kelly.

"Whatever!" Kelly crossed her arms, slouching back in her seat. "Are we almost there or what? This stupid shower thing better be something cool."

"Trust me, babe… it's totally going to be pretty sweet. I like, looked into it online and junk. This is one of those events that like, only comes around every hundred years or something. Totally, a once in a lifetime thing, you know."

"That doesn't mean it's going to be cool. And don't ever call me babe!" Kelly punched Trevor in the chest.

He pretended to wince and went in for a kiss. And just like that, they went back to swapping spit and most likely, Kelly's gum. Getting his hopefully soon to be fiancée's attention, Jared pointed to the back seats, and then shoved his finger in his mouth pretending to gag. It made Noel laugh, so he started to mimic Kelly by twirling imaginary hair on the side of his shaved short head. He danced in his seat pretending to blow bubbles and act ditsy.

Noel popped him on the arm.

"Cut it out and pay attention to the road." Her face was flush red.

"It doesn't matter anyway, because we're here!"

Jared drove past the open gates into the cemetery. Even though it was almost midnight and well past the hours of public access, the cemetery was always open. Saying that the grounds were neglected would be an understatement. The dilapidated fence that outlined the large cemetery was rusty and brittle. The last hurricane that had come through a few years back had done quite a number on the chain link fence. It was twisted, mangled and in some spots along the fence line, missing all together. The narrow road that Jared's VW Bug rolled down was bumpy and worn. Rather than a fine slab of cement, there was just dirt and loose gravel. The rocks pinged and popped under the frame of his car, as they came to a stop somewhere close to the center of the cemetery. Many of the headstones looked loose and the grass was high in some places. A cement bench lay on its side, broken in half. The flowers left by loved ones were wilted and long dead. Whoever had been in charge of upkeep had definitely fallen asleep on the job. The place was in bad shape. It always had been.

Cutting off the engine, Jared left the key in the ignition, so that his high beams would light up the area ahead. Cranking the music up as loud as it would go, he stepped out of the cramped car. Noel, Kelly, and Trevor followed, the sound of Norma Jean blaring across the field.

"Man, this place is like, totally a dump, bro," Trevor said, stretching his legs.

"You're telling me you have never been here before?" Noel was surprised.

Trevor shrugged.

"Come on… This place isn't a dump." Jared pulled Noel into his arms. "We come here all the time. I like it because it's peaceful. In the middle of nowhere. It's the perfect place for privacy." He kissed Noel on the forehead and scratched the shaved side of her head.

"Yeah," Noel agreed, leaning deeper into Jared. "This was the first place that Jared and I made love."

"You two are gross." Kelly put her hands on her hips and looked around.

"You hear that," Trevor said, bumping Kelly with his shoulder.

"Don't even think about it, pal." Kelly shoved him away. "I wouldn't be caught dead with my underwear down in a place like this. Might get a disease or something. That's so nasty."

Around them was almost pitch black. Aside from the light coming from Jared's car, there wasn't much light of any kind. Off in the distance, there was what looked to be a faint glow in the woods. Someone's house most likely. That was what Jared and Noel really loved about the place. There were no houses around and town was at least a fifteen-minute drive. They had slept at the cemetery on more than a few occasions and always woke up the following morning unnoticed. It was the perfect place to go when you wanted to see the stars. No manmade light was around to drown out the natural sky light. Tonight looked as if it was going to be another perfect night. There wasn't a cloud in the sky. Jared walked over to the hood of the car, popping the trunk and retrieving two blankets and a bottle of wine. He passed a blanket to Trevor and handed a blanket and the bottle to Noel.

"Wow," Kelly said. "Your car can run without an engine?" She peered into the trunk, truly amazed.

"That's right, Kelly." Jared patted her on the back. "It can also fly, like that Bang Bang movie."

"Jared…," Noel sneered.

He got the hint. He didn't know why Noel and she were still such great friends, although he thought it was cool that two people could remain friends for so long. Hell, he even wished he had a friend like that. In a way, he was jealous. But seriously, the two had little in common any more. And without saying it to her face… Kelly was dumber than a bag of rocks.

"No…," Jared smiled. "The engine is in the back where the trunk normally is. It's backwards."

"Ohhh…" She twirled her hair while chomping on her piece of gum.

Casually checking his pocket for the ring, a third or fourth time, since they had left for the show, Jared grinned at Trevor.

"So, what time is this shower supposed to start?"

Trevor looked at his watch. "Like twelve fifteen or twelve thirty, bro. So for sure, in totally like, no time at all, you know."

"Totally!" Jared mocked.

Noel glared at him again.

He blew her a kiss and she blushed, forgetting the outburst. Jared was like that to her. She was simply smitten with him. She didn't know a single person on the planet that could pull off a beard-Mohawk combo, and still look so damn hot. Sure, he was a bit too silly at times, but he had his sweet side too. She had just been accepted into the school of her dreams, and she just knew that the wine was his way to celebrate. What she didn't know was how he had found out yet. She hadn't told him. But then again, he was resourceful. Maybe, Kelly opened her big mouth and told him. Either way, she was happy to see that he was happy for her and that he would be taking the idea of a long distance relationship well.

"So…," Jared started to say. "If you don't mind, we are going to go off on our own and leave the two of you to it." He put his arm around Noel.

Trevor grinned, putting his hand around Kelly. She on the other hand didn't look very thrilled about being out in the cemetery.

"Aw, come on, Kelly," Noel said. "It's not a scary place, really. It's homey."

Kelly's expression went from nervous to frightened, just like that. Her eyes went wide, looking past her friends out into the darkness.

"Like, there's nothing out there, Kelly. Seriously." Trevor tried to comfort her.

"No…," She insisted. "I just saw someone out there!"

"Now you're just being ridiculous." Jared laughed.

"No, I saw something, I swear!"

The sound of something shuffled in the dark a little ways off, followed by a loud thud. Everyone but Jared tensed.

"It was probably a wild cat or something. It ran into some loose bricks by one of the plots and the bricks fell. You guys need to calm the hell down. I plan to have a good night. I don't need any of you being a buzz kill, just because you are afraid of the dar…"

A pale figure leaped out from the shadows.

Kelly screamed, drowning out the sound of hardcore music blaring from Jared's car.

An old man fell to his knees in the gravel right in front of the Volkswagen. Illuminated by the headlights, his clothes were muddy and torn. His hair was disheveled and he was out of breath. The man had to be in his late sixties. He was wearing a large plaid overcoat and jeans. When he reached up, leaning against the front bumper of Jared's car, something dark smeared across the bumper. The man was bleeding. He struggled to stand. There was blood all over his undershirt.

Noel gasped. Kelly and Trevor stepped back.

"Hey, buddy." Jared stepped forward. "Are you alright?"

As the man stood to his feet, he started coughing up blood, causing Jared to stop dead in his tracks.

"They're out there!" The old man's voice was weak and raspy. "We need to get out of here."

"Who's out there?" Kelly gulped, looking over her shoulder and into the looming darkness.

"The dead," the old man insisted. "They've come back. They've come back from their graves seeking revenge!"

Jared laughed.

Noel shoved him. "Now is not the time to be funny. The man is hurt. We need to do something."

"Listen old man," Jared said. "What the hell happened to you… for real?"

"They're out there. I'm telling you. The dead… they've come back!" He shivered in place, leaning against the car.

"What's your name?"

"Glen…," he said. "Glen Benta."

"Alright, Glen. You just need to calm down, okay. What in the world are you doing out here this late anyway?"

Whatever the man had seen, or had attacked him, had definitely done a number on his nerves. Resting against the car, he clutched his right arm with his other hand. It was then that Jared and the others noticed that the blood he was covered in was his own. The right forearm of his overcoat was soaked in dark plasma.

"I'm telling you…," the old man insisted. "They are coming. You need to turn off that radio. The noise will draw them to us. The graves… they have turned over in the graves. We need to leave!"

"All right. I've had enough of this." Noel stepped forward, grabbing hold of the old man.

"What are you doing?"

"What does it look like I'm doing, Jared? We need to get this man to a hospital."

"But I…"

"But nothing, Jared. This man needs our help! Now help me get him into the car."

"Fuck…" Jared looked up at the night sky, the anticipation of a perfect night destroyed. "Fine. Let's just get this over with. The closest hospital is at least thirty minutes away. Think you can hold on that long, old timer?"

The injured man nodded, forcing back a violent cough. Jared sat the old man in the front seat then turned back to his friends.

"Okay, look. I know that the bug is already cramped as it is, but are you guys going to be cool with sitting in the back with this dude? Because if not, Noel and I can take him to the hospital, drop him off, and come back and get you."

"Forget that," Kelly groaned. "You aren't leaving me out here. Are you crazy?"

"That's fine with me, either way. Just know that, with him in the back seat with you guys, you might get some of his blood on you."

Kelly sneered. "You have got to be kidding me."

Noel walked up beside them. "Whatever we're doing, can we please make a decision? That man is bleeding to death for God's sake."

"I'm fine with us just staying here and you coming back to get us," Trevor grinned, slapping Kelly on the butt.

"You would." Kelly snarled. "Pig!"

"Okay." Jared stepped forward shaking Trevor's hand. "It's settled then. We will come back and get…"

The car engine roared to life cutting Jared off.

"What the fuck!" Jared turned back to see his car taking off in reverse.

Gravel and dirt spun into the air like dusty smog. With the car fully backed out of the cemetery and onto the road, the old man kicked it into gear, careening down the winding road toward town. The sounds of hardcore music slowly grew fainter as the car drifted away in the distance.

"You have got to be fucking kidding me!" Jared said.

"Well, so much for like giving the guy a lift, right bro?"

"What are we going to do?" Kelly murmured.

"Does anyone have a phone?" Noel asked.

Trevor shrugged and Jared said no. Kelly insisted that she had hers on her, but she had it sitting in the back seat of the car. Noel patted down her tight pockets, pulling it free, then sighed.

"Battery's dead."

"Great," Jared said, tossing his hands in the air. "Just great!"

Darkness fell on the cemetery like a tangibly thick tar. Noel almost felt as if she could reach out and touch it like murky water. Trevor reached into his pocket and pulled out a lighter, but it didn't do much to push back the black. With the music, no longer there to cover the sounds of the wild, the cemetery suddenly felt eerie. It was as if a dozen unseen eyes were peering down on them. Things could be heard that weren't there before with the music up so loud. Things were moving.

The cemetery sounded *alive*.

"I don't like this, one bit!" Kelly griped. "I just want to go back home. I didn't even want to go to that stupid show tonight, anyway."

"Well, if it makes you feel any better, Kelly. I didn't want you to come along." Jared stepped away from his friends, starting to walk toward the road.

"Where the hell are you going?"

"We have three options here," Jared argued, his tempter high. "We walk all the way back to town. We sit tight and try to actually enjoy the stupid meteor shower, or we go to that house over there and see about using the damn phone! And I'm sure as hell not about to walk all the way back!"

Jared pointed toward the faint light off in the distance.

Noel had never seen Jared so angry before. In a way, it was scary, but she liked it. He was turning her on.

"I'm not walking through the woods. You can forget that!" Kelly crossed her arms, stomping a foot in the gravel.

"Oh yeah," Jared said. "You afraid of the big bad wolf?"

Then it happened.

Jared moaned at a sudden flash of movement.

One time, when Noel was a kid, she and her cousins would get on top of the roof to wait for her cousins' older brothers to get home. With water balloons in hand, they would laugh with excitement when sending over a dozen water balloons crashing down on their unsuspecting prey. Some of the balloons would hit their targets, splashing water across heads and faces. Other balloons weren't quite as accurate, landing in the driveway to explode into a gushing display of water and particle-plastic rubber.

That was what happened to Jared's head. Only, it wasn't water and shattered balloon rubber. It was blood, bone, brain, and hair that splattered across the gravel and dirt. A figure lunged out from the shadows tackling Jared to the ground. Off balance, the gothic punk rocker fell back, colliding head first with the rocky ground. Blood splashed out from his head on impact, along with the deafening crack of fractured skull fragments. Jared jittered for a moment on the ground, as blood spilled from his head, the frail attacker thrashing on top of him.

Overhead the sudden shower of starry meteors lit up the night sky, momentarily pushing back cemetery shadows. Noel started to scream, but Kelly beat her to it.

The living dead surrounded them.

TWO

Old man Glen Benta kept his foot to the floor, hardcore screaming music booming in his ears. Unable to hold back a fit of coughs, the car swerved on and off the road. Regaining his composure, the car continued at an easy ninety miles an hour toward town. The engine sputtered, giving out every bit of gusto it had to pick up speed. The man wanted more than anything to get clear across town, and as far away from that damn cemetery as fast as he could. He felt weak and he was losing a lot of blood. He had been the cemetery caretaker for over a decade, and had never seen anything like tonight before in his life. Sure, there hadn't been much upkeep in the last few years, but why should he have bothered? No one had visited the dead there in years. No one missed you when you were dead.

Now, with his hands behind the wheel of a stolen car, Glen began to panic. He had never stolen anything before in his life. He hadn't bothered anyone since his wife died a few years back. He just continued to do what they had always done; keep to himself. Living alone in that rickety old house three blocks behind the cemetery was their slice of heaven. A lot of times, he felt like he was one of the dead. No one cared about Glen, and just like that cemetery, no one ever came to visit him. Not even his children.

That was why he was so surprised when that racket started calling to him through the woods. Some stupid punk kids were at it again, vandalizing the cemetery property. Or even worse, tampering with the graves. Last summer, he had happened upon a few looters digging around and it took nothing to scare them off. That's all he thought tonight would be. The same old thing. Cut through the woods to the cemetery and scare those kids away. Maybe then, with the loud music gone, he could finally get back to sleep.

Glen's head raced with what went wrong back there. How could he truly believe what he had seen? The dead came up out of their graves, really? That just couldn't be. The funny thing was he didn't think of that at all. He could only think of his wife. She was out there buried alongside all those overturned graves of loose soil. Could she be out there? One of *them*?

Nearly to town, Glen simply wanted to get to the hospital alive. He had lost a lot of blood and knew it. He felt like he was going to faint at any moment. He gripped the wheel tighter, trying to focus on the road. The city streetlights were just up ahead. He was almost there. He was going to make it.

All of a sudden, the car dipped violently. He must have hit a pothole. The front bumper scraped against asphalt and his head crashed with the steering wheel and the roof. He felt something wet run down his nose and his head began to throb. His vision went blurry. With his foot still on the gas, the car sharply veered right and came to an abrupt halt.

Glen crashed forward into the windshield. His body blew through shattering glass like wet rags, rolling on the pavement in horrible pain. Despite the fact that he had just been thrown from the car, it was his arm where that damn thing bit him that hurt the most. The last thing he saw before blacking out was the city streetlight overhead and two figures looming over him. Whether or not they were dead, he couldn't tell. It all went black. He had made it into town.

The blaring sound of hardcore, scream'o music, no longer echoed out into the streets. It was instead replaced by the persistent hum of a fading steering wheel horn. Jared's car was totaled. The old man managed to skid off the road, sending the car straight into a power pole. Surprisingly, for how fast he was going, the pole held firm. The car did not.

"Is he dead?" Joe Montoya said.

Only twenty-three, he was greener than green behind the ears. Today was his first day on the force. A young buck with Hispanic heritage, Joe was determined to start with the right impression. He hadn't done so well. His partner and senior officer, Barrett Baily, wasn't nearly as young or inexperienced. He looked up from checking the old man's pulse, shaking his head. Barrett's face was flush with dread. Officer Baily didn't really understand why the precinct felt like he needed a partner. He hadn't had one in over ten years and it wasn't like Clarksburg, Virginia was a big town. Everybody knew everybody. He rubbed his thick mustache, knowing good and well that Joe got this job, simply because his uncle was the mayor. It was sad to see that, even away from the hustle and bustle, people could be promoted without any real effort.

"He's got a pulse… barely, but it's still there." Officer Baily clicked the receiver on his two-way radio, the small speaker on his shoulder crackling to life. "Unit two-twelve to dispatch, come in. We need immediate medical attention at the corner of Jenks Avenue and Fourth Street. It's old man, Benta."

"Shouldn't we move him or something?" Joe asked, clearly flustered.

"No…" Barrett was surprised. "You never move a body like this. He could have a neck injury. Didn't they teach you anything?"

Before Joe could respond, the radio sparked to life. "Roger that, Baily. An ambulance is on the way.

What's he doing in town? He hasn't been around here in years."

The officer didn't respond, still trying to figure that one out. Glen hardly ever came into town these days, not since his wife passed away. And one thing was for sure, he definitely didn't drive a Volkswagen Bug.

"Your wife called about two hours ago, by the way," the female radio responder said. "She said to pick up some milk on your way home tonight and that she was off to bed."

"Thanks, June." Baily said into the two-way. "If she calls again, let her know I got the message."

Glen opened his eyes. A fierce volley of coughs surfaced. Blood pooled at his lips after a volcano-like spray of red plasma flung into the air, only to splash back down on his nose and cheek.

"My wife…," he said with a gurgling rasp. "She's out there. She's in the cemetery with the others. They're coming back… They're coming back…"

"What's he talking about," Joe asked, leaning in, trying to listen.

"Glen's wife died a few years back," Baily offered. "She's been dead for a while."

"The dead… They have dug themselves free from their graves." Glen squirmed. "They're coming back for revenge. They're mad at us all!"

Both officers shrugged at one another, not sure what the old man was talking about.

"Lie still!" Officer Baily insisted. "You have been in an accident, Glen. Help is on the way."

Forcing the old man to remain on the ground, the officer dressed in blue, motioned his young partner over to help hold him. They didn't want to risk any further injuries. Baily was just glad to see that the old man was still alive. How he had survived crashing through that windshield was beyond him. In the distance, the faint sounds of a siren filled the air.

"You hear that, Glen?" Baily did what he could to comfort the old man. "Help's on the way."

Glen Benta finally settled, no longer trying to resist the officers. Joe stepped out into the street to wave the ambulance over. Still several blocks up the road, the siren grew louder.

"Now… Glen." Baily spoke calm, trying not to stir the old man up again. "Can you tell me where you got this car? This isn't your car."

Realistically, he didn't have to ask. He knew whom this car belonged to. It was Jared Garrison's car. That dumb punk was always up to no good. Throwing wild bonfire parties, vandalizing public property, and who knows what else. Baily wouldn't be the least bit surprised if the boy was into dealing drugs these days too. Baily knew one thing for sure; he would be there to catch that boy and see that he spent a few nights in the slammer. If old man Glen had Jared's car, then something was going on. If Baily went out to that old man's house and found Jared and his friends messing around, he would have their heads. He shrugged, then swallowed hard. If Jared was up to something tonight, that meant that Noel was with him. And if Noel was with him, then that could only mean one thing. Kelly was in trouble. He had no idea why his little girl hung out with those kids. They were no good. Officer Barrett Baily cringed at the idea that his daughter was out late tonight with any of those punk kids. Nothing but a bunch of trouble makers. Feeling uneasy about the idea, despite the fact that his daughter was old enough to make decisions and chose her friends for herself, he called his wife. Even though Kelly was nearly twenty-two, she still lived at home. Barrett didn't mind. He loved his daughter. She was daddy's girl. His hesitations and concerns were answered when his wife told him that Kelly hadn't made it home yet. It was normal for her to be out past midnight of course, but this was different. Baily grimaced, hanging up the phone. He had a feeling that he knew all too well where his little girl would be. And if she was in any real trouble, he wanted to be the first one there not only to protect her, but to also clear her name of any wrong doing. She was a good girl, unlike that friend of hers, Noel.

"The car, Glen… Where did you get the car?"

"The cemetery…," he winced in pain. "The cemetery is alive…"

"Stonewall?" Baily asked. "The one right behind your place?"

Glen tried to nod. His face crunched up in pain. The area around them grew louder with the wail of the ambulance call. Luminescent hues of reds and white flooded the dark streets.

"The dead… they came out of the graves. I saw it with my own eyes. I swear I saw it. They're dead. They're all dead. One of them attacked me…"

He tried lifting his arm, but was too weak.

"Who attacked you?" Baily asked. "Did that Garrison boy do something to you? What happened?"

Before he could reply, two medics rushed over shoving Officer Baily aside. While checking his vitals and securing him with a neck brace, the two men simultaneously counted to three, rolled Glen on his side and slid a metal bed under him.

"Can you help us lift him to the gurney?" One medic asked, looking at Officer Baily.

The three of them lifted Glen to the bed on wheels, while Joe Montoya stared with wide eyes. In a matter of seconds, they had him settled in place in the back of the ambulance. Gathering up their things, the two medics jumped back into the ambulance and were on their way. The two policemen watched as the ambulance raced down the road, slowly fading out of view.

And that's how it started in town. Once the ambulance was well out of view, Glen Benta died. But it wasn't long before he came back. Seconds, really. He lashed out, attacking the medic in the back with him. The medic never saw it coming either. Just when he was about to announce to the driver that they had lost him, his eyes opened. Only there was something different about them. They seemed empty and soulless. Caked with a milky white haze, he stared back for only a moment. Glen grabbed the medic by the shirt collar, pulling him in. The man never had time to scream. Glen's teeth sank into his jugular. The crunch of flesh and cartilage met with a spray of gushing blood from his throat. Glen forcefully pulled away the meaty flesh, clenched between his teeth. The medic's Adam's Apple tore free as skin stretched from his neck, splashing Glen's face with a wave of red mist.

Satisfied, Glen swallowed, and lashed out for more.

The medic fell back, grabbing at his obliterated throat. Instantly, his hand was wet and warm, as red ran down his arm. Weak and light headed, he fell to the floor in shock. Glen fell from the gurney, landing on top of the dying man, the driver totally oblivious. The ambulance continued down the street toward the hospital. But not for long. By the time the driver found out, it was too late. The ambulance came to a grinding halt only a quarter of a block from the hospital.

The feast began.

That's how it started in town. It spread like wild fire. First it was Glen and the two medics. From there, it was the homeless man on his way into the hospital, wanting nothing more than to sleep indoors for a change. It went from there to the nurse trying to stop what she thought was a drunken fight. Within the hour, it would spread through most of the hospital, then it would only have one place to go; the sleepy streets of small downtown Clarksburg, Virginia.

"Let's go." Baily's voice was stern.

"What about the car," Joe asked, still a little dazed. "We can't just leave it here like this. What if the power pole falls?"

"It's not going anywhere." Baily insisted. "I've got a hunch that we are going to find some trouble back at Stonewall."

"That old cemetery? Why are we going all the way out there? No one ever goes out there."

"Just get in the car, Joe." Officer Baily opened the driver side door. "Look, if it makes you feel better, call in to dispatch about the mess. Go ahead and get a tow-truck out here to clean things up. And while you're at it, let June know where we're headed and why. I have a feeling we are going to run into that Garrison boy and some of his friends."

They got into the patrol car and Joe did as he was told. The tow-truck would be along soon. For his first night on the force, tonight would turn out to be a pretty eventful night.

Too eventful for some.

With Officer Barrett Baily's focus on the road, his grip tight on the wheel and his teeth gritting even tighter, the patrol car left the scene of the accident.

What awaited them at the cemetery was only the beginning.

THREE

"Run… and like now, dude!" Trevor shouted.

"Oh my God…," Noel cried. "What about Jared? We can't leave him here!"

"We'll come back, I promise!" Trevor grabbed her leather jacket, pulling her away. "We got to go!"

Kelly began screaming, and didn't stop. Her cries were starting to turn into a rasping wail.

The short burst of light from the sudden meteor shower had passed, only lasting a minute. And a minute was all it took to see *them*. Over all, the cemetery was pretty big, especially for a town as small as Clarksburg. The wraparound fence line that bordered the property was nearly seven acres square. Most of that was filled with burial plots. Aside from the gravel drive, it was gravesite after gravesite. Noel wasn't much for math, being an art major in college, but she was pretty good at guessing. There had to be at least four-hundred gravesites per acre. Multiply that by seven, and you have a lot of buried bodies. The only thing was… none of them were under the ground anymore!

They were walking… *alive*!

Just in that short instance where the meteor shower lit up the night, Noel saw them. And she knew they saw her too. As much as she wanted to put away the idea that these people were dead, there was no denying it. Their bodies…they were distorted… and rotting. Right before Trevor had yanked Noel by the jacket, her gaze was frozen on her fallen boyfriend.

Bits of Jared's brain lay scattered across the asphalt. He wasn't moving. The thing on top of him… it was stripping meat from the bone with its teeth. Its thin body was pale and leathery like dried pig skins sucked tight to be bone. What clothing it was wearing was brittle, and covered in mud. The pants and jacket were remnants of a black tuxedo. The suit barely hung by its threads on the man's fragile bones. Looking closer, she could see that the man had no eyes. Its skull was bursting from the skin, the snarling grin on its face very apparent even in the dark. Hovering over Jared's lifeless body, the creature sank its teeth into his cheek. The pale ghoul's mouth smeared red like a mutilated clown. Tearing tissue from Jared's face, it swallowed in snarling satisfaction. The gratification only lasted a moment. It wanted… needed more. Using its thumb, the creature's overgrown and mud covered nail dug into Jared's throat. Puncturing the esophagus, blood gushed like water from a faucet. Red and white chunks of visceral gore peeled away as the creature pulled it free. The sound of grinding teeth and slurping grunts filled Noel's ears as she watched in horror.

Noel was oblivious to the hoard of undead looming in the shadows heading toward her. It was as if life had stood still. What she was seeing just couldn't be real. Jared wasn't dead. They were just laughing at how silly Kelly could be. They just went to an awesome show and were going to drink champagne. In no way could this be happening. The dead, slowly making their way toward Noel and her two friends were maimed worse for the wear. Years and years of rotting underground had taken its toll. The stench of rancid bile filled the cemetery grounds with the putrid aroma of death. If Noel's calculation was right, there had to be more than a thousand of them. It sure as hell looked like it when the meteor show came and went. However, just as fast, the darkness returned while she became preoccupied with her dying or dead boyfriend.

"Come on, Noel…" Trevor said again, pulling her forward. "We've got to get the hell out of here, bro!"

The first of a dozen zombies lumbered forward, breaking past the thick darkness. Its mouth opened wide with a hoarse moan that rattled dryly. Its head kicked back and its arms reached out toward Noel with long nails, like the ghoul still feasting on Jared. Bone protruded from splintered and decayed skin. Another stepped out into view close behind. It staggered forward, stumbling over a small headstone, crashing head first into the dirt and gravel on the drive's edge. Its head caved on impact, a dust cloud bellowing forth with rancid fumes of a decaying fungus. Even with its head obliterated, the creature struggled forward, eager to pursue Noel and her friends. Its attempts proved futile as it dug its fingers into the dirt, unable to pull itself forward.

As even more zombies stepped out of the shadows, one ghoul's foot landed right on the fallen brethren, instantly puncturing the center of the back. The sound of delicate bones shattering reached Noel's ears, helping snap her out of her daze.

The cemetery filled with the sound of snarling cries from every corner.

"Oh… my… God…," Noel finally realized.

Reality returned, the sound of Kelly's persistent screaming filled her ears. Trevor was tugging at her jacket and she realized that she had been holding her breath. Hearing the rapid sound of pounding feet, it took her a second to even comprehend that she had started running. In moments, she was heaving in deep breaths. She looked up seeing Trevor and Kelly ahead already in retreat. Trevor had a tight hold on Kelly's wrist.

"Where're we going?" she said between frantic breaths, jewelry jingling all over her body. "Wait for me!"

"There!" Trevor shouted, pointing toward the small glint of light leaking through the trees. "We need to get to safety. Call Somebody!" He managed to wheeze out.

Trevor looked back for a split second. Noel found out more than she wanted to know in that one moment. It was written all over the dudes face, a makeshift plethora of emotions. Fear stricken eyes went to her and then beyond, as if they were lost in a void of terrified expectancy. She didn't need to look back. She knew. She could hear them. They weren't nearly as fast, but that didn't matter. There were so many. There was no way they could run all the way back to town. They had to find a place to hide and call for help. Trevor was right. Looking through the thick tree line, Noel clenched her fists, hoping like hell that someone was home. If anything, she cringed, hoping that they had a working phone.

Luckily her eyes were finally starting to adjust to the darkness.

Ahead, Trevor called out.

"This way… I can totally like see a path through here!"

Trevor disappeared into the edge of the tree line, pulling Kelly along with him. Noel watched as her friend's blond hair and bright white skirt vanished into the brush. She was struggling to keep up, already feeling out of breath. She stopped for a second, placing her palms to her knees. Gasping for air, she frantically looked around. Ahead were the woods and not too far past that was the light from the house they desperately wanted to get to.

"Trevor… Kelly…," Noel called. "Wait for me!"

No one replied. Only the sound of fleeing steps faded away in the woods returning her call. Before she could call out again, something snapped close by. A twig or something... It didn't matter. She wasn't sticking around to find out, and bolted toward the woods edge at the same point that Trevor and Kelly disappeared. Instantly, she found herself inundated by bushes, briars, and tree limbs, beating against her attempts to move forward. Like the rushing fires of hell eager to swallow up a lost soul, the foliage engulfed her. She had lost the path.

"Trevor... Kelly... Help me!" Determined, she pushed forward despite the scrapes and entangling branches.

She felt her leather jacket tear, the sound of shredding animal hide reaching her ears between panicked breaths. She didn't care. She just kept moving. Finally, she broke through a small line of trees. What lay before her was a small one story run down house. The yard was a mess and the grass was way over grown. Birdbaths and piles of rusted junk lay scattered across the unkempt lawn. The front door was open, inviting sanctuary. Darting forward with high stepping stride, Noel rushed through the opened front door.

Her eyes scanned the room. "Trevor... Where the hell did you go?"

The door suddenly slammed shut, sending goose bumps crawling down her spine.

"Totally, woman!" Trevor leaned against the door, dread spread across his grim expression. "Scared the shit out of me jumping in here like that! Where the hell were you, you?"

"What do you mean... where was I?" She asked shoving Trevor. "I was right freaking behind y'all."

Noel scanned the doorway and Trevor still leaned against it. Something was missing. Kelly wasn't attached to his hip.

"Where is she?"

Nodding, still trying to catch his breath, Trevor motioned to the other room.

Kelly was sitting on the couch in the living room, looking like a statue with her expression frozen in disbelief, and hands limp in her lap.

"She alright?" Noel ran her fingers through her hair.

Trevor nodded. "Yeah, I think so, you know. And you… Like, are you okay?"

"I guess…" She stared at the wood floor, lost in thought.

Jared… Jared was dead and she watched it happen. That *thing* just tackled him to the ground. His head was cracked open like a melon. He wasn't coming back, and to be honest, she was still toying with the idea if this was all real. In a way, she expected Jared to come crashing through the door and for him and Trevor to burst out laughing, like they had both been in on some sick prank the entire time. But that didn't happened. Jared didn't come knocking, and she knew all too well that it wasn't a joke. He wasn't coming back. He never would.

At least not in life.

Noel fell to her knees, sobbing. With her face buried in her hands, the emotions flowed and the black-mascara that she purchased from Hot Topic began to run down her face. She wasn't sure how long she sat there like that, an emotional wreck. All she knew was that Trevor didn't try to do anything. He didn't try to console her. In a way she was thankful. She just needed to mull over the entire situation and let it all sink in. Hell, it was even possible that Trevor was able to read her and just left her alone because he knew she needed it.

But it probably wasn't that. He was probably in just as much of a loss for words as she was.

Eventually the tears stopped flowing, for that she was thankful. She looked up from her somber slump at the front door, surprised to find that Trevor was no longer leaning against it. Sniffling, she stood to her feet and made her way into the living room. Trevor was sitting on the couch with Kelly leaning deep into his shoulder. When she entered the room, he looked up acknowledging her presence.

The living room smelled musty and the lighting was dim. The furniture was rustic and old like something out of the early fifties. A taxidermy fox sat perched on the coffee table in the center. The fox was covered with dust and the table sat on top of a very faded rug. Its elegant pattern reminded Noel of the movie *Labyrinth*. The complex designs weaved in and out, crossing over one another. The only light in the room was a small lamp set on top of an end table between two rocking chairs. The lamp must have been what they saw from the cemetery, because it sat right in front of a window. Its curtains were ragged and moldy, the window open. A small gust of wind filtered into the room irritating Noel's sinuses.

"Way too much dust," she said under her breath, whipping the mascara from her cheek. Her eyes were swollen and warm from all the crying.

"What's that?" Trevor asked.

"Oh, nothing…," she said, finding a seat across from them on one of the rocking chairs.

"So…," Trevor started, his voice calm, not wanting to stir Kelly. He stroked her elegant blond hair. "I just wanted to like check… Make sure we are on the same page, you know."

Noel nodded, taking off her leather jacket to access the woodland damage.

"Are we all agreeing that we saw the same thing?" Trevor continued. "Cause I don't know what I saw. Like, maybe my mind was totally playing tricks on me. It can't be what I saw. Totally no way it was that…"

"No way it was what…" Noel groaned, tossing the torn jacket to the floor. "The dead, *alive*?"

She watched Trevor swallow hard.

"Yeah… that."

"I'm afraid so," Noel said, surprisingly calm.

"That's just not possible!"

"Well, I don't know what to tell you, man. We both saw it clear as day. They're freaking *dead*!"

"No… totally no way!" In denial, Trevor shook his head. "Not possible. Kelly told me your boyfriend liked to play cruel jokes. He's out there right now laughing his ass off at our expense."

Kelly whimpered, nodding in agreement.

Noel lost it.

"You have got to be fucking kidding me! Jared is fucking dead, Trevor! Look outside! We all saw the same thing. That old man that took off with the car had damn good reason. He ran into those *things*!" She stood up from the rocker, pointing out the window. Her septum ring jiggled as she shouted. "He isn't coming back and this isn't one of his pranks. You can't honestly tell me that you believe he managed to gather up all those people to play some ultimate joke. Well it's not a joke and I'm not laughing, am I?"

They both just stared back at her, jaws hanging.

"You know what," she continued to shout. "Maybe Jared was right about you, Kelly. You're dumb as fucking rocks!"

"Excuse me?" Kelly scoffed, pulling her face from Trevor's chest.

"Seriously… You're going to sit here and just deny what's happened?"

"Screw you, Noel!" Kelly defended. "We're all scared and you can't tell me you aren't either, okay. Just calm the hell down. You aren't helping us at all."

"You sure as hell aren't helping…" Noel started to charge forward, but recoiled. "Ahhh… What the hell is going on?" She screamed, addressing no one.

Trevor eased Kelly from his side, softly stroking her hair. She crunched up in the fetal position on the couch letting Trevor get up. He brushed his hand through his hair, clearly rattled. He sighed heavily, making his way over to the window. Stepping behind one of the rocking chairs, he pushed back the blinds to look outside.

"Well, what do you see?" Noel asked after a moment.

"Nothing…" Trevor whispered. "It's like, too dark, really. All I can see is the yard and the trees past that. It's too dark to see anything past the trees. They're too thick."

"Do you hear anything?"

He lifted his hand for her to be quiet a moment, and then shrugged.

"I guess that's a good thing," she exhaled.

"Okay…" Kelly finally sat up joining the living. "So, we are dealing with what we think we're dealing with, right? The dead are walking and all that. We agree that what that crazy old man was trying to say is true… They actually dug themselves free from six freaking feet underground. That still doesn't explain how the crap they were even able to start digging. How the hell did all of this even happen?"

"Thank you," Noel said. "Finally one of us is thinking straight." Her left hand slapped the leg of her jeans. "How the hell could this have happened and if we all agree that this is for real... then shouldn't we be doing something other than chatting it up? Last time I looked, those things were headed in this direction. Shouldn't we do something?"

"What... Like board the place up?" Trevor offered.

"I don't know!" Noel pulled at her hairspray stiffened hair.

"Weapons..." Kelly grimaced, still clinging tightly to the couch.

Just as Trevor started to step away from the window, something outside caught his attention.

"Oh, thank God," he proclaimed. "We're totally freaking saved, dudes!"

"What?" Both girls said simultaneously.

They both found themselves pushing the rocking chairs aside to get a look at what Trevor was seeing. Out in the darkness, beyond the yard and beyond the thick brush and trees, they tried to scan the bleak night. They didn't see it at first. Then the first zombie shuffled out beyond the trees and into the yard. Its body swayed limply with each step forward. The creature was naked. Its ribs were protruding from its sternum. As it stepped forward into view, Noel could see that its lower jaw was missing. Something in its place wiggled and squirmed like foraging earthworms. And that's exactly what they were. Worms feasting on mutilated and decayed tissue. Two more ghouls just as grotesque as the other stepped out from the tree line. Then four, and then six. Their moans filled the air as they slowly approached the house. Like a sea of rancid remains and undead sand, the dead poured out before them.

Kelly screamed.

"Oh shit..." Noel said in horror.

"No… Not that," Trevor said, still sounding hopeful. "Out there… Look!"

In the distance Noel finally saw it. The lights were far off, but still there all the same. The blue, reds, and whites flashing as they rolled down the street toward the cemetery were unmistakable. The cop car was driving in from town and they could see its lights through the thicket.

"Hey… Over here!" Noel shouted, leaning out the window. "Please help us! Over here!"

Her exasperated flailing was useless. They were too far away.

"They can't hear you." Trevor pulled Noel from the window. "We need to figure something out until the cavalry comes!"

"What do you mean?" Kelly gasped. "We're saved. They're coming to get us the hell out of here!"

"That may be true," Trevor agreed. "But what good is that going to be if *they* get to us first?"

Noel shuttered, looking out the window at the approaching ghouls. So wrapped up in the idea of help on the way, like Kelly, she suddenly forgot that they were so close. She slammed the window shut, and then picked her jacket back up putting it on. She looked around frantically for something, anything to use in defense. There was nothing. She wasn't some CIA operative from some Rambo movie and had no idea what to do. She was a college student about to transfer to the Savannah College of Art Design. It wasn't like she had a gun crazy dad that raised her to be a tom-boy either, having grown up with two sisters and a single mom. Life was simple and this was anything but. Finally, something in her head snapped together like long, lost memories or a sober relapse.

"Weapons!" She snapped her fingers.

"Right, dude!" Trevor agreed.

"Oh my Lord!" Kelly shouted, still looking out the window. "They're at the door! What do we do?"

The door shook on its hinges.

Kelly started screaming.

"Get the door," Noel insisted, rushing to it to keep the dead from getting in.

Trevor was right beside her pressing against it while the door violently shook in place. The wood creaked and groaned against the persistent pounding.

"It's not going to hold!"

"Tell me something I don't know!" Noel shouted over Kelly's screams. "The back door. We need to get out of here. We can't hold up much longer. There're just way too many of them."

For a moment, Trevor looked around assessing the situation, then agreed. She was right. They had to move. It wasn't safe here. The door wasn't going to hold them off for long, and it would only be a matter of time before they were overrun by the masses that hadn't even made it into the front yard.

"Okay…" Noel said, pressing against the jittering door. "On the count of three, we both break from the door."

Trevor nodded.

"Once we break," she continued. "You grab Kelly. We bolt for the back and on the way I will try like hell to get us some kind of a weapon. A broomstick. Anything… Cool?"

"Yeah, like now or never, bro!"

"1… 2… 3!"

They dashed forward. As they agreed, Trevor ran back into the living room and grabbed Kelly by the arm. Still wailing like a maniac, she didn't resist. He pulled her along, heading toward the back of the house. Noel darted toward the opposite side and into the kitchen. Exactly where she wanted to be. Flipping on one of the light switchers, the room lit up.

"Come on… come on… Give me something. Anything!" She shouted to herself.

Not quite satisfied, she yanked a large cooking knife from the old wooden sheath. Although she was hoping for something a little more long range, it would have to do. Swinging it twice for good measure, she started her way back to the living room. Just as she reached the main entryway, the front door caved in. The bolt hadn't held and the hinges were too worn and rusty. The door fell flat to the floor before her, sending in a heavy gust of wind.

Startled, she stepped back, gripping the knife at the ready just as the first undead creature lumbered into the house. Noel ran forward, wanting to pass them before there were too many. As she darted past, the lead ghoul snarled with eager excitement. The stench of rot filled her nose making her wince with watering eyes. It reached out just as she passed, grabbing hold of her shoulder. Quivering with fear, she reared back with the knife in hand. Hovering right over her, the zombie snarled wide, pressing forward. Its potent breath assaulted her in the face almost knocking her clean off of her feet. She persevered against the nausea as bile brewed in her belly, and lashed out with the knife, stabbing the ghoul's throat. The gray, leathery tissue sliced like thick jerky. Expecting a gruesome flood of blood and plasma, Noel reared back, shocked. Nothing but dust and brittle tissue bellowed forth from the gaping puncture.

The creature didn't let go.

Noel pulled away screaming, dropped the knife and squirmed to be free of the leather jacket. The sound of metal meeting wood clanged as the heavy knife reached the floor. Slipping from the jacket's sleeves, she ran into the living room. As much as she hated to see it go, a present from Jared or not, it wasn't that important.

She quickly reached the back door, finding both Trevor and Kelly standing there looking out into the gloomy night. She was surprised to see that they had waited.

"What happened to the weapons?" Trevor grimaced.

She shrugged, frantic.

"They got in, bro?"

"Yeah," Noel nodded, scanning the backyard.

The coast looked clear.

"What the hell are we waiting on?" Trevor demanded.

The sound of over a dozen zombies staggering through the front door and into the house filled their ears. They were getting closer. Something fell, giving way to a loud *thud* somewhere in the living room.

"That was in the living room!" He cried. "Like, totally down for a plan right about now, you know!"

"Fuck if I know," Noel said. "All I know is we should try to get to that cop car!"

"Okay…," Trevor sighed. "Let's do this."

Noel glared long and hard at Kelly. "Are you ready to do this?"

Kelly didn't respond. She just stared off into the nothingness that was her hopeless situation.

"Kelly… Are you in there?" Noel grabbed her best friend, shacking her senseless. "I'm not about to have you slow us down. You going to keep up or not?"

"Yeah…" Kelly whimpered.

Noel nodded at Trevor, who met eyes with the gothic girl. He reached back grabbing Kelly by the arm, knowing that was what Noel was suggesting with the nod. Her arm was raw and dry like sandpaper, feeling cold like the deep soil of the earth. He looked up and saw Kelly and Noel stepping out into the yard. Still standing at the door he gasped, swallowing so hard that he almost swallowed his tongue. The thing's wrist started to crumble in his grip. Dust seeped free from the crackling skin between Trevor's fingers. A worm broke free through the dead tissue crawling across his hand. His eyes went wide with fear. Still standing at the back door, the creature lunged forward. Its throat was freshly slit. Worms and white chunks of dry puss slid out from the open gash. Worms fell to the floor as the creature leaned forward, its teeth meeting the fleshy area of Trevor's forearm.

Trevor screamed out in pain.

FOUR

"You think that old man is going to be okay?" Joe Montoya asked.

"What… old man Benta?" Officer Baily said, driving up to the cemetery entrance. "Honestly, kid. I don't know. He is pretty old. Hell, I'm pretty old too, and don't know how I feel about living through a wreck like that and I'm ten years younger than Glen. He looked pretty bad. Lost a lot of blood."

"I know," Joe agreed. "I've never seen anything like that in real life before. I almost threw up!"

"Well…" Baily stroked his thick mustache, and then licked his thumb rubbing the moisture into his left eyebrow. "It's times like these that you need to keep your wits about you. I haven't had any real problems with that Garrison boy before… but for some reason, I just have that feeling tonight."

"Oh yeah?" Joe sighed, checking the side mirror.

"Yeah, Joe. And if old man Benta doesn't end up pulling through the accident, I'm going to have Jared's head! He's up to something. I just know it."

"Jared?"

"Garrison… Jared Garrison." Baily shrugged. "Are you taking *any* of this in, Montoya?"

"Yeah… I am!" Joe jerked his head back against the headrest. "I'm not a little kid…," he mumbled.

"What's that?"

"Nothing, Baily. Don't worry about it. Let's just check things out and call it a night." He looked at his wristwatch. "We're supposed to check in at the station in less than an hour. I don't know about you, but I'm ready to call it a night."

Joe Montoya didn't understand why things had been so hard for him at the precinct. So what if his uncle was the mayor? He worked just as hard if not harder than anyone else to get where he was on the force. And if he had it his way, in ten years he would be well beyond the point of patrolling the streets in a cop car. Officer Baily was just giving him a hard time because the old fart didn't like how fast he was moving up. If things kept advancing at this pace, Joe would be his boss in five years. Then, he'd put Baily behind a desk. The jerk deserved to be a pencil pusher.

Joe realized that he was a newbie, but it was his first freaking day on the job. Baily needed to let up some and give him a break. Just because he was the shortest cop in Clarksburg, didn't mean he couldn't hold his own in a brawl. He couldn't wait for the moment when he saved his partner's ass. Maybe then, Baily would soften up a bit.

The car stopped at the cemetery's entrance. Baily left the siren and flashing lights on along with the headlights. Unlocking the shotgun strapped in the center console, Baily checked the chamber for shells, and clicked the safety to off. Nodding at Joe, he stepped out, slamming his door shut.

"Man… Maybe Baily is just uptight," Joe said before getting out of the car. "The shotgun… really?"

He stepped out, closing the door and un-holstering his sidearm, leaving the safety on. One thing that annoyed him was cops leaving on the flashing lights. It was unnecessary in his opinion and often just gave him a headache. He looked up to see Officer Baily leaning down and looking at something in the middle of the road. Baily's back was a flash of cascading reds and blues. His silhouette danced on the gravel in rhythmic stride with the lights. With the shotgun in one hand, he reached for the bulky flashlight at his hip and shined the beam to the gravel and dirt at his feet.

"What is it, Baily? What do you see?" Joe asked, still standing beside the car door.

"Come take a look." Baily waved him over. "Blood and fresh tissue of some kind. And look there…" He waved the light forward. "Footprints everywhere. Something went down here and we need to find out what. I've been in this business for a long time, son. And if I had to guess… this is old man Benta's blood. There was a struggle. You see all these footprints?"

Joe nodded.

"There has to be several dozen separate tracks here." Baily continued, pointing his flashlight back toward the cemetery entrance. "Looks like they're headed out toward the woods."

Nearly every zombie that had fled the cemetery in pursuit of Noel and her two friends were already too far into the woods for them to see. There were those closer than either suspected, immersed in the darkness. If Baily would have scanned the area with his light, he would have seen over a hundred shadowy figures pressing forward toward old man Benta's house.

But he didn't.

He stood to his feet and panned the light to the left and right. The cemetery was in shambles. The gravel drive was covered in countless steps. Upon further inspection, they noticed the graves. The soil was overturned, not on just one… but all of them.

Joe was overcome with disbelief as he stepped away from the patrol car to get a better look. Even the tops of almost every headstone had at least one or two muddy prints.

"Are you believing this, Baily?"

The older officer didn't say anything. He just kept looking around and shining his flashlight across the field of graves.

"How could someone have dug up all of these graves in one night?" Joe asked. "How many acres is this place?"

"Seven," Baily said, still stunned. "Seven acres."

"Wow," Joe gasped. "That has got to be something like eight or nine hundred graves. That's impossible for someone to dig up in one night, right?"

"I… I don't really—"

A groaning hiss cut Baily off. It was coming from near the car. It was then that Joe realized they had walked a lot farther from the cemetery entrance than he realized. The car had to be at least fifty feet away.

"What was that?" Joe said. "Man, this cemetery crap gives me the creeps. Can't we call for backup or something?"

"I heard it too," Baily said, shining his light toward the car. "And no… we can't call for backup. We are the backup. It's after midnight, remember?"

"Yeah, don't remind me," Joe grimaced.

"Well, you going to go check it out?" Baily insisted.

"Me? You're the one with the light and the shotgun!"

They heard it again. The groan was human but unnatural. It was more of a rasping wail than a cry for help. Baily gulped and eased his way back to the car. It was then that Joe realized Baily was just as unnerved as he. All this time the old man was showboating about how much of a badass he was and here he was, just as uneasy. Following behind Baily, Joe shook his head in disapproval. Baily was just a pushover that didn't realize it yet.

They slowly crept around the car toward the eerie sound, unable to see what was making the noise. The groaning turned into rustling.

"Holy Crap!" Joe dropped his gun.

The pistol *thumped* hard at his feet in the loose dirt.

It was dead!

Baily stepped back. The creature lay on its stomach unable to move forward. Its head was caved in from where it had fallen and its back looked as if it had been kicked in. Its skin was pasty white with rot and decay. A rancid jaw rattled back and forth biting at the air when it lifted its head. As it strained further, its neck snapped with a teeth gritting *pop*, severing the head from the spine.

Joe stared wide-eyed. The thing was clearly deader than a doorknob and yet its teeth were still chomping like no tomorrow. Its eyes were black cavernous, rotting voids of scarred and scratched skull. The stench of bile wafted in the air.

Baily covered his nose with his sleeve, shining the flashlight down on the grotesque monstrosity. Even with its body separated from the skull, the arms dug forward in the dirt, hoping to advance.

Joe vomited.

The splash of warm wet chilidogs plopped across his boots and the grass before him.

"Back up!" Baily shouted. He lifted the shotgun and aimed it at almost point blank range on the creature's face. It bit down on the barrel. Brittle teeth sickly cracked against the steel.

Joe stepped back, the deafening blast sent his heart nearly into his throat.

When the dust, dirt, and gravel settled, only tiny bits of debris and skull fragments remained.

Baily lifted the flashlight, making a full scan of the cemetery. In the distance, he saw three shadowy figures coming toward them.

"Hey… you!" He shouted. "Stop right there!"

Joe's eyes darted to where Baily was aiming the shotgun.

"Shit, son. Pick up your damn gun and get in the game!"

"Yes… yes sir…" Joe's voice wavered, looking down at the gun and the headless ghoul lying beside it. "What the hell is going on here?"

He bent down and picked up the gun.

"Hey… I said stay where you are! That's an order. I'm Officer Baily of the Clarksburg Police Force! Halt!" Baily shouted.

Terrified, Joe looked up at the figures heading toward them. The gun shook in his grip as he pulled it from his side and took careful aim.

Then it grabbed him. The undead *thing*, even without a head… it reached up and snatched Joe by the wrist.

Joe screamed, falling back on his butt in the grass. Without even thinking it through, he aimed the pistol and fired. He was confident with a firearm, thanks to time spent at the gun range with his uncle and the training at the academy. He had even ranked almost top of his class when it came to accuracy, but this… this was different. He had never shot flesh before. He had never inflicted pain on another person before; alive or dead.

Joe felt bile fill his throat again. He swallowed hard, rapidly pulling the trigger. The back of his throat burned with acidic recoil. In sporadic succession, bullets tore through the undead monster. Grime and dry, meaty, rotting tissue gushed into the air like a cloud of putrid dust. The body jittered with each loud report, as the bullets tore through brittle bone. Joe just kept firing. Baily didn't stop him. He was busy aiming the shotgun out into the darkness.

Twelve shots later, Joe's arm felt numb and his wrist felt warm. The gun clicked empty. His ears rang and his eyes focused on the creature at his feet. For a moment, he thought it had been enough. But it wasn't.

The thing started moving again!

"What the hell is going on?" Joe shouted.

He looked up to see Baily still taking aim on the approaching figures. Two females and one male shambled forward, filing between headstones and unearthed soil. The lead female was wearing what once was a long flowing gown. Originally white, it was now a dusty rust color. Its majestic bead pattern across the front was reminiscent of something from the nineteen forties. The bottom of the dress was torn, revealing knee caps with the skin peeled away. Her hair was matted and thinning, showing a cracked skull underneath. Clotted grime and puss pooled from her eyes. In her excitement, she lifted her arms toward Joe, bumping into a headstone. The jolt shook her slightly, but she maintained her balance enough to move forward. Just after, her left hand fell to the grass from the wrist. Joe panicked, aiming his pistol and pulling the trigger. Nothing happened. It clicked empty.

"Reload your weapon, Joe!" Baily pumped and fired a round.

The dead woman's dress shredded into pieces, scattering into the wind and pulled away in the night. The woman fell forward as bones, dirt, and dust splashed out behind her onto the other two approaching ghouls, colliding violently with a headstone at her feet. Bones separated from bone, sounding like a set of old wooden chimes as her severed parts came to a rest in the grass. The noise was so great that she might have groaned on impact, but it was too hard to tell amidst the sound of crashing bones against cement and earth. The parts of her that were left intact tried to continue forward, but were not capable of making any progress.

Stepping past the fallen female, the other woman and dead man shambled forward past her. Stepping on her fragile bones crushed them, and fragments of tissue spurted in the air at their feet.

Joe's hands shook with fear as he toyed with his pistol, frantic to reload. Baily kicked the stock of the shotgun open dispensing the two empty shells. So preoccupied by the two ghouls, they didn't realize that the sounds from their firearms had drawn the attention from a great number of the zombies not yet in old man Benta's house. Changing direction, they meandered blindly back through the woods and toward the cemetery. Those not yet in the woods were already in hot pursuit and starting to get close enough for the two men to see.

The men were so flustered that they were oblivious to the growing sound of eager grunts and moans heading toward them from the direction of the woods.

It finally came to Joe in a flash!

In training, under high-pressure situations, reloading had always been much easier and he didn't understand why he was having such trouble with it now. The clip slammed home, bringing its satisfying *click* to Joe's ears. Quickly, he stammered to his feet and aimed the pistol at the closest ghoul. But before he could pull the trigger, Baily's shotgun went off. Startled, he almost dropped the handgun again. He looked at Baily. With the shotgun at his hip, his eyes showed shock. Joe could tell because the man's eyes were wide, which was uncommon for the squinty eyes of the old man. His crow 's foot wrinkles on the side of his eyes smoothed for a moment. They returned the second the shotgun went off again. His eyes squinted tight as the gun recoiled, his grip firm.

"You need to focus!" Baily shouted, starting to reload.

Joe's gaze went back to the two ghouls approaching. They weren't there anymore. Instead, there were just three big piles of rot infested bones squirming with worms and maggots. At first, Joe thought that was all that was moving, but it wasn't. The bones were too. It was as if they were trying to reconnect with themselves and move forward. Nothing happened though. The bones just rattled around like an agitated infant not yet able to crawl or walk.

Joe gasped and sighed heavy all in one. He looked to Baily who now had the shotgun reloaded. He imagined that he probably had the same expression as his partner. Baily's jaw hung in frozen awe.

"What the hell just happened?" Baily said.

"I have no idea," Joe whispered, his focus falling to the ground. "They were dead?"

"Yeah… I think so, Joe. I think so."

"Is that even possible?"

"I wouldn't think so… But I've been wrong before." Baily's eyes never left the squirming piles before them. "I don't imagine it could be anything else but that. You see what they look like. They *are* dead! Shit… they're still moving for Christ's sake."

Officer Baily shoved the shotgun forward, pointing its barrel at the things he had just shot. Joe watched, swallowing hard. Acidic leftovers churned in the back of his throat with a burning sensation. He wished they hadn't stopped at Sonic for those dogs. He pressed his hand against his stomach letting out a belch. It made him feel better for the moment.

"How in the world could this be happening?"

"Beats me," Baily said, still staring.

"Well, shouldn't we call this in or something?"

"And say what, Joe? June isn't going to believe a word of it. Hell… I wouldn't even believe a word of it had I not been here to see it. We can't call this in. Not yet."

"And why the hell not, Barrett?" Joe stepped forward, stern and confident. "If all of these graves were dead people coming to life, then somebody has to get back to the station and—"

"You think I don't know that, boy?" Baily stepped forward, pushing Joe with the butt of his shotgun. "I'm the one in charge here. Not you. I'm the one with years of field experience. Not you! Or have you already forgotten that? Never address me by my first name. I've told you that! It's Baily… Officer Baily. Got it?"

Joe nodded, taking a step back. "Yeah, but…"

"No nothin'! You got that? My little girl is out here somewhere."

Joe stood stunned.

"We can't just leave her out here."

"But…," Joe started. "How do you even know she's out here? This is a pretty remote place to end up at in the middle of the night."

Waiting for Baily to reply, Joe rattled about with the idea that maybe Baily was talking about a different daughter than the one he had met. Did he have a child buried in this cemetery and the old cop was talking about finding a walking dead person? That was just crazy.

"I just know... okay!" Baily grunted. "That bug that old man Benta was in back at town."

Joe nodded.

"Well, that was one of her friend's cars, okay... And, I know that they were together tonight. We have to find them. We just can't leave them here. We can't leave *her* here!" Baily squeezed the shotgun tight, grinding it like he was giving it an Indian burn.

"Fine..." Joe stepped forward easing the shotgun free from Baily's clenched fists. "We can scout around out here. That's fine. But I'm not about to do a damn thing until we call this in. And since you see it so important to remind me that you're the superior officer, guess who's going to make that call... You!"

Baily sighed, letting go of the gun.

They looked silently at one another for a moment or two, and that was when they heard it. The rustling of what had to be more than a dozen footsteps in the high grass was accompanied by one loud and unnatural hum. Joe looked up, following the noise.

He froze.

Like the steady hum of a lawn mower as it grew closer, the dead groaned in unison. With the first dozen or so zombies in the lead and less than forty feet away, Joe shoved the shotgun back into Baily's hands. The dead were uncomfortably closer to the car than either of them. Baily and Joe both gulped as more than a hundred zombies poured from the woods.

"Move!" a shout rang out. With one foot in front of the other, it took Joe a second to realize that it had been him.

They needed to get to the car before it was swallowed up by the dead. The last thing he wanted was to end up on foot, waging war against these creatures so far from town. It would be suicide. With pistol at the ready, he aimed and began to fire. He held his nerve this time, making each shot count as best as it could. With each pull of the trigger, bodies jolted and jittered. His small 9mm was no shotgun. It wasn't doing much damage, let alone sending any of them to the ground. His third shot hit one zombie square between the eyes. The things head jerked back pretty hard, but that was about it. It didn't stop coming as bits of its skull splintered into the air.

Joe jumped across the hood of the car, sliding across to the passenger side. He had always wanted to do that, and now, with the situation around them progressing, he didn't even enjoy the experience. He was scared out of his ever-loving mind!

The closest zombie lumbered forward with anticipation, picking up pace. Its arms reached out grabbing Joe's hand.

He reared back, kicking out as hard as he could. The brittle creature fell back, its bones folding with the forceful blow. Another ghoul instantly took its place as it fell to the gravel. Decomposing, walking corpses engulfed the car. Joe turned to get the door, and in his panic, could see Baily climbing into the driver's seat. He heard the door slam shut. Not looking back, he yanked the passenger door open. As he reached back to pull the door shut, a grotesque figure fell in with him. The door slammed on its thin frame, sending dust into the car. More arms began to reach in.

"Go… go, go!" Joe shouted, trying to keep the creatures at bay.

The engine roared to life and Baily slammed on the gas. A dozen ghouls collided with the hood, reaching their destination. Gravel and dirt sprayed from the wheels as they connected with the earth. The car sped forward, leaving most of the ghouls behind. But Baily would have to turn around. Aside from the path that led through the woods, there was only the one entrance to the cemetery. As he maneuvered the car while breathing heavily, Joe grunted and wrestled to close the door. The zombie in the car was stuck between him and the door. Its teeth gnashed in front of Joe's face. Joe did his best to keep the monster at bay with his arms.

The creature found its moment and came down fast and hard with its mouth wide. Its teeth clenched tight on Joe's shoulder. Shouting more out of fear than pain, he kicked hard, shoving with all he had. The zombie fell away landing on the pavement. Its head erupted in a putrid explosion as the back tire rolled over it.

Joe slammed the door shut and the car collided with the still growing horde of dead walkers. The car shook, as bodies collided with the moving vehicle. In seconds, the car was on the road and out of the cemetery. Baily turned off the siren lights, shooting a wide-eye look to Joe.

"You alright?"

"Yeah," Joe winced, grabbing his shoulder. "Damn thing bit down on my two-way."

Joe pulled it free from its perch on his shoulder. The radio was practically shattered. No longer useful, he tossed it to the floorboard.

"Damn things bite hard," Joe said, trying to force out a smile.

It never surfaced.

FIVE

"We need to keep moving!" Noel grunted, pushing Kelly forward.

"You didn't hear all of that shooting?" Kelly whined.

"That doesn't matter. We can't go back that way!"

"No shit, bro." Trevor wheezed, feeling dizzy.

"I think they're still following us," Kelly cried, trying to keep up.

Noel could have sworn that he was right behind her when they had broke away from the house into the back yard earlier. He hadn't been and it was that sudden yelp that startled her into looking back. His cries sent chills up her spine, and aside from the fact that she felt frozen in terror, she reacted without considering the consequence. Surprised, she felt something within take over.

Trevor wasn't looking that great and Noel was glad she went back from him. As she looked him over, the thought of what happened flashed through her mind again.

She looked up to see Trevor still standing at the back door wrestling with the same creature that she had lashed out at with the kitchen knife. As he struggled, she saw even more zombies reaching the door from inside. Without thinking, Noel had dashed over to help. She didn't know where the strength came from. By the time she reached the back door to aid her friend, she had a large branch in one hand the size of a baseball bat. The bark was dry and it roughed up her palm as she swung it as hard as she could. The branch snapped in half, sending bits of mulch and wood chips into the air. The zombie that had a hold of Trevor let go, falling back and into the house. She didn't want to stick around. The thing was already starting to get back up and more of its undead friends were right behind it. They all snarled with excitement the closer they got.

She snatched Trevor up from the high grass and pulled him away from the house. She saw it, but did her best not to panic. Trevor's forearm was split wide open and dripping in blood. The wound was so deep that she could see the layers of pulled skin revealing bone. The loose meat wiggled as she pulled him to safety. She swallowed hard, trying to keep her stomach contents down, and managed to pull Trevor more than halfway through the yard before he collapsed to the grass. He pulled her down with him as he fell. She tried with all her might to lift him to his feet, but he wasn't moving. He looked like he was about to faint and his complexion was pale in the moonlight. She slapped him in the face to keep him from passing out.

"Come on, Trevor. We can't do this right now!"

She looked back at the house, panic gripping her so tight that she lost her breath for a moment. Three zombies were already in the yard, shambling forward and more than a dozen were struggling against one another to be the first through the door and into the yard. The lead ghoul was the one that had taken a chunk of Trevor's arm. Not only did she beat it with a branch, she also sliced its throat. These things weren't going to give up. Red plasma pooled from the dead things lips as it shuffled forward, a grin of satisfaction lingering in crimson.

Trevor wasn't moving. He was too heavy for her to lift.

"Kelly... help me!" Noel shouted.

She looked around but didn't see her friend. Just when she was about to accept that Kelly had left her high and dry, the blond crashed down at her side to help lift Trevor. With one arm under a shoulder, the girls lifted him and forced him forward. The lead zombie was only a few feet away and would have had them, had they delayed a minute longer. But they moved on just in the nick of time. Jogging as fast as they could, Trevor struggled to find his footing, only pulling his weight every couple of steps. They managed to carry him for half a mile, but it was becoming too much. They weren't even sure where they were exactly. The yard of the house had led through a small line of dirt roads that veered left and right seemingly forever. But they were persistent in sticking to them.

It was then that they stopped, no longer able to see their pursuers. Trevor fell to the ground, weak from the loss of blood. Noel felt bad for him, but was thankful for the momentary release. Her shoulder was starting to get sore and tired. She wasn't sure how much longer she was going to be able to carry him.

"What the hell are we doing?" Kelly pulled at her hair looking around. "We're in the middle of nowhere! Can't you call someone?"

"No. My phone is dead," Noel reminder her. "Being in the middle of nowhere is the least of our worries. Look at Trevor. We need to do something for him. He's going to bleed to death."

And just like that, she remembered. She wasn't a medic by any means, but it wasn't rocket science either. She leaned over Trevor, asking Kelly to give her a hand as she lifted him up.

"What are you doing?"

"We need to take his shirt off," she said, starting to lift it over his head. "I'm going to use it to stop the bleeding. Other than that, I honestly don't know what else we can do, other than get him to the hospital."

With the shirt in hand, she instantly saw what had attracted Kelly to the soon to be ex-boyfriend. He was totally ripped. Taking the shirt in one hand, she then put one of the sleeves under her foot and tore it free.

"Hey, that was his favorite shirt," Kelly protested.

"Honey, I don't think he's going to care one way or the other at this point. Look at him."

Kelly shrugged.

Noel went to wipe the area before she tied the fabric around his arm, but it was pointless. His wound was covered in dirt and grime. The shirt was in just as bad of shape. She brushed it on her jeans then tied it in place. The shirt soaked instantly. Then she tried to coax Trevor into walking on his own.

"Here… Help me get him to stand up."

The two were able to lift him back to his feet.

"Okay, Trevor. Think you can do this? We can't carry you. I know you lost a good bit of blood, but it wasn't that bad. Really…"

As much as Noel was just trying to encourage him, in a way it was true. It wasn't the loss of blood that made him so weak. It was the shock and the massive rush of adrenaline from the spark of pain that had him on the verge of passing out. One time, when Noel was jumping on the trampoline with some friends, she fell off and scraped her elbow really bad on some rocks. Just the pain alone from hitting her funny bone was enough to make her want to pass out. So she knew what Trevor was going through… kind of. Now was not the time to lose it. He needed to man up and come back to life, for himself, and for them. There was no telling how far behind those *things* were.

"Well," she said, lightly slapping him on the cheek.

"I'm like totally cool, you." Trevor grimaced, clearly still in a lot of pain. He forced back a cough, then said, "Let's just like get the hell back to town, you know."

Noel smiled, happy to see him coming back around and on his feet by himself. Satisfied that he could maintain balance, she left him on his own and scanned the area.

The dirt road was dark and narrow. The trees were high and thick on both sides. If the way they had come led to that old house, then the way they were going had to lead somewhere. She knew that much. But where was somewhere?

"As much as I am onboard with getting back to town, which direction are we even headed?"

"What about the cops?" Kelly said. "What happened to finding them? My dad is a cop! He can help us get out of this."

That was Kelly for you. She always pulled the card about her dad being a cop. The town was small and she used him to her advantage all the time. It was her way to score all kinds of things. It was basically, *give me this or I'll tell my daddy*. Noel hated that about her, but had to admit it had come in handy a time or two when scoring the better deal on where the good parties were at.

"That sounds nice, Kelly… but do you see any flashing lights around here?" Noel said. "We are on our own. We can't go that way!" She pointed the way they had come. "And guess what… that is where our cop friends were."

"But…" Kelly lowered her head and remained quiet.

"And besides," Noel continued. "Didn't you hear all of that shooting. Sounds like they had their hands full anyway. As eager as I am to get around some people with weapons, it sure as hell didn't sound like I wanted to be where they were! I'm with Trevor. We need to get back to town. We need to get him in to see the doctor, and then as much as telling the cops sounds like a good idea, I am pretty sure they already know. They were the ones doing the fucking shooting… remember?"

"Yeah," Kelly said. "But which way are we even supposed to go?"

"Actually…," Trevor groaned, gripping his wounded arm with his free hand. "I like totally think I have a good idea of where we are?"

"Yeah?"

"Me and some of my bro's come through here mudding sometimes, you know." He looked around. "If we keep going this way, we should come across a three-way fork. From there I'm pretty sure I can get us back to the highway. But even still, we are a long way from town. On foot, we are looking at an hour."

"Well… it doesn't look like we have much of a choice at this point." Noel rubbed the shaved side of her head. "Think you are going to be able to make it, Trevor?"

"I'll try," he said. "Let's just like take it slow, okay."

She nodded. "We can do that. Let's move before we end up with unwanted company. And if you feel like we need to stop, just let us know, okay?"

Trevor started to grin, but it quickly turned into a wince from sharp pain.

"Seriously," Kelly grumbled. "If I knew we were going to be doing a lot of walking tonight, I wouldn't have tagged along."

"If any of us knew what we were going to get into tonight, I don't think any of us would have come, Kelly." Noel glared at her.

They started to walk and from what she could tell, Trevor was going to be all right. He still looked really pale and was obviously in a load of pain, but he'd make it. Her only concern was his wound becoming infected. It was covered in dirt and grime and the gash was wide open. If they didn't get him into the emergency room soon, he could be in a lot of trouble. That kind of stuff going untreated could kill you. At least, that was what she thought. In the end, she wasn't sure. She felt bad for him, watching him limp along beside her. She was surprised to see that Kelly didn't seem the least bit concerned for her boyfriend. With Noel in the middle, Trevor on one side and Kelly on the other, Kelly hadn't stopped to console him not once since they started walking. With one foot in front of the other, she just kept her arms crossed; an irritated expression gripped her smug face.

Noel wondered what Kelly was stewing about. Sometimes she could be hard to read. If she wasn't concerned with Trevor's well-being, then why in the world would she be dating the guy to begin with? She laughed to herself knowing good and well she already knew that answer. Then the silent laughed turned to gentile sobs. Jared was gone. He wasn't coming back. How was she supposed to feel about all of it? It had happened so fast, and she was still struggling to process the whole thing. She thought of his smile and the quirky little mannerisms he had that always made her grin. Silent tears ran down her face.

She pushed the thoughts of him away, not wanting to break down for a second time tonight. Instead, she focused on the narrow dirt road, one step in front of the other, one foot at a time. As they walked, things were quiet, and Noel knew that Kelly and Trevor were probably just as lost in thought as she was, unable to process everything going on.

It wasn't until Trevor suddenly stopped that Noel realized they had been walking for quite some time. She looked up, taking her eyes away from her shoes. Just as Trevor had predicted, she found herself standing in the middle of the dirt road, the three-way intersection a major relief. They weren't lost. She was thankful that one of them knew where the hell they were.

"See…," Trevor coughed, favoring his right side. "I totally told you I knew where we were going, you know."

"So what," Kelly said. "I say we're still lost. There aren't any street signs."

The road veered off in two separate directions from the way they had come. Kelly was right. There weren't street signs or markers of any kind. They could be anywhere. Noel decided to give him the benefit of the doubt. She believed him when he said he knew. Sure, she didn't really see Trevor as much of a four-wheeling mud runner, like all of the other rednecks in this town, but who was she to judge? She had only met the guy a week before when Kelly started dating him. She never took the time to really get to know any of Kelly's guys, because they were always so short lived. But out of all of the guys she had brought around, Noel felt like she had this one figured out. She was wrong. The guy looked like he shopped at *Pac Sun*, and the way he talked suggested that the guy at least skateboarded on occasion. But mudding, really?

It didn't matter. Kelly needed to look at the brighter side of things and realize that Trevor was at least trying.

"Shut up, Kelly." Noel grimaced. "At least one of us knows where we are. He's your boyfriend. If any of us should give him a chance, it's you." Noel shook her head in distaste then looked to Trevor. "So, which way from here?"

He looked around for a second.

"Well… like…"

"See!" Kelly clapped her hands together. "We're lost. That's just great. We've got some dead people crawling up our asses and we get lost!"

Noel ignored her. "So, which way is it, Trevor?"

"This way… Yeah, totally, sure it's this way, bro."

"All right then. This way it is."

Noel pressed forward in the lead, taking the road on the right like Trevor had suggested. She just hoped that he was correct, because he sure as hell seemed unsure. The last thing she wanted was for one of those *I told you so* moments from Kelly. Any time a situation like that came around, the ditsy girl wouldn't let it go for weeks.

Leading them down the dark, narrow dirt road, Noel occasionally looked back to make sure Trevor was holding up. They hadn't been walking for very long and he was already starting to take a turn for the worst. She found herself needing to slow down, because he was starting to have a problem with keeping up. Seeing Kelly not at all interested in his well-being, boyfriend or not, drove Noel mad.

Kelly just stomped along, both arms overlapping one another. She simply seemed livid with the idea that her night had been ruined. The girl probably didn't even give a shit about what happened to Jared. What could she do? Noel couldn't change her friends. They were who they were. Noel sighed and just kept on walking in silent disappointment. It was so dark that it was hard to tell how long the road was or how far they had to go. Other than the light shining down from the moon and the stars, there was none. A thick blanket of gloom wrapped around them, the night far from over.

"God... How much longer are we going to have to walk?"

"Shut the hell up, Kelly." Noel didn't even look back. "Jared is dead and Trevor isn't doing so well. You need to just be thankful we even made it out of there, all right!"

"Oh, you're one to talk! Miss I got my life figured out art school blobb-adee-boo! Just because you are actually getting out of this shitty little town unlike the rest of us, that doesn't make you special. I'm getting really tired of you bossing me around!"

Noel stopped dead in her tracks and turned around.

"Excuse me? What the hell are you talking about?"

"Don't play dumb, Noel." Kelly balled her fists up and perched them on her hips. "You know exactly what I'm talking about. Ever since you got into that dumb school you think you're better than the rest of us. Well, you're not. I'm going to get out of here too. I just haven't told you yet. Just because you got some fancy break, doesn't make you my boss. All you have done lately is tell me what I can and can't do."

"Wow..." Noel was speechless.

"There... I said it!" Kelly jerked her head back, her long blond hair fluttering off of her face.

"You are ridiculous, Kelly. You know... Jared was right about you all along. You are a selfish little brat that is just jealous of me. You always get things you want. Dad this and dad that. Big freaking deal. Your dad is a cop in this small town. Wow... that doesn't make you the queen of Clarksburg. And lately I have been telling you what to do because it's saved your ass." Noel pointed at Kelly, stern and clearly agitated. "I don't know if you noticed... as a matter of fact, I know you didn't notice, because you were freaking livid. While I was trying to keep us out of danger, you were screaming you fucking head off. You are nothing but a lazy whore!"

Noel had instantly regretted it as soon as she said it. But it was true. This was honestly what she thought of her friend. She had just taken this long to say it to her face. They had practically grown up together and did countless sleepovers, playing with Barbie dolls into the morning. They had talked about sharing an apartment right after high school and that nothing would come between them. But that was when things changed. Everything changed in high school. They both made new, separate friends, and started to drift apart. It had been Noel that did her part to retain a relationship, but in the end, it had only become work. And when she and Jared started dating, it all just went downhill from there. Kelly started going crazy with almost every guy she ever hooked up with. And unfortunately for them both, the sleazy trend just continued on after high school was well over.

"Take that back!" Kelly pouted.

"I'm sorry… I… I didn't mean—"

"Shh…" Trevor cut her off. "Do you hear that?"

The girls both fell silent, stricken with sudden fear.

"What?" Noel whispered.

"Shh… Listen," Trevor said. "It's like coming from up ahead."

At first Noel didn't hear anything. She saw it first. A light far off in the distance was headed toward them. It was a car. She breathed a heavy sigh of relief. In that single second it was almost as if her entire world had been lifted from her chest and freed into the air to never bother her again. Suddenly her cheeks were hurting and she realized it was because she was grinning so hard.

"We're saved!" Kelly started running forward. "Thank you, God!"

They were spotted and instantly the night was flooded with luminescent blue and red. It was the cops!

The car pulled up and Kelly's dad jumped from the driver's seat to greet them. A short Hispanic officer that Noel had never seen before stepped out of the passenger seat wielding a pistol.

"Oh, thank God you're alright, baby." Kelly's dad rushed to her embrace and then looked around. "I am so glad I found y'all. Don't ever scare me like that again."

"Daddy," Kelly said, looking up at him from within his arms. "The people from the cemetery... They..."

That's all she could muster. She folded, too emotionally weak to utter another word. She burst into tears.

"I know," Baily said, stroking her hair. "We were there. Let's get you home. It's okay, honey. Daddy's here now." Comforting her, he looked around. "Noel, are you alright?"

Noel nodded, eager to get in the car and get the hell out of there. They had gotten lucky and she knew it.

"Trevor is hurt pretty bad. We need to get him to the hospital," she said.

"What happened?" Baily asked.

"You said you were there. Do you really have to ask?"

"Right...," Baily nodded. "Well, let's get this young man back to town then."

He opened the back door to the patrol car ushering his daughter in. "Joe, help that boy into the back seat."

Joe did as he was told, assisting Trevor into the patrol car.

"Where's Jared?" Baily rested a hand on Noel's shoulder.

All she did was shrug, and then sighed and looked to the ground.

"Say no more." Baily frowned, and assisted her to the car. "We will talk on the way."

He closed the door and climbed behind the wheel. At first the car ride was silent and eerie. Noel, feeling safe, finally let herself really shut down. Her body felt tired and her soul felt heavy. Her muscles spent from the journey and the fight. At this point, all she wanted to do was go to sleep and wake up tomorrow to start life anew. She slumped low in the back seat and let her thoughts drift away through the trees and the night sky that passed in her window.

It was Joe that finally broke the silence.

"What in God's holy name were y'all doing out here tonight?" He turned, addressing no one in particular.

"The meteor shower," Noel whimpered, her eyes not leaving the passing scenery in her window.

"The what?" Joe asked.

"Honestly I don't know much about it. There was some crazy meteor shower tonight and after the show we went to, we decided to come out here and watch it. Trevor is the one that knows all about it." She looked to him hoping he would jump into the conversation, but he didn't.

Instead, he lay leaned against the door on the other side, Kelly between them. His eyes were closed and he was slouched pretty low. Hell, she didn't blame him for conking out like that. He must have been feeling weak. There was no telling how much blood loss he had sustained. She swallowed hard thinking about his dirty bandage. The shirt wrapped around his arm was no longer its natural color, but rather a dark brown. She didn't want to touch it, but imagined that had she done so, blood would have seeped from the torn, soaked fabric. He would be alright though, she hoped. They were saved and on their way to getting him some help.

"The meteor shower," Noel replied, looking at the Hispanic officer in the front passenger seat. "Honestly I don't know what is going on. And judging by your expression, neither of you do either, do you?"

Noel had never ridden in the back of a cop car before. Jared had on occasion and had shared a slew of stories about it. One thing that she found odd was that Jared said every cop car had a metal grate separating the back seat from the front. This one wasn't like that at all. It was like a normal car, just for cops. There was some fancy computer stuff in the front between the seats along with a shotgun locked into place by some kind of holster, but no grate separating the good from the bad, or whatever it was for.

"No...," Joe confirmed. "We tried calling in to the station about what we encountered, but June hasn't responded to our radio calls."

"Who's June?" Kelly asked.

"The lady running dispatch back at the precinct, honey." Baily replied, looking into the rearview, and taking his eyes away from the narrow dirt road for only a second.

"I take it that's not a good thing," Noel said.

"No, that's not a good sign at all." Joe's eyes went wide. "I've tried calling her a few times."

As Baily weaved through the narrow dirt road back toward civilization, Joe filled the girls in on everything that had happened. How they ran into old man Benta, and how the VW bug was totaled and how they came out here expecting to find Jared and some other kids vandalizing or stealing from the old man's house. He told them how they almost didn't even make it back into the car when all of the dead suddenly walked up on them in the cemetery. Whatever the hell was going on, it was something really bizarre.

She had only met this cop and she was already starting to like him. He was closer to her age, which she could tell, and despite the stereotype, he was being open and honest about the situation. As much as it scared her to know that he was scared, there was something about it that also comforted her. It made her know that he was real. Someone that could be counted on.

Finally having her turn, Noel stared out the window explaining what had happened with them and how Jared was attacked.

"But, we didn't see any bodies…" Joe grimaced, referring to what happened to Jared.

Baily glared at Joe.

"… well, none that hadn't come back from the dead that is," Joe reiterated.

And all the while, as they finally made their way onto the main strip of road that would lead them into town, no one realized that Trevor stopped breathing.

Nearly ten minutes or more away from the hospital and what could be the young man's savior, it didn't matter.

Trevor was dead.

SIX

Clarksburg was rotting from the inside out with putrescence. What started at the hospital had quickly made its way beyond its fortified structure and into the streets. There was something oddly different about the dead that roamed the streets in town, compared to their rancid brothers in the outskirts of town near the cemetery. It had to do with the bite. Something transferred into the blood of the victim.

A dormant cell had awoken from the gates of hell. Or did it? No one knew. Moments after the nurse tried to stop what she thought to be a drunken fight between two homeless men, she was victimized as the reward. The ER waiting area was a massacre of bloody violence that spread like wildfire through the hospital. The elderly, the sick, and injured had no chance. Some of the others, such as the nurses, and visitors, at least had a chance. But by the time the enormity of the situation was realized, the undead cannibalistic mob had grown into an uncontrollable number.

Unlike the rotting dead back at the cemetery, the creatures were anything but slow. The halls ran rampant with chaos as the hungry undead feasted on the living. Those that were eaten were reanimated back to life to eat too. The transfer time was much faster.

Old man Benta had been bitten in the cemetery next to his house, and managed to drive for ten minutes before being found. By the time he was in the ambulance, more than thirty minutes had passed since he was bitten.

It happened much quicker at the hospital. Almost as soon as the heart stopped beating, the victims would awake again as anew. Something beyond evil. Something no longer dead. The growing numbers added exploded exponentially.

They ran the hospital halls belligerent with rage and hunger for flesh. One nurse had managed to avoid being attacked by hiding beneath the counter under her desk. Equipped with nothing for defense but a broom handle, she patiently waited for her chance to flee. But her luck didn't last long.

As a group of zombies wrestled with a flailing victim, one of the ghouls fell over the counter and discovered her hiding place. Without hesitation, the woman struck the creature with the broom handle. As the creature lashed out toward her with blood covered teeth, the tip of the broom struck home hitting it in the eye. She drove it forward, feeling the soft tissue of her attacker's eye socket give way. The eye exploded in a bloody spray of muck and gore. The broom handle snapped as it sent the creature motionless to the floor. She looked down at it in horror. The splintered handle protruded from the man's eye. Blood pooled from the wound to the cold tile. She didn't know what to do. She just stared at the unholy sight, terrified, and decided to go back into hiding. That would prove to be her biggest mistake. She should have taken the chance to leave when she had it. It wasn't long before the creature began to move again. It started to lift itself up, but it wasn't the same. It was slow and struggled with its coordination. The creature stood to its feet and meandered slowly about in the confine of her work space. It acted as if it was unaware of her presence. It just shuffled around, bumping into chairs and the counter. When she felt like she could make a break with the thing ambling away, she took it. She darted out from under the counter. Just as she thought she was free, the zombie turned toward her. The splintered broom handle still stuck from its bloodied eye socket. Excited, it lashed out and managed to grab the neck of her scrubs. She screamed and fell, after slipping in the bloody mess on the floor. The creature fell on her and began his ravenous feast. Her scream never reached the air. As soon as she fell, her head hit hard against the tile and knocked her unconscious. She was one of the lucky ones.

And that was just how it was. The monstrous horde spilled out into the streets. Those that were able to defend themselves didn't last long. Zombies scoured the streets in search of two-legged sustenance. Those that fell to the hand of the living eventually got back up to shamble aimlessly in their lost pursuit of fresh meat. There was no stopping them.

How can you kill something that is already dead?

The gas station attendant across from the hospital was one of the first to go. He never saw it coming. He stood behind the counter, sipping on the Dr. Pepper that he had neglected to pay for, while flipping through one of the many porno magazines that lay on the rack behind him next to the plethora of cigarette choices. He scratched at the slowly growing bulge in his pants and flipped the page.

The front door crashed open, making him slam the book closed, and dropping it to the floor. Expecting to see another insomniac customer stepping in to get a few six-packs of beer, his eyes went wide. More than half a dozen, blood covered men and women rushed in, fully enraged. He didn't have a chance.

The first one was on him before he could press the emergency button beneath the counter or grab the revolver. It wouldn't have mattered if he had. Unfortunately for him, it was not a painless death.

Gnashing and thrashing teeth pulled and tugged as more than one set of hands tore muscle from bone. When he returned to his new existence, the dirty magazine at his feet was forgotten and covered in his blood. He climbed over the counter eager to join the chase.

The hungry, living dead engulfed the small town of Clarksburg.

Tina Smothers lived alone a few blocks away from the hospital and had worked there for more than thirty years. She was retired and nearly eighty-five years old now. She was a tuff old woman. So when her puppy, Snowball, suddenly wouldn't hush from barking at something outside, it was no wonder she woke up and proceeded to check it out. Nobody was going to be snooping around in her flower patch and get away with it. That, and she needed to appease Snowball so that he would calm down and let her get back to sleep. With her walking stick in one hand, she made her way onto the porch to shoo off whomever it was that was bothering Snowball.

"Get out of here," she had shouted into the darkness, waving her walking stick in the air for good measure.

That was all it took. Before Tina died, coming back to be one of them, she felt her bones break as she was tackled to the ground by two zombies. She winced as her hip dislocated and several of her ribs cracked as she collided on her backside. What came next was even worse. The first one bit down hard on her throat. She winced, blood pooling in her mouth. Blood and viscera wallowed forth from the wound. The zombie hovering over her followed the first bite with another. Blood bubbled in the open wound as she drowned in her own bile.

And then there was Tom. It wasn't someone rustling about in his flowers outside that woke him. No, he had a habit of waking up suddenly in the middle of the night. The doctor had called it night terrors, but he knew better. It was God. It was God showing him things. Others told him he was just being crazy. A little bit much of a fanatic. But what did they know? They were probably all headed to hell. Above his bed, was the crucified image of Jesus dying on the cross. And next to his nightstand laid the Bible. But not just any Bible, the NKJV, and nothing else. He'd have it no other way. Of course he was a fanatic. What forty-seven year old, Pentecostal preacher wasn't? He sat up pulling the covers free from his sweat covered body and planted his feet on the warm carpet. He rubbed his eyes with his palms and looked at the clock. It was getting pretty close to one in the morning. At least tonight the dreams had taken a while to wake him. The night before, he was up by eleven.

No matter. He wiped the cold sweat from his head and stood to his feet making his way through the dark and into the kitchen. If God wanted him awake, then it was for a good reason. It was time to pray and maybe even do a little reading. For the last couple of weeks, the nightmares had gotten worse. Aside from feeling a little sleep deprived during the day, he had taken advantage of his time awake in the middle of the night. One thing was for sure, his sermons had gotten quite better, having had more time devoted to reading and reflection. This was a good thing in his eyes, mostly because attendance had been down for some time. What wasn't down, though? When the economy crashed, everything was affected by it. Including church attendance. If he could just get the people coming, into giving just a little more, maybe, just maybe, they could meet the fundraiser goals for the year. The church building was in bad shape and needed to be remodeled. If anyone knew that, it would be Tom. His father's father built the church with his own bare hands. It was the most recognized icon of the community. He hoped all of the extra time spent awake would pay off in his attempt to turn things around for the church.

Wearing nothing but his boxer shorts, Tom's bare feet slapped against the cold tile in the kitchen as he retrieved a glass from the cabinet. There was no time that wasn't the right time for a nice glass of cold milk. He was in luck. There was enough left in the carton for one serving. Satisfied, he gulped it down and sat the glass on the countertop. The glass meeting the surface of the counter broke the silence. Tom ran his fingers through his thin, gray hair.

He crept down the hall past the framed pictures of him and his wife, who happened to be away on a women's retreat. He smiled, examining the photo for the billionth time. Her hair was long and brown and her dress made her body look perfect in every way. They never had any children, although not for lack of trying. They even prayed that God would give them a son. But, if it was going to happen, it would be His time and not theirs. It never came. He didn't blame God and tried with all he had to not blame his wife. It was hard sometimes. He loved her dearly and couldn't wait for her to come back home. Reaching the living room, he turned on the light and sat down at his favorite spot, the Lazy Boy, worn and old from over a decade of use. Had he owned a television, he might have turned it on. But he didn't. Everything on it was corrupt and filled with the sins of the earth. No, he had something much more entertaining than that. He had God's blameless word.

He leaned the recliner back and picked up his reading glasses and the Bible that lay next to them. There were Bibles everywhere in his home and just about all of them got a lot of use, especially the one that sat next to the toilet in the master bedroom.

He sighed heavy, and then closed his eyes.

"Okay, God. You woke me. Show me what you have for me this night… Amen."

He opened his eyes and began to flip through the holy book's golden trimmed pages. As he read the sanctified word, he held the cross necklace around his neck for comfort. At first, he opened to no page in particular, scanning its red words amidst the black text. It wasn't long before he found himself reverting to his favorite passages in the book of Psalms. He read there for more than half an hour taking no notes. He really didn't need to, having memorized many of its passages. It wasn't long before he found himself nodding off again, still sitting in the recliner.

It wasn't until he fully fell asleep that the thick book in his grip slipped free, falling with a loud *thud* to the floor. The sudden sound jarred him to attention. For a moment, he was unsure of his location, the surroundings were unfamiliar. He thought he had still been asleep in bed. But as his eyes adjusted to the bright light, he remembered that he had gotten up and entered the living room to read. He wondered how long he had been asleep in the chair. He rubbed his eyes and started to stand. His bare back and legs stuck to the pleather chair as he pulled away.

Finally finding his footing and peeling himself free from the chair, Tom adjusted his boxers and walked over to the window. He smiled at the portrait of Jesus that his wife had gotten him two years back for their anniversary. It was almost as if Jesus was smiling right back at him. He pushed back the curtains to take a look at the front yard. If there was anything that he took away from his old man before he passed away, it was that a church can live or die based on location. He smiled, knowing that this is what had kept the community of believers alive for so long. His house was in the same neighborhood as the Clarksburg High School and the massive lot that his window overlooked next to the house was the church. He was proud of it. Sometimes too proud. If there was one thing he loved even more than his wife, it was living on the same land as the church.

He smiled at it while peering into the darkness. The streetlights illuminated the small building and its large steeple. The large wooden cross at its peak stood tall and firm, being lit by the florescent lights it contained. He smiled with satisfaction. Keeping that thing lit might have been a major expense for the church, but it was worth it in his eyes. Jesus was the truth and the light, and that light never wavered. And so, neither would that community steeple. Along with the streetlights, the steeple helped light up the church's small parking lot. Tom liked that it was always lit. It made things easier for him to check out from the comfort of his home without going outside.

"You know…," he said out loud. "Between you and me, God. We are going to turn this town around. You just wait and see."

His eyes burned, making him realize that he needed to get back to sleep and get some shut eye. With a heavy yawn, he started to push the curtains back into place and go back to bed. But suddenly, something outside caught his eye.

A figure darted across the church's parking lot. Running like they were injured. Just as they disappeared around the church building and out of sight, another figure followed behind in pursuit. There was no questioning that someone was being chased. Tom felt his chest tighten and his throat tensed. He tried to swallow, but it felt clogged. He watched in disbelief as the two disappeared behind the church.

Tom darted into the kitchen and snatched up his phone from the wall. About four years back, the church was having a lot of problems with the homeless sleeping in the parking lot, so he had the local law enforcement number along with the fire department and a few numbers of some of the Deacons on the refrigerator.

He dialed the police department. Holding the phone to his ears, he waited, but nothing happened. The phone was silent. He tried the number again, but there was nothing. The phone was dead. That wasn't good. He tried a few of the numbers on the fridge and came away with the same problem. The lines were down. He bit his lip looking around. He was getting too old for any of this.

"Okay… Okay…," he told himself. "What would Jesus do?"

He stood there for a moment and shook his head.

"I can't believe this. You are going to owe me big time," he said looked to the ceiling.

He ran into his bedroom and threw on a pair of sweatpants. He slipped into the Velcro-shoes he bought from Wal-Mart for ten bucks and then grabbed the baseball bat from beside the bed. Gripping it tight, he was glad that his wife had been so insistent about feeling better with a weapon near in case of emergency.

He wasted no time. There was no telling what was happening out there. Some poor woman could be getting raped, or even worse, murdered. It had been a very long time since anything as hideous as a murder happened in Clarksburg, and Tom would be damned to hell if he was going to let something like that happen on *his* church property.

He reached the front door and kicked it open. The cool night air felt moist against his bare back and chest. He gripped the aluminum bat tightly. The damp grass folded under his frantic steps.

He crossed the lot and reached the church parking lot. His steps instantly grew louder against the less forgiving cement. His shadow stretched the closer he got to the looming streetlight and the corner of the building. He bit down hard on his lip, feeling something wet and warm in his mouth. It tasted of iron. His palms were sweating and his heart was racing with fear as he rounded the corner. A large shadow from the building made it hard for him to see anything. He didn't need to. He knew they were still there. He could hear them. He stopped dead in his tracks and let his eyes adjust and to keep his presence unknown.

What he heard was ungodly.

Wet sloshing and slurping filled grunts filled Tom with grief. With the bat tight in his grip held above his head, he slowly eased forward to get a better look. A figure came into view amidst the shadows. He had been right. The woman was in danger. A large man was on his knees leaned over her doing God knows what. The woman lay on her back and all Tom could see was her legs and part of her dress.

He muttered a silent prayer while clenching the cross around his neck, and then moved for a clearer view.

It took Tom a second to build up the nerve, but he finally spoke up. "Hey… you," he said. "What do you… think you're do… doing?"

The attacker didn't respond to Tom's call. Instead, he just kept doing whatever it was that he was doing. Tom felt sick to his stomach. He had never been in a physical confrontation in his entire life. He had no real idea what to do. It was obvious in his voice. He gripped the bat tighter and waved it in the air for the attacker to see.

"Hey now… I… I said…" Tom found his voice. "What in God's name are you doing to that woman? Answer me!"

In a way, Tom hoped that startling the man into realizing he had been caught would just make him run off for fear of being caught. But that wasn't what happened at all. The man slowly stood to his feet. Tom instantly regretted putting himself in this situation. He estimated the man had to be twice his weight.

"Now, I'm not looking for trouble, Mister." Tom shoved the bat forward as the man turned around. "You hearing me? You leave right now, we will forget this whole thing. Now go!"

The man didn't leave. He started toward Tom.

Through the shadows he could see the man's gruesome features. Tom almost dropped the bat. The man snarled wide eyed with a rancid grimace. His face was covered in blood and as his mouth was opened wide. A large meaty chunk fell from his lips into the grass at his feet. The man rasped an angry warning.

"Hey pal, I don't want—"

The man lunged toward Tom with hands raised. Tom screamed and swung the bat as hard as he could with his eyes shut. His hands stung as the bat made impact. He opened his eyes back to see that he made contact with the head, knocking him down into the grass. Blood ran down the side of his head, his hair already matted with red gore.

"Oh my God, I'm so sorry…" Tom said, but the man began to get up again. "Don't move!" he shouted.

He didn't listen. It was almost as if Tom's sense of primal instinct kicked in. It was like a hedge of angles had taken over guiding his hands to strike again, and again. As much as he would refuse to admit it later, the rush of adrenaline that had filled his being with each strike excited his mortal bones. He felt more alive.

The bat came down a third time and hit him in the head again. Blood splashed into the air as the bat connected with the dying man's skull. Tom looked down to see that the man's features were distorted and maimed. He had done a number on this poor man. Tom dropped the bat feeling weak.

He stepped away from the man and braced against the building, trying like hell not to pass out. Tom vomited the milk into the grass and then looked at the dying man again. He no longer moved or breathed.

It wasn't until the woman abruptly sat up that Tom even remembered that she had been laying there. What he saw made him gasp for breath. One of her eyes was hanging limp from its socket and her bottom lip had been peeled free like an orange skin. Her smile never wavered. As she stood to her feet, he called out. How could someone abuse another human in this way? He looked down at the man he had just killed, and felt totally justified.

"Hey, I'm here to help," he muttered as she reached out and wrestled him to the ground.

The bat fell from his grip as he collided with the damp earth.

"What's your problem, lady?" He said, franticly keeping her at bay.

Her teeth snapped violently together trying to get close to his face. He pushed hard making her fall away. Tom took the opportunity to stand and grabbed the bat at his side. His body raced with adrenaline and fear, not actually sure what was going on. He looked up and panicked. Not only was the woman finding her footing, but the man that he had bludgeoned was getting up as well. His head bobbed left and right as he began to slowly stand.

Tom turned, heading for the church doors and muttering memorized scriptures.

"Behold, I give you the power to tread on serpents and scorpions and over all the power of the enemy and nothing by any means will harm thee… He gave his only begotten…"

Tom reached the church's front double doors. He flipped the key pad to the alarm system open and looked back. The woman was rounding the corner and headed toward him. No longer clouded in a shadow of darkness, the streetlight illuminated her mangled flesh. Not only was one eye hanging on her cheek, but the other one was gone, devoured. Blood and plasma ran down her chin onto her neck from the open gash that was her peeled lower lip. She reached out toward him, several of her fingers missing. Her dress was covered in dirt and what looked to be her own bodily fluids.

It was then that he realized that he was covered in it too. When she had tackled him to the ground, her gore and bloody mess had gotten all over him.

"Stay back!" Tom shouted, trying desperately to key in the code to unlock the church doors.

He heard the door lock click. It unlocked. As he stepped through the double doors, he saw the dead man finally shamble into view from the corner of the building. Its staggering steps were slow and unnatural. Something was definitely wrong.

"God, please help us all," he said as he slammed the doors shut just before the mangled woman reached them hoping to get inside.

SEVEN

"Yes… and for the third time, we did not, I repeat, did not see your boyfriend's body at the cemetery," Officer Baily insisted. "If it had been there, then maybe it got moved before we showed up."

"That just doesn't make any sense," she said, perturbed.

"What I don't get," Joe started, "…is how the meteor shower had anything to do with raising the dead. It's not like some space rock landed in the cemetery giving off some strange cosmic life force. You said that those *things* were already out of the graves by the time the shower actually lit up in the sky."

"I know… I know…," she replied. "I don't get it either. Honestly, what the hell else could it be? Trevor was saying something about it being one of those rare showers that only happen once every hundred years or something."

The streetlights and billboards pushed back the darkness of the rural landscape leading toward the town that was lit up like the Fourth of July. Baily kept his hands firmly on the wheel and looked toward the back seat for a moment.

"Speaking of Trevor, how is he holding up, honey?"

Kelly didn't look at him. With eyes forward, she said, "Fine. He's fine."

"Okay, well, we're almost there. Daddy's going to drop him off and then he'll get my little baby doll home and tucked in."

She rolled her eyes and looked away. "Dad… don't talk to me like I'm a three year old in front of my friends."

Baily started to reply, but stopped when his gaze returned to the road and the town came into focus. What he thought were the lights of the town shinning in the sky, turned out to be several of the buildings lit up in flames. Now he understood why he was unable to contact June.

The patrol car rolled into town with the passengers staring in disbelief. With his jaw dropped and his grip tightening even more on the wheel, Baily let up on the gas to access the situation.

"Look over there. That might explain a few things." Joe pointed toward the Volkswagen Bug that they had found old man Benta driving.

"That's Jared's car," Noel said.

The front end of Jared's Volkswagen was mashed up against the phone pole and crushed in the rear by a wrecker displaying *Buck's Towing* painted on the side. Buck wasn't in the driver's seat. The pole leaned so far to the side that it looked like it was going to fall to the ground at any moment. The electrical lines drooped and crossed, sending sparks shooting through the air. Two figures crouched over something large enough to be a body among the shower of sparks, paying no heed to the patrol car as it passed by.

Small one-story mom and pop shops that lined the downtown area of Clarksburg, normally calm in the dead of night were in turmoil. Tammie's Hair salon's front window was a shattered mess, leaving shards of sharp glass on the sidewalk. Next to it, the front door to the antique store that specialized in assortments of yarn and crafting fabric was wide open and teaming with people. The feed store on the opposite side of the street appeared to be secure, until the roof started to smolder and catch fire. Buildings were damaged up and down both sides of the road.

"So, you think the phone pole back there was the problem with—"

"No, Joe. I don't think that's what caused the communication problem with June. We are using radio waves, not the…," Baily stopped, distracted by a large mob of people that ran frantically across the side street ahead.

Shouts and screams roared in the distance. Baily brought the patrol car to a dead stop.

"Well… If that ain't what's keeping us from getting in touch with June, then what is?" Joe said.

"… Wait, what?" Baily said, still focused on the mob that had just dashed past them.

"June… Why can't we get a hold of her?"

"Really?" Noel scorned. "Do you really have to ask that right now? Look around, man! What the hell is going on?"

Joe's eyes went wide with the ensuing chaos. "I… I just don't understand. How could this have all happened so fast? We were just here less than an hour ago helping that old man into the ambulance. I just don't get—"

The blaring horn from a white, unmarked van cut his words short. It swerved back and forth swiping parked cars on either side as it careened toward them. Kelly screamed. It lost total control and slammed into a Sedan. The van rolled over and slid upside down with a deafening screech before coming to a stop. Baily, Joe, Noel, and Kelly sat in silence and waited for something else crazy to happen.

But it didn't.

"We've got to go check this out," Baily said as he reached for the shotgun.

"Are you out of your mind?" Noel protested. "You can't go out there!"

"Noel's right, Dad." Kelly reached up grabbing his shoulder. "Don't go out there."

Baily looked back, his brow creased. "We have to. Just sit tight."

Kelly slumped back into the seat, giving up on the idea that her old man would listen.

"Okay, Joe. You ready to do this?"

Joe didn't speak. He just removed his firearm from its holster and gritted his teeth. He was with Noel and the blonde. Screw going out and being killed. That was crazy. He was too young to die, and for the first time ever, he was beginning to think that following in his great grandfather's footsteps into law enforcement wasn't such a great idea after all.

"All right, let's do this," Baily said, opening his door and stepping out.

Joe looked back at the girls. Noel tried to force a smile, but it just made Joe feel even worse about the predicament.

"Hurry back…" Noel managed to mutter.

Joe didn't hear her. He was out of the door heading toward the van and his commanding officer.

Noel watched in horror as the two police officers slowly edged their way toward the side of the van. As they drew closer, she felt her heart grip tighter insider her chest. She just knew that something bad was going to happen. Someone or something was going to jump out and attack. She just knew it.

As they reached the van, Baily waved Joe over to take a closer look. Noel realized that she had been holding her breath.

"We don't have time for this shit," she huffed, looking to Kelly. "We need to get Trevor to the hospital."

She looked at Trevor and was relieved to see him shift his weight in the seat, counting him among the living.

"Glad to see you're coming back around. You had me worried for a second there."

Trevor stretched his arms to the side.

"Ewww... Gross," Kelly squirmed. "Get your nasty, blood rag arm off of me!"

Noel started to laugh, but her laughter quickly turned to a harsh gulp. Something was wrong with Trevor. His skin was chalky and his eyes were fogged over in a milky white haze. His lips stretched open and he lashed out with a hand.

"Ow! What the hell is the matter with you?" Kelly shouted, pushing Trevor away. "Let go of my hair!"

Before Noel could make a move, the unthinkable happened. Kelly grunted an abnormal moan as blood sprayed Trevor across his pale face. Noel screamed bloody murder as she watched Kelly's neck run red with plasma. Kelly began to go into spasms as Trevor dug his teeth deeper into her face. Noel heard cartilage snap as more blood spewed across the seats and onto her lap. Trevor pulled away again with something meaty in his mouth. As Kelly jittered in her seat, Noel watched as Trevor pulled at the chunk with both hands. He pulled it from his mouth. His hands were covered in blood as it ran down both elbows. It looked like Trevor was chewing on an ear.

Noel screamed again, and reached for the door.

"Help me, please!" she shouted.

The door wouldn't open. The handle shook back and forth, but the door wouldn't budge.

"Please..." she shouted. "Oh my God!"

Still fighting with the door, Kelly fell against her, her dead weight limply sagging to one side. Trevor pressed against Kelly even more as he tore into her chest and pulled off her blouse. The fabric ripped; sending a few buttons into the air. With her bustling breasts partially revealed beneath the frilly-laced black bra, Trevor sank his teeth into her meaty flesh. Skin and leathery tissue peeled free as he chomped.

"Help me," Noel continued. "Dear God… Get me out of here!"

The door still wouldn't open no matter how hard she banged against it. With Kelly leaned against her and Trevor pushing Kelly forward, Noel became pinned against the door. Gunshots rang and she had no idea what was going on outside. One loud report was quickly followed by another amongst shouts of protest.

Wet slurping grunts and smacking forced her attention back to Trevor. Blood was flying everywhere. It wasn't until droplets speckled across Noel's chest that the young gothic flipped. She screamed one long shout of terror while pushing with everything she had. With her hands on the back of Kelly's head and shoulders, she pushed them both toward the other side of the back seat. She fought her way toward the front seat, those doors wouldn't be locked. Her hands felt wet and warm, but she didn't want to think about it. She just needed to get the hell out of the car before Trevor got a hold of her too.

With Trevor finally pressed against the door, Noel climbed forward between the two front seats. Screaming, she felt Trevor grab her leg. She kicked hard enough to break free. Refusing to look back, she reached the front passenger side door with her right hand. A figure loomed a few feet outside the window. It didn't matter. Being out there would be better than being stuck in the car. She opened the door and stumbled out. The figure grabbed her by the arm and violently pulled at her with rage.

She screamed, nearly fainting.

"Come on," Joe said, pulling her from the car.

His voice was a fresh sound of assurance. As Joe helped her to her feet, the car door slammed shut behind her. She looked back to see Joe kicking it with his foot. The firing continued, making Noel look toward the van. Baily was slowly back stepping and reloading the shotgun. One of the people he had just shot was starting to get back up and several shadowy figures were surfacing in the distant darkness.

"We've got to move on!" Joe shouted at Baily while grabbing Noel by the hand.

"I can fucking see that, Joe. Get back in the car!" Baily aimed the shotgun toward the looming figures.

The loud report reverberated off the street corner and the surrounding buildings.

"We can't!" Noel shouted.

"What the hell are you talking about?" Baily said, firing another shell.

Noel looked back at the car just as Trevor's arm smeared blood across the front windshield from inside. His arm and hands were covered in red, spreading even more gore along the glass as he thrashed in his attempt to get out.

"Where's Kelly?" Baily shouted.

Noel nodded toward the slightly rocking patrol car and Trevor inside, belligerent with rage.

"My daughter's in there!" Instantly forgetting the figures that he had just shot, Baily ran toward the car.

Noel froze in horror. She was starting to feel like the tide had turned and now she had become more like Kelly. Unable to keep it together, just as Kelly had done in the old house, Noel stood paralyzed by what her eyes forced her to watch.

Baily swung the driver's side back door open, removed his sidearm, and aimed it into the vehicle.

"I'm going to save you, baby!" He shouted.

What was happening inside the car was hard for Noel to see because of all of the smeared blood. But what she did see she would never forget. Baily pulled the trigger and Trevor's head jerked back violently. It sent a volcano of brain, matted hair, and skull fragments splattering onto the rear glass from the back of Trevor's head.

With Baily no longer manning the street, Joe stepped out with pistol at the ready. Checking the safety, he aimed it at the walking dead that approached. Each shot was surprisingly precise and calmly executed. Like it mattered. With more than half a dozen ghouls coming from behind the van and the neighboring street corners, Joe's take downs didn't amount to much. The ones that struck home sent bodies down, but not for the count. One thing that he quickly noticed was that the second time they got up after being killed, they were much slower. With even more still pouring into the streets, he changed his tactics to only firing at the runners. One after another fell with the squeeze of the trigger. All head shots as the target. It was only moments later, when they rose again to shamble forward. Joe put three shots to the head in one and all it did was struggle to maintain balance. They were unstoppable.

His gun clicked empty. He reached for another clip while dispensing the empty, then drove the new one home, all in one fluid motion.

"Um… We have company," Noel whimpered between Joe's shots.

More of *them* were closing in from behind about five blocks away. Noel could see shadowy figures bobbing back and forth in the shadowy street. The night was playing tricks on her. She didn't like not being able to actually tell how many were coming.

The shadows cast from them by the overhead streetlights made her instantly lose count. It didn't matter. Their numbers were overwhelming.

"Joe…" She panted.

Joe fired two shots into the crowd by the van, and then turned to see Baily pulling something yellow and red from the back of the patrol car. It was Kelly.

"What the hell happened?" Joe shouted.

"… Joe…" Noel's insistent voice and frantic demeanor finally got the young cop's attention. "Look there! We need to go!"

"Holy crap!" Joe aimed toward the oncoming mob, hesitated, and then lowered the gun. "There's too many! Get back in the patrol car!"

"Over my dead fucking body!" Noel shook her head, wide eyed and still frozen in her boots.

"We don't have time for this!" Joe said running to her side, and grabbing her by the arm.

The ones that could run would be on them in a matter of moments. Their horrendous grunts and hissing filling the night air. Joe looked into the bloody, gore-covered car, then back at Baily who was holding his daughter in both arms. Her shirt was torn and she was covered in bloody bite marks. He looked back to the van, the dozen or so shambling ghouls still a good distance between them. The other side wasn't any better. More figures were appearing, some fast and some slow. In just moments, their numbers had seemed to double.

"What the hell do we do, Bai…" Joe's words were cut off by Baily's brutal scream.

With his daughter held tight in his arms, she awoke to new desires and hungering sensations. Her teeth sank into the side of his neck, puncturing his jugular. He tried to pull her away but her teeth just clenched down even harder. Baily fell to his knees, his little girl still resting in his grip. As she pulled away, the skin on his neck stretched, suddenly snapping free like the rubbery tissue it was.

"Baily!" Joe shouted, letting go of Noel to rush to his aid.

As Joe rounded the car, Baily fell to the ground. When he got to his partners side, it was already too late. Baily's eyes were locked in a death stare as he lay on his back. His daughter, eyes milky white, reached into his torn throat with her bare hand. Joe watched and nearly vomited as Kelly reached deeper and deeper. With her arm nearly to the elbow, she pulled something free from inside. Red and meaty in her grip, she bit down on it to satisfy her need.

Joe covered his mouth with his sleeve, aimed the gun, and fired. The side of Kelly's head erupted in a wave of reds and blond hair as she slumped to her side. The meaty intestinal muck that had been in her hands fell to a wet slap against the gravel.

"Oh, my God. You shot Kelly!"

"It wasn't her… Now come on. We have to go like you said."

"Where the hell are we going?"

"Anywhere but here," Joe shouted, rounding the car again and grabbing her by the wrist. "Let's get the hell out of here!"

Joe scanned the street left and right. Between him and Baily, most of the zombies coming from the north near the van were slow. Their odds were better heading in that direction. He wanted to take the car, but Baily had the keys. He didn't think he could get Noel into the blood bath that covered the car's interior anyway. With a firm grip on Noel's wrist and at least half a dozen plastic bracelets, Joe pulled her away from the patrol car and toward the van. With one foot in front of the other and his pistol aimed to kill, he only took shots when necessary. Already realizing that head shots would do nothing to slow them down; he aimed for the kneecaps as he ran. With each shot, legs pivoted in a bloody display of flesh and bone fireworks. These things, these creatures didn't seem to exhibit any sense of pain. He cringed with each pull of the trigger.

Finally reaching the street corner just past the white van, Joe took an immediate right down the side street. He turned back firing three more shots into the crowd and then picked up his pace. From behind, at least thirty ravenous cannibals both slow and fast, were closing the distance.

"Let go of me," Noel panted as they ran. "You're hurting my arm."

Joe didn't hear her. He was too busy trying to escape. She pulled against him, trying to break free from his grip. He looked back, but not at her. A few runners appeared around the street corner directly in front. Joe let go of Noel and took his pistol in both hands. With his footing firm and his grip steady, he took aim. The gun kicked in his hands and the bullet sent the lead ghoul to the ground. He fired again and again. Two more down. Then he waited. With his weapon still at the ready, he waited, expecting more ghouls to pour out from the street corner. His prediction had been right. Four more brutally grotesque figures joined in the chase. With arms raised and angst in their frantic voices, three rushed forward. The fourth of the group slowly shambled in pursuit. Joe fired three shots. Heads jittered back as blood and mucus sprayed from their backsides, sending each creature down momentarily.

As Joe aimed on the fourth, much slower monster, Noel grabbed him by the arm. His shot went wide, ricocheting off the metallic stop sign at the street corner.

"Forget'em!" Noel shouted, trying to pull Joe away. "We're going to run out of ammo. Then what? Let's get the hell out of here and find somewhere to hide or steal a fucking car or something!"

Joe glared at her with stern eyes. He had hardly ever missed a shot… ever. It was then that he came back to reality and realized that Noel was right. They were outnumbered and he needed to focus on staying alive rather than going commando. He checked his hip. There was one full clip left and he knew he would have to make it last.

"All right…" He said, watching the ghouls he had just shot start to get up.

"What the hell do we do?"

"You know how to hotwire a car?"

Noel's expression confirmed that she did not.

"Well, the precinct is all the way across town from here. Initially I would say we head there. But that's too risky. Let's just find somewhere close by that we can hold up until we figure out what the hell is going on. Maybe we can reach someone that does."

"Like who…," Noel grimaced.

"Hell if I know. The National Guard or the reserves or something. Anybody." Joe looked back at the ghouls slowly closing in. "We'll figure it all out once we get out of the open!"

She nodded in agreement then started running again. With Joe in the lead, Noel did her best to keep up. He was a much faster runner than she was. With the night sky swallowing up the street corners and creeping places, they ran down block after block on edge, fearing that something or someone would jump out at any moment. Their footsteps were loud against the pavement, echoing in the darkness. Before long, they found themselves no longer on the main street and were in the back streets of the Clarksburg's neighborhoods. Surrounded by homes and fenced in properties, Joe looked for any sign of life and hope. But there were none. Had he seen a house light on or someone moving about beyond closed curtains, he would have stopped instantly to seek refuge. There was none of that.

Clarksburg at this point felt like a ghost town. Noel started to feel fatigue in her legs. They burned with throbbing fire.

"I... I can't keep this up," Noel gasped.

"Come on... We can't stop now." Joe looked back, slowing down.

"Let's just pick somewhere and get out of sight." Noel's hands fell to her knees as she tried to catch her breath. "Any place is as good as any, right?"

"I guess so," Joe said looking around.

Before them was the Clarksburg high school, and beyond that, a small glowing cross peeked out over its high buildings. Joe was never much for religion or the fanatics that came along with it, but the first thing he thought of seeing a church, was the word *sanctuary*. He wasn't sure why, but it seemed like just as good a place as any. At least the light was on. Maybe that meant that someone would be there.

"Come on," he said looking back at Noel, knowing good and well that she didn't have much left in her for running. "Just another block, I promise."

They started jogging again, a little slower this time for Noel's sake. Sticking close to the school building as they skirted across the lot, they did their best to keep to the shadows.

The night was still young, and just beginning for Noel and Joe.

EIGHT

Tom was starting to grow very weary of the constant banging against the church's double doors. The hinges rattled as the two ghouls outside persistently pleaded to be let in. They had been at it for quite some time and didn't seem like they would be letting up any time soon. By now, there could be more. Tom didn't know and he didn't want to find out either. He tried ignoring their insistent banging and bellowing calls.

It wasn't working.

"… and I promise, we will make things right." He had been praying, his focus broken. "Would you please shut up! I'm trying to talk to God for you. Maybe if you had spent more time in here, you wouldn't be out there now!" He shouted, frustrated at the dead outside.

His impatient ramblings only ensured them of his location, making them grow more excited. Their banging and determined flailing grew even more resolute. Truly irritated, Tom slammed his fist into the pew's soft velvet cushion. He couldn't do this. Not now. Had the rapture happened leaving him here all alone to suffer and perish with the wicked? Is that what it had come down to? Deep down, Tom knew that he had been destined for something great, but not this. He didn't want this. He wanted to be home with his Father and Lord. He wasn't up for the challenge. And besides, if this truly was the end times and the true rapture, it was nothing like what he expected. Those people out there were something straight from hell. Not from this world.

Tom sat in silence for a moment hoping to hear God. Then it clicked, making him laugh. He grabbed the Bible at his side and flipped through the many pages to the back of the book. It took a minute to find what he was looking for, but once he did, he smiled and laughed some more. As he read the words before him, he thought of the man's skull that he had obliterated earlier and how even after death, he rose again for revenge.

"In those days men will seek death and will not find it; they will desire to die, and death will flee from them." He looked up having read a passage from Revelations. "Is this it, God? Is this what you meant by these words? Nothing can kill them, can it? But why, God… Why? Why have you forsaken me like Christ in this place? I've been faithful. I've come in here every Sunday for the last ten plus years, speaking your word and your will. If anyone deserved to be taken before all of this, it's me. But, never the less. Your will be done in Heaven as it is on Earth. Let it be your will and not mine."

Tom closed the book, laying it at his side on the pew. He looked around taking in the church's four walls. This had been the church his grandfather built, his father pastored, and now he was its caretaker and soul speaker. A lot had happened here while growing from a young boy. He looked to the pulpit, reflecting on the many sermons he had preached in his days. He thought of all the people who had left a few years back when that new church opened across town. He glanced at the five stained glass windows that lined the wall on either side of the pews. He had gotten a good deal when he had them installed, just after taking over for his father.

He had never been able to match his father's fiery sermons on Sunday mornings. Tom grimaced, feeling like that was a large part of the church's issues. A major reason as to why so many members had fallen to the wayside after his father had passed away. All he wanted was to measure up to his old man's successes.

He sighed, stood to his feet, and walked up onto the stage.

Behind the pulpit was a large wooden cross hanging on the wall. The plush red carpeting that ran along the floors ran up the steps all the way to the back. It was a perfect match for the padding that they had decided to use for the pews. Around the cross on both sides was one large stained glass mural of light beams. The glass was perfectly placed making the cross look as if it were illuminated by God's glory. It was a beautiful sight when the sun fell, shown dead center. But now, in the pitch black of night, there was no light from outside seeping in. The glass mural looked eerie and bleak like his fallen friends outside at the door.

With his hand resting on the wooden podium like he had done more than a thousand times, Tom stared down the empty pews. The doors at the end shook, fists pounded violently against them. Although he had stood in that very spot countless times, he could never say he had ever done it wearing sweatpants… or shirtless for that matter. The thought made him giggle. He smiled, thinking up the different reactions he would have gotten from some of the church members had he been caught preaching in his current wardrobe. He ran his fingers through his thinning hair and clenched the cross around his neck. If God had him stay behind, after the rapture, then it was for a reason. And he was determined to figure out what that reason was.

Closing his eyes, hands still firm on the podium, he prayed "Our Father in Heaven, hallowed be your name. Your Kingdom come, your will be done, on Earth as in Heaven. Give us today our daily bread.

Forgive us our sins, as we forgive those who sin against us. Lead us not into temptation, but deliver us from evil. For the Kingdom, the power and the glory are yours. Now and forever. Give me strength this day. I honestly can't say I know why you would leave me and take so many others. Please, God. Give me a sign... Amen."

Practically on cue, the report of gunfire echoed outside. Startled, Tom opened his eyes, focused on the double doors before him. He swallowed hard, not realizing that his teeth were grinding. He stood frozen for a moment, and then another shot rang out, instantly splintering a dime-sized hole into one of the doors. Something slammed hard against the door. Another shot went off. He ducked low behind the pulpit.

"This is God's house," he shouted. "Leave now for the wrath of the Lord is at hand!"

Tom was surprised to hear someone actually shout something back. Another shot went off followed by an abrupt slam against the doors. Then the pounding started up again. But it was different. More controlled. More human.

"Open up!" A man shouted, between the beating fists. "We've got company!"

"Go away!" Tom insisted.

"Come on, man. Let us in. We got some of those things tailing us!"

The pounding continued.

"Open the damn door or we're going to break it down!" A female demanded.

Two more shots went off.

Tom clinched the necklace in his fist wondering what he should do. For all he knew, these people were crazed just like all the rest. It made sense. Anyone not taken up as a part of the rapture were without God's mercy. And for that, they probably wanted in to kill him and burn the place down. As he sat contemplating his options, the pounding outside grew more aggressive.

He had no time before the decision was made for him. Three quick burst of gunfire sent wood chips flying off the doors, as they swung open. A short police officer led with a weapon in hand, a girl following behind. Their expressions were frantic with fear. The unexpected guests had triggered the alarm system with their anxious entry. A high, pulsating squeal filled the air.

"Help us block this door!" the policeman yelled above the alarm, aiming his gun outside and firing off a few more shots.

The moans of the monsters rose in the distance as the policeman fired. Tom saw a figure out in the parking lot fall. What was going on here was just mad. How could any of this be happening? These people were defiling God's holy place.

"Hey, he's talking to you, dude!" The satanic looking girl said while trying to shove a pew in front of the double doors. "You think we can't see you hiding up there on the stage? Get your ass over here and help me move this!"

Her hair was cut strange and all of her clothes were black as were her lips and eyes. Tom's stomach turned. He had only seen people like her in the Mall a few towns over and had never liked the feelings he got from them. They always looked on him with judging eyes. Like they knew he was God's warrior.

"Get over here, man!" The cop shouted, holstering his gun and slamming the double doors shut. "Help us move these pews. They're going to get in if we don't…"

The doors shook on their hinges, and the first of many ghouls reached in. Joe leaned against the door, shoving the mangled hand back out. He closed it, leaning against it with all of his weight. Noel was too weak, too small to move the large wooden seat across the thick red carpet. Joe tried to reach out and help, but the hinges shook hard, almost pulling from the door facing.

Tom breathed heavily. He didn't know the girl or her cop friend. Maybe they weren't like the two monsters that had chased him into the church. Maybe they were his reason for being left behind. Maybe God had set it forth for him to help these two find what they were looking for. He let go of the cross around his neck and stepped out from behind the podium.

"I'm… I'm Pastor Tom…"

"No offense pal, but now's not the time for introductions." Joe waved him over. "Help her move that pew over here. We need to barricade this door!"

The doors kicked open a little, pushing Joe away. Two pale, blood covered hands reached in. Joe stepped away, letting it open all the way. Two zombies lumbered into the church, their bloody bodies leaking into the red carpet. Joe yanked his pistol free and fired. It did nothing, the safety had accidently been engaged.

"Fuck…," Joe said, looking down to remove the safety.

The lead ghoul fell on Joe making him fall to the floor. Noel screamed, while darting from the entryway. The loud report of Joe's gun echoed inside the church. The ghoul on top of him went limp. He aimed the gun at the door, hitting the second creature right between the eyes as it rushed in. Its head kicked back, a quarter-sized hole blown out. Blood dripped down its nose. Its legs buckled and the lifeless body dropped to the carpet. Joe slid out from under the rancid, unmoving corpse.

"Help me move these outside before…"

"Before they get back up?" Tom said, stepping forward to help push the two bodies outside.

"Yeah…" Joe cringed, grabbing one of the bodies by the legs.

The two men grabbed each body, throwing them to the steps outside. After they tossed out the second corpse, Joe looked out into the church's parking lot and beyond. More of the undead were coming. The alarm acted like a beacon giving away their location.

Joe stepped back inside shutting the doors. In a matter of minutes, they had five pews piled up on one another to secure them. Joe still felt a little uneasy about the barricade and recommended that they move the piano that was perched atop the stage to the back of the church.

"That's not going to do any good," Tom said. "It's on wheels."

"Good…" Noel said. "It will be easy to move. Once we get it over here, who said it's going to still need the wheels?"

Without the old man's consent, Noel and Joe rushed over to the piano and pushed it off the stage.

"Be careful with that," Tom insisted. "That piano is older than both of you put together!"

"No offense, dude." Noel pulled her black hair from her face as she pushed the piano. "Either help us or get the hell out of the aisle. You're in the way!"

The best leaders lead by serving, Tom nodded.

He stepped aside letting the piano pass and then jumped behind it, helping his new friends push it toward the door. Its wheels were stiff as they rolled against the carpet. Reaching the door, Joe leaned against the piano with everything he had.

Initially, Tom grimaced at the idea of damaging such a wonderful family heirloom, but life is more important than any material possession. Tom pushed harder. The piano tipped forward and crashed down hard against the stack of pews. The sound of colliding keys and the piano's insides jittered about as the large instrument rested on its side, becoming a part of the barricade.

All three of them slumped to the carpet. The pounding at the door was starting to grow. The alarm continued to beep its loud waves of pulsating irritation.

"That thing was fucking heavy…" Noel took a breath, catching a look from their new friend. "Sorry… I mean… *freaking* heavy."

Tom ran his fingers through his hair. "Yeah, you're telling me. I haven't moved that thing in probably five years."

Tom was about to say something else, but Joe grabbed him by the shoulder.

"Before we really get into all of this, can we please do something about that noise? That alarm is only attracting more unwanted attention. There is no telling how far that sound reaches into the neighborhood."

"My Lord… Of course… of course…" Tom stood to his feet, walking over to a small booth by the door.

Behind the booth was a soundboard for the church's small sound system along with a computer and lighting switches. The little nook was the church's electrical heart, so to speak. On the wall at the far side of the booth, Tom flipped open a plastic lid and pressed a few buttons. Sliding the lid closed, the alarm was no more.

"How's that?" Tom asked, shaking his pinky in one ear. "Any better?"

Joe nodded, helping Noel to her feet. "Hi… sorry about the door," he said and pointed at the barricade. "My name is Joe Montoya, and this here is Noel. I never did get her last name."

"It doesn't matter," she said, shaking hands with her new shirtless friend. "You can just keep it simple. Noel is fine."

"I'm Tom… I'm the pastor here… or well, I was."

With the alarm no longer booming in the background, the growing pounding at the door seemed louder. Confident that the dead outside couldn't get in, Tom steered them through another door that led to a narrow hall reaching the back of the church. To the right was a set of gender specific bathrooms. To the left there were two other rooms, probably about the same size as the restrooms. One room looked like a small office that had the words *Pastor Tom* on the door. The other was clearly a play room for toddlers and younger children. The room was small, but looked like it had a lot to offer in the way of children's entertainment.

"Here, step into my office. Take a load off and have a seat."

The office space was small, making the oak-wood desk seem much larger than it actually was. On one side of the desk was a very expensive looking brown leather chair and a book shelf behind that. The shelf was loaded with books by authors that Noel had never heard of. On the wall beside the shelf were plaques with Tom's name engraved on them, along with a framed newspaper clipping.

As Noel sat down, she said, "Don't take this the wrong way, Tom… but, do you always strut around in here after hours with your shirt off?"

He laughed, taking a seat. "Oh… no, young lady. It's kind of a long story."

"Young lady? Who is this guy, the Pope?" Noel thumbed at Tom while smirking at Joe. "Noel is fine."

"Okay, *Noel*. Well…" Tom sighed. "It's rather obvious as to who I am." He waved the contents of his office. "And I see that you are a cop."

"Yeah," Joe said, "believe it or not, today was actually my first day on the freaking job."

Tom nodded his sympathies. "And what about you, Noel. Who exactly are you?"

"What do you mean, who am I?"

"You know… what do you do?"

"Art major. I'm going to school."

"A muse," Tom smiled. "We are all muses in one way or another, are we not?"

"I don't mean to butt in, but…," Joe said, changing the conversation. "Do you know at all what's going on out there? What happened here, to you? What do you know so far about anything?"

"You know…, Joe. I can tell I am already going to like you." Tom leaned back in his chair, putting his hands behind his head. "Straight to the point. No beating around the bush. I like that."

Noel rolled her eyes, but only Joe caught that she had done it. She couldn't stand religious people. They were always so damn judgmental. Joe smiled at her in an attempt to have her at least give this guy a chance.

"Well… What happened? Obviously, something went down. You aren't wearing a shirt and you're covered in blood. And it's obvious that it isn't yours. I may not be a detective, but it doesn't take a rocket scientist to put two and two together. Those *things* out there drove you in here, didn't they?"

"If you got my story figured out already, then why not skip the pleasantries and let's hear yours."

Joe glared at Tom from across the desk.

"Okay, look. I feel like we are somehow getting off on the wrong foot. You should be thankful, I even let you in here."

"You didn't!" Noel insisted. "We had to knock the damn door in ourselves!"

Tom threw his hands up in surrender. Things were going south and quick. He closed his eyes and thought about it for a moment. Noel was right. He hadn't let them in, which definitely gave them the wrong impression about him.

"You're right." Tom said calmly. "I'm sorry. I truly am. And I wouldn't doubt it if I have to answer for that when I finally do get to go home to the Lord. I should have let you in. But to be honest… I was scared. Scared out of my mind in fact."

Tom proceeded to explain to them about his earlier encounter with the man who attacked the woman, and how she changed and attacked him. He explained that he wasn't sure what was going on and that he had been too afraid to even go out the back door back to his home across the parking lot. He even divulged his theories about it being the rapture and that he had been left to deal with this seven year terror. He was excited to meet them, because that clarified a lot regarding those assumptions. If what was happening was everywhere, he was worried for his wife who was only a few counties over at a women's retreat.

Joe accepted his apologies for both him and Noel. Tom's fear was understandable. Had he been alone holed up in a secure place, he couldn't say he would have let anyone in either.

Having heard how much Tom cared for his wife, Noel felt a lot better. It let her know that he was a real person, not like so many of those other church goers, only eager to increase attendance. As much as she didn't want to, Joe encouraged her to explain what had happened to them at the cemetery. She was about to begin, but lost it when her thoughts returned to Kelly, Trevor, and… Jared.

"What's happening?" she whimpered between sobs.

With his hand on her back, Joe comforted her.

"For these are the days of vengeance, that all things which are written may be fulfilled."

"What?" Noel looked up, her eyes swollen and red.

"Luke 21:22," Tom said with a grin. "What if what's happening here is for a reason? What if it's part of God's judgment to man?"

"But what about the meteor shower?" Noel asked. "Could that have something to do with it?"

"God's wrath can come in many forms, little lady." He paused. "Sorry… Noel. In the end times, a lot of crazy things are going to happen. Like the dead coming to life. You know… the Bible says that in the end, man will seek death and not find it. They will cast themselves upon the stone and not die. I honestly think this is what's happening."

"I don't know what I believe," Joe said. "Meteors or the bible. At this point, all I care about is what we are going to do from here. There is no telling how many of *those* creatures are still headed this way."

"What makes you say that?"

"Because, Tom. That alarm was pretty freaking loud. And if it were up to me, we would think about what we are going to do and move on, before too many of those things come around for us to handle."

"Well, whatever we do, I want to get to my wife."

"You said so yourself. She is pretty far away. Before we do anything drastic like that, I'm with Noel. I want to figure out what the hell is really going on here and maybe get in contact with someone that can help."

Noel smiled, pushing back her tears. She liked seeing that Joe had her back. At first, she hadn't liked Tom, but the more they talked, he seemed all right. A little set in his ways, but alright all the same. She smiled at him too, glad that she found a new friend. She just hoped that they would make it through the night. Even with the door to the office closed, more than fifty square feet between them and the dead at the front door, she could still hear their persistence. The whole thing just made her uneasy.

"So… Joe. You seem pretty confident about all of this…"

"Confident? What the hell makes you say that? I'm on pins and fucking needles here."

Tom grimaced.

"Sorry… *freaking* pins and needles. What makes you think I have it figured out?"

"Honestly, I don't," Tom said. "But I guess a part of me just assumes that if any of us has it together, it's you. You are the one with the gun and the badge."

"This is true," Joe smirked.

He took out his gun and checked the clip. He only had three bullets left and one final clip with twelve rounds in that. He grimaced, slamming the almost empty clip home.

"Do you have a working phone?"

"Sorry, Joe. I don't. The lines are down. I tried it a few times, here and at my house."

"Your house?"

"Yeah, you weren't listening when I mentioned that I live just next door?"

"Please tell me you have a car," Joe said.

"I do. Full tank, the last time I checked too."

"Well, if y'all are up for it," Joe said, standing to his feet. "I say we go on a little road trip!"

"To where," Noel inquired.

"The precinct house, for starters… I think we'll be able to figure out what's going on from there. That, and I would feel a hell of a lot better with some more guns and ammunition."

"Only if I get a gun too!"

"At this point, Noel. I don't see that being a problem."

"Well, it beats sitting around here, right?" Tom pushed his chair back, standing up. "I need to get next door and into a shirt anyway."

Tom forced out a smile hoping that the remark would have made his new friends laugh. It didn't. They just looked him once over, in an odd and silent way agreeing with the statement. As they exited the office, the mood changed and the feeling of safety no longer was present. The sound of the dead outside grew louder as the three survivors quietly crept down the narrow hall.

With Pastor Tom in the lead and Joe following up the rear, Noel rubbed her burning eyes, fatigue starting to really catch up with her.

The last place she wanted to be was back outside with *them*.

NINE

"And when did you say these reports were coming in?" Benjamin Watts demanded.

Benjamin was the CEO and head director of Golden Arches Co. in West Virginia, otherwise known as the *G.A.C.*. They were the fastest growing fast food chain in America, next to Burger Queen. That didn't matter though, because competition was a good thing. It kept businesses from resting on their laurels.

The average *G.A.C.* factory processed nearly five hundred thousand pounds of meat per day. That much couldn't be said for the competition.

Ben was over six feet tall and had an athletic build. He had class, boyishly good looks, and of course… money. His hair was dirty blond in color and cut short to perfection. His eyes were light green and his completion fair. He presented himself in a way that demanded others to perceive him as being successful. His handsome features only added to his allure.

In truth, Ben was a workaholic. The exorbitant amounts of time he had put at work paid off. Although, the higher-up's loved him, those that worked for him felt just the opposite. He was rude, easy to anger, and never appreciative of their efforts.

Benjamin had earned his way to the top at the ripe age of 28. In just ten years, he had worked his way up the corporate ladder, going from a factory maintenance hand to plant manager. Buying a large share of stocks in the company had bought him a seat with the big boys. It was his instinct and willingness to take chances that pushed him to become head CEO of the lead factory in West Virginia. The factory was new, only two years old. As CEO of the plant, against his wishes, he was forced to also act as head director of the new factory. The hours were long but the pay was amazing. If things worked out as he planned, he would be able to retire in the next five years. He was proud to say he would be the first Watts family member to retire before the age of thirty-five. It was of the upmost confidence he believed that nothing would be getting in the way of that goal. Nothing.

"Answer me when I'm talking to you, woman!" Benjamin demanded.

"It's… umm… it's been more than a few hours ago, sir." Chelsea cringed.

She hated herself for taking the job as this swine's assistant. The pay was great and during the interview, Mr. Watts had been such a gentleman. She learned quickly that it had all been a front. Aside from his constant disrespectful demeanor, and caustic attitude, his sexist ways were constantly pushing her to the edge. Had she not been locked into that damn mortgage, she would have left a long time ago. The last six months had been hell, but she did her best to bite her tongue and get by.

"And you are just telling me this now?"

What Chelsea wanted to say was how she had tried to call him earlier, but he was too damn stubborn and never seemed to answer his cell after hours. How he could expect her to be on constant call and him not, was beyond her.

"I'm just finding out about it myself, Mr. Watts. Honestly," she said.

"Unacceptable!" Benjamin shouted, slamming the glass of bourbon onto his table.

Chelsea winced against the sound of colliding glass and wood. Benjamin's office was unnecessarily large. The walls were plain, white lined, with various framed photographs. Each picture was of Benjamin shaking hands with random people of power throughout the world. The head CEO of Econoline, Disney, the President of the U.S., and more. The room was mostly empty. One small chair sat in front of a desk that had a minibar on the side, which was where Chelsea was now sitting next to Benjamin. His chair, like the room, was much larger than the one she sat in. The wall behind Benjamin was made of solid glass, which overlooked the factory's meat processing area. With his office on the second flood and the entire plant at ground level, he was able to overlook every little thing that happened in the plant.

"But…" Chelsea started to say.

Benjamin pushed his chair back and stood to his feet. Making his way to the minibar, he topped off his bourbon, and then made his way to the window. With his nose almost touching the glass, he looked down on the hundred-plus employees who worked third shift. He hated coming into work this late, but sometimes he just had to. He had no choice after catching word of what happened, he got up out of bed and came down to the factory. Everything on the ground level seemed to be running smooth. With tired bags under his eyes, he took a sip of bourbon.

"Who authorized this little mishap?" Benjamin asked, not looking away from the window. "We need to clear this all up tonight."

You mean to tell me you are going to do what you always do, Ben? Place the blame elsewhere? Really… you wouldn't be that shallow would you? You don't remember signing off on waste management contracts that allows countless pounds of contaminated meat to be dumped into the Elk River to cut financial corners? It's not connected to the drinking water, you had said… Chelsea thought, rolling her eyes.

The relatively new factory was fifteen miles south of Clarksburg in the outskirts of Stone Wood, near the Stonewall Cemetery. The Elk River was a narrow waterway that ran past the factory, alongside the cemetery and even worked its way through Clarksburg and the surrounding cities. It had been a major tourist attraction for hikers and canoeing campers for over a decade, but that had been shut down shortly after the Golden Arches Co. established itself in the area as the largest factory in southern West Virginia. Not only did the factory buy up most of the land south of Stone Wood, they also purchased a major chunk of the Elk River. It was quickly closed off to the public. Within the first six months or so after the factory began to manufacture its product, the local area tried to stop it, wanting back the rights to use the section of purchased river. The public protest was brought to a quick end. Ultimately, the factory had given more than half of the Clarksburg area and beyond the potential for new job opportunities. With the economy in its current slump, that wasn't something to pass up. Needless to say, *G.A.C.* won and the people were silenced by the State. Money bought power. Benjamin knew how to play that game all too well.

"Well…" Benjamin said, turning away from the window and sitting back down behind his desk.

"Honestly, Mr. Watts… I don't know."

"Who is the floor manager tonight?"

Chelsea gritted her teeth. Benjamin wasn't about to pin this mess on someone else. She looked down at the manila folder in her lap, thumbing through. After a moment of scanning the third shift manning list, she looked up.

"Paul Tanner. He's worked for the *G.A.C.* for more than twenty years. His life is invested into this company. He's the best we have."

"That's too bad," Benjamin said between sips. "Go get him for me."

"You can't fire him!"

"Oh, I am going to do more than fire the man. I woke up for this. Someone is getting fired. Do you want it to be you? Now, do what I tell you, woman!"

Chelsea's jaw hurt. She had been grinding her teeth. It was something she found herself doing when she was in this man's presence. Well, she was finished with bending to his every whim. She was going to stand up for herself and for the loyal employees of this corporation.

"No… I…" Her voice wavered.

Benjamin leaned back in his seat, surprised. No one had ever talked back to him like that.

Finding her voice, she continued. "No. I'm not going to go get that poor man so that you can fire him for a mistake that *you* made! This is a result of pouring our waste into the river, not the result of some shift manager. He has a family and kids in college. We can't just drop people at a whim, just because you are losing some shuteye."

Benjamin smiled. He was getting an erection. Her sudden outburst was something he had never expected from the little red head. It also helped that one of the reasons he had hired her, was because she was easy on the eyes. Sure, she could stand to change it up a little with the wardrobe. Something a little less was always better. He had hinted at it a few times, but she never did get it. She was plain in his eyes. But that could easily be changed, if she just wore something a little tighter, and more revealing. Hell, he'd even consider giving her a raise then.

"And…" She continued, not realizing that Benjamin was smiling at her. "If you don't recall, it was you that decided it was best in the interest of the company to dump our excesses into the river… Not Paul the shift manager! I think you need to man up, Mr. Watts, and either admit that you made a bad decision or get off your ass and clean this up yourself!"

They sat in silence for a moment. Chelsea swallowed hard wondering if she should have opened her mouth. She was going to be fired, she just knew it. As nice as that sounded, because she loathed Mr. Watts, she couldn't afford to lose her job. The room grew thick with anticipation. Her palms began to sweat. She crossed her legs, feeling uneasy about the way Benjamin was looking at her. She had no idea how he was going to respond.

He remained calm, just the opposite of what she expected. Benjamin took one massive gulp of bourbon and sat the empty glass down on the desk. He leaned back in his chair and smiled.

"You know, Chelsea. No one has ever stood up to me before. I like you. I can see now why I hired you. You've got guts." Benjamin rose from his chair, grabbed his empty glass, and walked over to the minibar again. "You want me to make you a drink? You know, now that I think about it… what are you doing tomorrow?"

"Have you heard anything I've been saying?" Chelsea tossed the manila folder onto the desk and jumped to her feet. "We have been dumping contaminated meat into the Elk River for the last three months and it's finally come back to bite you on the ass! People are getting sick. Real sick, Benjamin!"

He grinned, taking a sip of his newly filled glass. She had never called him by his real name before. Always Mr. this and Mr. that.

"First time you've called me that before."

"What?"

"By my first name…"

"Uhhh…" Not even realizing it, the pen in her hand flew across the room softly hitting Benjamin in the chest. "Wake up, Mr. Watts. Clarksburg and the surrounding area are under attack by the town's people, because of mad cow or some shit. And it's your fault. Do you even care?"

Benjamin went back to gazing out the window at the floor below. Chelsea walked over to the bar, picked up her pen, and turned to walk out. She had enough of his crap. He was a self-centered, egotistical prick. Then it came to her. Just as she reached the door ready to leave the office, she took in a deep breath and sighed.

"Just think, Benjamin. What is going to happen to this company after an investigation?"

He ignored her.

"Just think…," she continued. "Just think what is going to happen to you and your precious retirement when they find out that you caused all of this and did nothing to clean it up!"

Hell, you're probably going to jail, dumbass. She thought. *Ehh… who am I kidding. You've got enough money and friend power to get around that.*

Realistically, Chelsea knew that this thing was way bigger than Mr. Watts or anything he could do about it. In fact, she had already taken the initiative to contact people at Corporate. Apparently, something similar to this had happened in North Florida a few years back and they had a cleanup crew to take care of things. Based on the call she made to Corporate, some specialists were already on their way to the Clarksburg police station to set up base and hopefully have everything cleared up by sunup. More than anything, she just wanted to see Mr. Watts realize the errors of his ways. Sure, once this was all over and cleaned up, he could be the one in front of the camera signing all of the insurance checks. And yes, he would do it with a smile knowing that it wasn't doing anything to damage his personal pocket. She just wanted for something in him to change. She wanted that smile to be genuine when he did the right thing.

"Well…," she said, standing at the door. "You going to do something? I've already called Corporate and have a…"

"You *what*?" Benjamin yelled in surprise and turned away from the window.

"That's right," Chelsea pressed her firsts to her hips. "Corporate is already on the ball and you're not. How bad does that make you look?"

Benjamin laughed. "And you made the call?"

"I did."

"Well, in that case. It doesn't make me look bad at all. You're my assistant, which means I had you make the call. Good job at making me look good." Benjamin went back to overseeing the workers on the first floor, all hard at work. "Come here, Chelsea. Come look and see what I see."

Hesitant, she stepped away from the door and made her way around the large desk. She walked up beside Benjamin, whose breath reeked of alcohol and lack of hygiene. Standing close to him, she could tell that he was tired and a lot more irritated than she realized. She looked out the large window down at the first floor. It was a view she had seen more than a hundred times since starting her job with *G.A.C.*.

Over nearly a hundred workers, all wearing white coats, gloves, hard hats, and masks were busy about the factory floors. All they did was process meat twenty-four seven. The area below the office was nothing, but large machine after large machine, pushing meat into grinders to be turned into fast food patties or processed chicken nuggets. The thought of food processed like this made her cringe. Shortly after getting the job, one of the first things Chelsea did was stop eating the stuff. It made her sick just thinking about it.

The contaminated food was even worse. She had never been to that part of the factory and had no intentions of ever going. That was where they sorted the stuff that had spoiled. She covered her mouth with one hand.

"You see all these people, Chelsea?" Benjamin put his hand on her shoulder, squeezing unreasonably tight. "They would be nowhere without me. They would be nothing. Have nothing. This *town* that you're so worried about would still be the nothing that it was, had I decided to not move this plant here. You know how many jobs I've provided this dead city and all its weak little towns around it? Do you know how much I've offered them? I'm like God to these people." He pointed down at the workers below. "Today I am their king. Tomorrow... when all of this is cleaned up and blown over, I will be their hero. And you know why? Because you made that call."

He turned his attention to her, resting his hand on each shoulder. She lowered her head, swallowing hard. He always made her feel uncomfortable. It was easy for him, and right now was one of those times.

"I'm glad you called Corporate... I am."

Benjamin leaned in and embraced her with a hug. He liked the way her breasts felt against his chest, as he squeezed her tighter. He smelled her hair and caressed her back with soft intent, then pulled himself away smiling at her. This type of appreciation was something she had never seen him display before. Being honest with herself, she wasn't sure how to take it. In was kind of frightening in a way.

Benjamin slapped her across the face. The sudden *smack* resonated throughout the large office. His hand came away revealing a rosy red cheek on her left side.

Chelsea winced from the unexpected pain. She pulled away, her eyes starting to swell. She was stronger than him. She didn't need to show her weakness.

"Don't ever go over my head again! If I want Corporate's involvement, then I will let that be known. Do I make myself clear?"

She didn't respond, still shocked that he had actually raised his hand at her.

"Come here…" Benjamin leaned in and took another breast filled hug. "I'm sorry. I didn't really mean that. It's just that I had to make you realize how serious I am about my job. It means a lot to me that you showed initiative. Really, it does. But… next time… I don't care how important it is. Don't wake me up in the middle of the night for *anything*. I need my beauty sleep. Not all of us are blessed with great looks like you, Chelsea."

"Yeah," she sighed. "I just want to help you do a great job. You mean a lot to this community. The Golden Arches Co. has helped rebuild hope for the people here."

Yes, the factory had provided many jobs in a sinking economy for Clarksburg and the surrounding area, but that was unimportant. What she said was a lie. She hated him. And no one ever raised a hand to her. Ever! She wasn't about to sit by and let that slide.

At this point, she was ready to quit right on the spot. There was only one thing keeping her from doing it now, and it wasn't her bills. Fuck that. Clarksburg had always been her hometown and somebody needed to do something. If anyone was going to be there to make sure this thing got cleaned up, and that Mr. Watts would be there to take the fall, it would be her. She would see to that, if it were the last thing she ever did.

She leaned in, forced a smile, and then kissed him on the cheek.

"Well, there's no point in getting to bed… *yet*." She winked. "I've already called your personal pilot in. Like you, he was a little cranky to pull out of bed this late. But… he's here. Even though we have some cleanup crews already setting up base at the Clarksburg police station, I think it would be good if you at least made an appearance. Show Corporate that you're at least concerned and ensure the locals that this kind of thing isn't going to happen again."

It took a little coaxing on her part, but after nearly ten minutes of pleading and subtle seduction, Benjamin was on the factory roof and in the helicopter. Thankfully, he had a lot to drink already; otherwise, Chelsea wasn't sure she would have ever gotten him to go.

Other than the pilot always being a little on the cranky side, Chelsea enjoyed her experiences in the air. The helicopter smell reminded her of her dad, a machinist, after a long day at work. It reminded her of him. She thought it was cool wearing the headgear and being able to talk over the sound of the propeller. It always made her feel like she was in a movie. Her first time riding in a helicopter was with Mr. Watts. If there were anything she was going to miss once she did finally tell him off, it would be the flying.

With the chopper in the air, they started toward Clarksburg. The moon was bright, revealing the world and the ground below in a luminescent hue of greys. It was just bright enough to see everything as they flew overhead. Chelsea watched as the helicopter drifted over the drop zone that had caused all of these problems. A large series of pipes that were connected to the factory ran down a narrow fenced in field to eventually drop off into the Elk River. As they passed over it, the contents of contaminated bile still poured from its pipes. Chelsea cringed. The idea that she was associated with the people who were damaging the river she grew up on made her sick to her stomach. The helicopter followed the river for a while, and eventually gave way to the cemetery and Clarksburg beyond that. The town was in ruins. Buildings were ablaze and people ran wildly in the streets. If they were looting or not, she couldn't tell. One thing was sure, she was surprised to see that so many people were out of their homes this late at night.

"We's got a call comin' in from the cleanup crew in Clarksburg." The pilot said, breaking the silence.

Chelsea's heart skipped a beat. The pilot's words were clear in her headset as if he were sitting right on top of her. She looked to Benjamin to take the call, but he waved her off. She scowled at him, and then took the call herself. Leave it to Mr. Watts to pass the actual work onto others.

"Put it through," she said, then stared at Benjamin knowing he could hear everything. "This is Chelsea, Mr. Watts' assistant."

"Hello. I caught word that Mr. Watts was headed here to assist in the cleanup. That's good to hear." The male voice on the other end said. "Unfortunately, I do have some news. Bad news."

"Oh…" Chelsea said.

"The reports that we were getting in of people becoming sick is much worse than we could have ever imagined. And with that, I am only calling to give you a heads up."

"Thank you," Chelsea insisted. "But I believe we are already aware of how bad the situation is and we should be there shortly."

"Really?" the man said. "Just what have you heard so far? Because with the way things are right now, it could take weeks to get all of this cleaned up."

"What do you mean?"

"We can't get in and do our job when my men are in danger. That's what I mean!"

"You mean the reports of violence?" Chelsea curled her brow.

"You really don't know do you?" the man on the other end of the radio said.

"Look, I understand that the river has become a big problem and a lot of people have gotten sick. Some have even resorted to violence, but there is no reason this should take more than a day to fix." Chelsea insisted.

The call went silent for a moment. Chelsea shrugged her shoulders at Benjamin, and then looked to the pilot. The pilot was too busy flying the chopper, so she looked back to her boss.

"Look…" the voice finally came back. "I make it my business to go in and clean up Corporate America's fuck up's. I've made it my profession. But in over a decade, I have never seen anything like this. These people aren't just resorting to violence. They are eating each other, for Christ's sake. In the last hour, I have sent out three teams to survey the total damage. I've only heard back from one of those teams. And you aren't going to believe this when I tell you, but… two of the members of that team are dead!

We're not built for this kind of shit. We're a contamination cleanup crew, not a fucking military outfit. If you think that I'm going..."

His voice trailed off, filling the headsets with static and muffled banter. The last thing any of them heard was what sounded like muffled screaming. What sounded like a gunshot filled their ears then the call ended.

Chelsea swallowed hard and looked to Mr. Watts with terror showing in her eyes.

Benjamin smiled, looking at her chest and not her face. He could care less

TEN

"What kind of a car do you drive anyway, Tom?" Joe asked, standing at the church's back door.

"Nineteen-eighty-two GMC Truck… Why?"

"Just wondering what we are looking at here." Joe said. "Is there going to be enough room for all three of us inside? I don't want any of us getting stuck in the bed to potentially fall out. Last thing we need is a ridiculous accident like that happening."

Tom nodded. "Yeah, tell me about it. No, there's enough room. It will be a tight fit, what with it being a stick-shift. I'm sure we can make it work."

"Window…" Noel slightly raised her hand.

"You're the shortest. Sorry, but that kind of automatically disqualifies you."

"Look who's talking, Joe. And it doesn't even matter. I called it!"

Joe's grin turned sour. His eyes squinted down at Noel as if to burn holes through her. She just smiled back, cocking her hip for emphases. Tom shook his head at them both, knowing that they were probably somewhat close to the same age.

"Look," Joe said, his playful demeanor demolished. "Once I open this door… We follow Tom. Try to stick to the shadows, and for God's sake, please keep quiet." He looked at Noel's plethora of jewelry and gothic accessories. "The sooner we get into the house, get what we need, and get out the better."

Noel and Tom stared blankly.

"Also…" He continued. "Tom, do you have any weapons in the house? Guns, preferably?"

"Sorry, but no. It took my wife five years to talk me into putting a bat next to the bed."

"That's better than nothing," Noel offered.

"True," Tom agreed, looking down at the bloodied bat in his hands. "But, this is the only one I have. We never had kids, so there was no need for sports equipment, you know. We tried, though…"

Noticing that Tom's attitude had suddenly dropped to super negative, Joe patted him on his bare back and smiled.

"Hey, look at it this way, holy man. At least, you only have your wife to worry about in all of this shit. Right?"

Tom just shrugged making Joe feel even more uncomfortable. Maybe he should have just kept his mouth shut.

"What if we turn the alarm back on?"

"Why the hell would we do that?" Joe asked.

"Because," Noel said. "It would cover our noise and possibly even attract all of the others from town to this location. When we leave, they could possibly end up heading this way and make it safer for us out there."

"Hey," Tom grinned. "That actually sounds like a good idea."

"Sounds like a good idea and is a good idea are two totally different things." Joe ran his hand through his hair. "Glad to see you have your thinking cap on, Noel. But, I don't want to attract any attention. Period. We don't know what we're going to get into next door. Let's just keep it as quiet as we can and move on."

"But…"

"But nothing. Between now and when we actually get into Tom's GMC, I don't want to attract any… not any attention."

Noel sighed. "I guess you're right."

"Okay," Joe finally said after a moment. "Let's do this. Just like we said. Steady, quiet, and in the shadows. We are going to be right behind you, Tom. Noel, I want you to follow up behind Tom and I will be close behind. No matter what happens, don't stop. You got me?"

They both nodded, tension twisting their expressions.

"Alright then…" Joe turned the knob opening the door. "Let's move!"

The door opened up to the darkness. The back of the church building was nothing, but grass with a path that led to a few small trashcans. Ignoring them, Tom darted across the grass at a steady jog. His house was just across the way, but seemed so much farther in the dark. Their near silent steps were almost instantly met with those of another. Joe looked up to see a mangled pursuer in the parking lot dashing toward them. Their location had been compromised. At full sprint, the creature howled a guttural moan. As it crossed the parking lot, several ghouls rounded the church building, after leaving the double doors.

"Go! Go! Go!" Joe shouted.

Noel looked back and started to slow down, but Joe caught up to her and pushed her forward. Noel watched Joe bring his pistol to the air. With one foot franticly still in front of the other, she put her hands to her ears. It really didn't help. With Joe practically hovering over her, pushing her to keep going, the gun's report blasted in her ears. Her ears rang and her head blurred for a moment. Joe shoved her hard sending her falling forward. She fell to her knees. Expecting to land in the cold and damp grass, she fell onto soft carpet. She looked back, seeing Joe fire another shot outside, then slam the door shut. The lights went on and she found herself in Tom's living room.

Joe stepped forward to help her to her feet.

"Sorry about that."

"It's okay," she groaned from a little carpet burn on the knees. "I kind of blanked out when you started shooting."

"No big deal." Joe holstered his firearm. "Here, help me move this couch in front of the door. We need to get back on the move as fast as we can. They know we're in here and it's only a matter of time before they decide to come crashing in through one of the windows."

The sudden bash at the door startled Noel into action. The pounding fists came much sooner than she had expected. Frantic, she helped move the couch. In three quick strides, they had it in place. It wouldn't hold for long, but it would have to do.

"Should we do something about the windows?" Noel asked, terrified by the idea that one would shatter at any moment.

"Not really enough time. We need to get those keys to the truck and get the hell out of here before the house is totally overrun."

Joe and Noel made their way into the kitchen, feeling it a little safer with the lack of windows.

"Where did Tom go?"

"I saw him go down the hall," Joe said. "I think he went to get the keys and to change. Just give him a second."

"You make it sound like no big deal." Noel found a seat at the bar by the refrigerator. "You do realize those things are going to get in here in any moment?"

"Just calm down, girl. Yes, I realize that, but we still need to keep our cool. Running around like a chicken with its head cut off isn't going to help anything."

"Yeah…"

Joe found a seat next to her and they sat in silence for a few minutes. Aside from the banging at the front door, which was starting to become a regular sound, they could hear Tom shuffling through things in one of the rooms. They looked around taking in the feel of the holy man's house. It was clean and well kept. Noel pulled a large Bible to her, thumbing the pages.

"What do you think of Tom, anyway?"

"Ehh…" Noel opened the book. "I don't know. Seems cool to me. Honestly, I am used to people like him being super judgmental. Tom doesn't seem that way. He seems honest. I like that about him."

"Yeah, I can agree with that." Joe rested both elbows on the bar, still looking around. "He means well for, sure."

"Definitely," Noel agreed. "So do you think what Tom was saying is true? The end times and stuff?"

"I don't know. What do you think? You seem to have been thinking about it."

"A little bit, I guess. What if the Christians were taken up and we are left here to suffer forever? You know… that thing Tom said. That we will seek death and not find it. It makes sense. Everybody that dies is just waking back up!"

"That is true, Noel…" Joe put his hand around her. "But how does that explain what happened to you and me at the cemetery. How does that explain the dead coming out of their graves? It's not that I don't believe the end-times are possible… It's just that my parents were church goers and because of that, I read a lot of that book. I don't recall anything about the dead coming to life and eating everybody."

"John six-fifty six." Tom interrupted.

"What?"

"He who drinks my blood and eats my flesh abides in me and I in him."

Joe gave Tom a distained look. "That doesn't count, Tom. Eating Jesus' flesh and the dead coming back and ravaging on us is nowhere near the same."

"But it's still in there…" Tom laughed, stepping into the kitchen.

With the asinine grin across his face, Tom waved the truck keys in the air. He was wearing a white shirt with the words *John 3:16* in bold print. The shirt was tucked into his loose fit jeans and nicely topped off with the black suspenders. His belly pocked out over his belt. In his other hand was a golf club.

Noel busted out laughing.

"What's so funny?"

"Nothing," Noel said. "Those suspenders look pretty sweet."

"Oh? Would you rather I go change into my spandex pants and dye my hair green?"

Tom was hoping for her to laugh some more from the comment. She didn't. Her head went low and all she could do was think of Jared and his silly green hair. She bit her lip and closed her eyes, and shoved the holy book away from her.

"What did I say?" Tom mouthed to Joe.

Joe shrugged.

"Well here, Noel. I thought you might feel better with this."

She looked up to see Tom handing her the baseball bat, no longer covered in gore.

"I even cleaned it up for you."

She forced a smile. "Thanks…"

"Never have been great at golf, but I'm feeling like I've got a lucky strike a comin'." Tom lifted the club accidently bumping it to the ceiling.

Noel's smile returned and Joe laughed as dust fell in Tom's eyes.

"Enough horseplay. Let's get going before we regret it." Joe reached out for the keys. "No offense, but I'm driving."

Luckily, the truck was parked inside the garage. The garage was attached to the house. They didn't need to go outside to get to it, which explained why Joe hadn't seen it when they ran up to the house earlier. The cab was a tighter squeeze than Joe would have liked. Noel gave him a stern look, having somehow managed to still get stuck in the middle although she had clearly called the window seat. With Joe driving, Tom was too tall to take the center seat. His legs would have gotten in the way of the gearshift. The car smelled of pine and mothballs. Neither Joe nor Noel was surprised when Noel had to move a Bible aside before she could sit down. The upholstery was worn and cracked loose in areas by years of sun exposure. Although old, the red truck cranked up with ease which made Joe feel good about their trip. The tank was full just as Tom had promised; another plus.

Turning on the headlights, Joe nodded at Tom. He reached over Noel clicking the garage door opener on the visor. The door creaked and groaned its electrical protest as it slowly rose revealing more than one set of anxious legs. The garage door jittered as it lifted. The motor groaned against the pressing bodies.

"Let's send 'em back to hell!" Tom grinned.

With the door fully elevated, five mutilated and mangled figures raced forward, colliding with the front bumper of Tom's truck. Their features with illuminated by the headlights showing a tattered mess of bloodied gore. Noel jumped in her seat at their cries. Joe reached between her legs, knocking the shifter into first. The vehicle bucked, then jumped forward catching traction. Five ghouls instantly became two as the truck sent three to the ground. Rolling over their bodies, the truck bounced about as it moved forward. The sound of bones and meaty pulp reached their ears as they rolled over the dead. The other two that remained held tight to the hood. Shoving into second gear, Joe pushed the gas pedal to the floor.

The truck raced out and into the street where more of the dead were waiting. Joe had been right. That short amount of time that the church alarm had been on wasn't a good thing. It had attracted an overwhelming number of runners. As he swerved, trying to shake the two zombies off the hood, his eyes went wide with fear.

The street was crowded with active bodies.

Having been to many hardcore and metal shows with Jared, Noel looked out at the street and could instantly tell how many were chasing toward the truck. On several occasions, Jared had lost his share of ten-dollar bets to her for guessing what the turnout was at some of the shows. She had been amazing when it came to guessing head counts.

Looking at the overwhelming horde, she whispered, "Good God. There's got to be eighty of them…"

"Well, let's not stick around and let it turn into a hundred!" Joe groaned, gripping tighter on the wheel and shifted into third gear.

The truck picked up speed in a collision of bodies. The sudden jarring impact sent one of the hood riders to the ground, but the other held firm trying to climb its way up the front of the truck. It snarled with bloody, menacing teeth. The truck shook violently as is became swallowed by a wave of pressing arms and beating fists. Determined not to let up, Joe dropped it back into second and gave it everything the little truck had. Bodies were pushed aside as the truck rushed through the crowd. For a brief moment, Joe thought that with the help of the mob, the zombie still holding tight to the hood would be pulled away. But that didn't happen. Breaking through the horde, the creature still held firm. The truck broke free from their growing numbers, picking up speed after shifting gears and heading down the narrow suburban street.

Noel cringed; finally taking a breath, she looked in the rearview mirror. More than half of the dead they had just plowed through were in hot pursuit. She was thankful that the truck was much faster than they were. Ahead of the truck, a large cluster of ghouls was closing in. The herd was much smaller. The truck passed out of their reach. Finally, easing up emotionally, she looked down at her right hand realizing that she had been holding onto Tom's arm. Looking from her hand to him, Tom smiled. When she let go, his arm went from white to red, then back to its natural color. She hadn't realized she had squeezed him so hard. He didn't seem to mind.

"Sorry," she said.

"It's alright," he nodded, rubbing at the bruised limb.

Suddenly the truck turned hard right and then regained control lining back out on the road. Noel screamed, looking up at the street. The creature was still on the hood trying to climb toward the cab. Its blood covered arms and hands smeared the hood as it clawed its way forward.

"My bad," Joe hissed. "Trying to shake this damn thing."

The truck slowed. Joe put the truck in neutral, popping the clutch. With no ghouls in sight, the truck slowly rolled to a stop. Joe took out his handgun, rolled down the window, and aimed.

"Get the hell off of my truck!" The loud report made the gun kick in his grip.

The shot hit the creature in the face, sending a spatter of blood both out the front and the back of its head. Brain and matted hair blew out the back and the right eye exploded. The ghoul slumped limp with a loud *thump* on top of the hood. Joe looked around checking the street for zombies. He didn't see any. He looked at Noel and Tom wearily, then opened the door stepping out. Grabbing the immobilized ghoul by the jeans, he pulled it from the hood. The body fell flaccid to the road. Joe didn't waste any time climbing back into the truck and getting it back into gear. As the truck picked up speed and the hood rider finally taken care of, they headed for the police station as planned. Before turning on one of the adjacent roads, Noel looked in the rearview mirror and what she saw was at this point not at all surprising. The creature that Joe had just shot was working its way to its feet.

The GMC turned left down the side street toward the main streets of downtown Clarksburg. With the neighborhoods slowly giving way to small mom and pop shops, the passengers were quickly reminded of the mayhem that had so quickly engulfed their little town. Tom, on the other hand, had not yet taken sight of these terrible things. He gasped, finally realizing how bad things had gotten so quickly.

It was Tom that was the first one to finally break the silence.

"I hope you don't mind my asking, but… What do you think we are going to gain from going to the police station? Things are obviously really bad here. Because of that, I don't want to waste any time that would be better spent trying to find my wife."

With his eyes on the road and a strong grip on the wheel, Joe said, "Something like this doesn't just happen overnight without someone knowing something about it."

"So…" Noel mumbled.

"I just think that," Joe continued, swerving around zombies in the street. "There's really no reason why we should have lost connection with June back at the precinct. I think something's up."

"What do you mean?" Noel asked. "Of course, the police station could have lost contact with you. This is a small town, Joe. The station was probably overrun with cannibals just like the rest of town. You didn't get through to June because she was too busy eating somebody!"

Joe sighed.

"She does have a pretty good point." Tom frowned. "But so do you. I agree… Something like this doesn't just happen. Either somebody knew it was coming or is behind it. But what in Christ's holy name could have caused something like this other than God himself?"

"Man," Noel breathed. "The human race is pretty screwed up."

"Regardless of what's caused all of this, I hope we find out at the station. And if the station is overrun, hopefully, we can at least get in there and get some firearms."

"Then what?" Tom leaned forward looking at Joe.

"If we can't figure out what's going on there, we're shit out of luck. I guess all there is left to do is get the hell out of town." Knowing what Tom was thinking, Joe said, "And what better place to go from here than to pick up your wife."

Tom smiled. "Okay, good."

"I don't know why you're smiling. Your wife could be dead!"

"Noel! Come on." Joe insisted. "Really?"

"You know it's true. I just don't want him to…"

The sudden sound of a roaring helicopter cut her off. They all leaned forward trying to look beyond the trucks roof. The night nearly engulfed the black aircraft, but its few blinking lights gave away its location.

"Man, they're flying pretty low." Noel pointed out.

"Yeah, and it looks like they are headed in the same direction as us."

"Think they're going to the police station too?" Tom asked.

"I don't know," Joe said. "I haven't seen a helicopter like that before. Doesn't look military."

"Well… speed this puppy up and see if we can't figure out where they're going to land." Noel demanded. "You're the one that thinks we should figure out what the hell is going on, Joe. Take some initiative and put the pedal to the metal!"

As much as Noel liked what she said, because it made her seem like she was on the same page with Joe, she wasn't. She saw that helicopter as her chance to get as far away from Clarksburg as she could. As much as she missed Jared already, and was worried for her parents, worrying wouldn't do anything. She needed to get out before it was too late. Even though, none of them really knew what was going on, she felt one thing was certain. The longer they stayed in Clarksburg, the harder it would be to leave.

Joe kicked it into gear and started down the road, picking up speed. Pushing nearly ninety miles an hour, Joe's expression showed focus. There were still dead meandering in the streets and off in the distance, doing God knows what. The streets were a blood bath of chaos and destruction. With a firm grip on the wheel and only about four more miles between them and the police station, he hoped with everything that he had, that whoever was in that helicopter was there to help.

ELEVEN

Benjamin's helicopter had no problem landing on top of the police station. The station wasn't designed to accommodate such landings, but the pilot managed to bring it down just fine. The noise that the helicopter generated while in the air had attracted a lot of undesirable attention from people meandering aimlessly in the streets. With the propellers winding down and the engine off, Benjamin, Chelsea and the pilot all stood at the rooftop's edge. They looked down at the precinct parking lot and the streets past that.

"What are they all doing?" Chelsea asked.

She crossed her arms and huddled lower to stay warm. The wind wasn't blowing strong, but it was blowing enough to send chills up her spine. With it came the stench of putrescence and rancid bile. She wrinkled her nose against the stench.

"I don't like the looks of this at all," the pilot said, scratching his stubbly chin.

In the street, more than three dozen people were shuffling their way toward the station. They were coming from all directions. As much as Chelsea knew why they were acting strange, she didn't understand what was wrong with them. Sure, the company had made a mistake by contaminating the river water, but it wasn't like that was a source of drinking water for Clarksburg. Besides, even if it did mix with the drinking water, people wouldn't be acting like this. Sure, some upset stomachs and poisonings. But not this. Not battered and maimed disfigurement. It just didn't make sense. The idea that they were attacking one another didn't add up either. And if the reports mentioned that, then why weren't these people attacking each other now. They weren't attacking each other at all. They were just shuffling around in the street, getting closer to the building. It was as if their minds had turned to mush or something. Directly below, at the police station's double doors, Chelsea watched as close to twenty men and women were eager to break inside. They pounded against the doors with irritated protest. There was something unnatural about their moaning taunts. It was then she realized those out in the street were making their way over to join in with those at the double doors.

"Man, what the hell's wrong with these people anyhow?"

"They're being overly dramatic. That's what!" Benjamin said, patting the pilot on the back. "Let's just go downstairs… give a little face time and call it a night. I don't know about the two of you, but there's no reason why this couldn't have waited till morning."

Chelsea crunched her nose in disgust. He couldn't be serious. There was something seriously wrong with these people.

"Introduce myself to the cleanup crew," Benjamin said, pointing down at the vans in the parking lot. "Show a little sympathy and face time, then go home. Who's with me?"

Down in the parking lot, along with the handful of parked patrol cars, there were two large yellow charter vans. On the side of each van there was a logo of planet Earth. Beneath that were the words *Global Waste Extractions*. The *G.W.E.* had been around for a long time cleaning up messes of almost any kind. They had been there for the relief efforts of hurricane Katrina, the BP oil spill off the coast of Florida, the Tsunamis of Japan, and countless other disasters that required cleanup. On more than a dozen occasions, corporate America had called *G.W.E.* to take care of their messes before anyone ever became aware there even was a mess. They had been there when Universal Electric had a power plant meltdown in Ohio. But no one ever heard about that. No one ever heard about what happened in Georgia with the drilling industry in 2008 either. That's all because the *G.W.E.* had done their job; and done it well. Here they were now in the middle of the night in a nowhere town, making the big bucks to clean up other peoples mistakes. Benjamin's mistakes.

"I'm up for that," the pilot grinned. "Let's do this. The sooner we's get back in the air, the sooner I can get back to the Misses."

"See… he's on board." Benjamin smiled, yet irritated that he wasn't at home asleep. "Let's get this over with, Chelsea."

She sighed, and followed behind Benjamin and the pilot. They made their way through a door on the roof, down some steps, and through a few hallways. As they worked their way through the maze that was the back off the police station, Chelsea couldn't help but feel uneasy. Something much worse was going on here than any of them could ever realize. The closer they got to the front of the building, the more her stomach tightened and her throat tensed. The persistence of those outside grew louder, making her sick to her stomach.

After passing what looked like storage lockers, a few bathrooms and a hallway that led to the holding cells, they reached their destination. It took trying a few locked doors and some uncertainty, but they finally made it.

The door opened out revealing a large room with half a dozen desks. Two rows of three. Each desk had computers with various pictures and post-it notes making each desk its own. The ceiling was low and the panels were old and moldy in some spots suggesting water leak issues. With Benjamin in the lead, they made their way down the center aisle. At the end of the two rows of desks, the room veered right. It opened up to another, much smaller area near the buildings double door entrance. The dead outside couldn't be seen, but they could definitely be heard.

"You must be Benjamin." A tall man with dark hair said just as they entered the room.

He walked over shaking hands with the three new arrivals. His wardrobe was all white except for his black boots that tucked his white jeans into them. The only thing on his white shirt was the *G.W.E* planet logo on the left of the chest. Standing up next to Benjamin and the pilot only made him look even bigger. Chelsea instantly noticed his hand when he walked up to them. Having shaken everyone's hand with his left made it a dead giveaway. His right hand was bandaged and tucked away in his pants pocket. Before she could ask about it, he started laying out the details of what had happened to them so far. She cringed with every word he spoke. This was no normal waste management spill. This was something much worse.

"Hi, I'm Dane. The one you corresponded with not all that long ago. As you can tell, the situation is bad." He motioned toward the entrance to the station. "So bad in fact, I would implore you to involve higher authority. The National Guard or someone of that nature. People are killing each other out there and it has been more than an hour since I have received correspondence with several of my cleanup teams. Cleanup teams that were escorted by at least one local law enforcement member, I might add."

"First of all, Dane…" Benjamin's voice was very insistent. "The last thing we are going to do right now is involve someone like the Na…"

As he was still talking, Chelsea drowned out his voice. It was something she could do on command. He just had that annoying arrogance about him that anyone in their right mind would learn to shut out. She looked past Benjamin, who was being very stern with this Dane character. There were only two other people in the room. One was a very large, heavyset woman sitting behind a desk. Chelsea guessed that her name was June. The nameplate lying on the desk gave it away. Beside her, also on the other side of the desk was a frail old black man. They both seemed utterly terrified, huddled together. On over, there were two doors in the room. One obviously led to the lobby and the main entrance and the other was a smaller door. This made Chelsea assume it was a maintenance closet or even a bathroom. It wasn't labeled as anything so there was no telling. What made Chelsea stop breathing for a moment was the smear of blood on the unmarked door. It caught her attention instantly. She looked at it again, then at the heavyset woman, and back at it again. June's frightened expression locked eyes with Chelsea. June nodded at the blood smeared door, then at Dane, who was still listening to Benjamin rant on and on about power hungry nonsense.

"… and that's going to be the end of it!" Benjamin was saying. "Not another word on the matter. We take care of this ourselves and that's that. Got it?"

"You're just being a…" Dane started to bark back, but Chelsea cut in.

"Not to be rude… but, what happened to your right hand?" She then nodded at the door across the room. "And is this it? Is this everyone in the police station? What happened?"

Dane looked back at June and the old black man. "Yeah, we're it. When my crew got here," he said glancing at his watch. "More than an hour and a half ago… I had two teams of three. Each team has their own van. June over there was nice enough to call in some of the policemen that were off duty. We had at least one cop per team. But that was more than an hour ago. The only team I've heard back from didn't have that much in the way of luck." He frowned.

"What do you mean," she asked.

Dane lifted his right hand from his jean pocket. It was bandaged well… but was soaked with blood.

"The team leader was the only one that made it back alive."

"Oh, this is bullshit!" Benjamin insisted. "I'm not about to sit here and hear these lies."

"Shut up, Benjamin. Let the man talk!" Chelsea pushed past her boss to get a better look at Dane's hand. "You need to re-bandage this."

"I am aware of that." Dane said pulling away from her. "Like I was saying. Kyle, the team leader, made it back. But he was the only one. The two other members and the cop were gone. When we finally got him out the van and into the station, he was ballistic. Saying things…"

"Like what?" The pilot asked.

"That the people out there weren't just attacking each other. But that they were dead. But not just dead. Returned from the dead!"

"Yeah, right." Benjamin threw up his hands. "You can't be believing this shit."

"Go on…" Chelsea said, ignoring Benjamin. "What else happened, Dane?"

Dane stepped over to the desk that June was hunkered down behind. He leaned against it pulling a pack of cigarettes from his left pocket. It was obvious that he was pretty shaken up, something Chelsea didn't notice about him when he first introduced himself. He packed the cigarette box twice, and then pulled free one smoke. Not offering one to anyone else, he stuffed them away. He came away with a lighter. The embers of paper and tobacco came to life as he inhaled. With a bellow of smoke exiting his lungs, he took a moment to speak.

"You hear that out there?" Dane asked, nodding at the noise out front. "The little bit of noise we made outside helping my team leader out of that van was what brought all of them out here. And now... now, they won't go away. It wasn't until we had Kyle out of the van that we realized we were starting to gather some attention in the streets. Luckily, we got him back inside safe. There were seven of us including Kyle then." Dane took a deep breath and looked back at June and the old black man. "The crowd. There were too many of them. The three cops that were here tried to hold them back. But their persistence didn't matter. It wasn't until the first cop shot someone that we knew it was serious. There was blood everywhere and people were falling left and right."

Chelsea gasped.

"Yeah... but that's just it. They didn't stay down. They got back up. I'm talking headshots and still getting back up. Who the fuck does that? Needless to say... the three cops with weapons held back and bought us some time to pull Kyle inside. They didn't make it."

"And your hand?"

Dane shrugged then glanced at the door across from them. Leaving the cigarette between his lips, smoke pouring from his nose, he massaged his right hand. His expression suggested it was uncomfortable, but tolerable. Chelsea swallowed hard. She was smart enough to put two and two together. Kyle, this so called team leader wasn't around. She looked at the blood-covered door with fear. Her heart felt like it was in the back of her throat. Her eyes burned and she felt herself getting dizzy.

"Yep… you guessed it." Dane puffed on his cigarette a few times then looked at the bloody door. "Kyle's in there. Shortly after we got inside and did what we could to barricade the entrance, he flipped out. I mean more than normal. Hell, if I was out there and got attacked, I would flip out too. But this was different. He changed."

"What the hell's ya mean, *he changed*?" The pilot groaned; his eyes wide with shock.

"When we pulled Kyle out of the van, he was pretty banged up. He stayed conscious long enough to tell us about being attacked by the river front. They were assessing the spill zone for contamination levels. What it was is… and then …He was dead! I swear… he was fucking deader than a damn door knob."

"Sounds to me like we're just wastin' time here." The pilot interjected. "I say we get back to the roof, get in the chopper, and get the hell out of here!"

Dane busted out with a fit of coughing. Taking one last drag from the spent cigarette, he dropped it to the cold tile floor and mashed it under his boot.

"I'm with this guy. Getting out of here is the best idea I've heard yet." Dane said.

He stood up, pulling himself away from the desk. The sudden sharp pain in his hand made his face crunch up.

"You weren't done telling us what happened," Chelsea demanded. "What happened with Kyle and your hand?"

"Well," Dane sighed. "After we realized that Kyle had quit breathing, June over there…," he said pointing at the heavyset woman. "She and the old man helped me lift him. We were going to move him into the other room, you see."

"Let me guess…" Benjamin said, sarcastically. "He woke back up?"

"Exactly!" June said.

Everyone in the room suddenly turned to her with undivided attention. Chelsea could tell that it made the overweight woman uncomfortable. Her face went flush and her lips sealed shut as if she wished she hadn't opened her mouth to begin with.

"Come on… You can't be serious!"

"No one asked you, Mr. Watts." The pilot glared.

"Yeah…" Dane continued. "We had him up and were moving him into the other room when he woke up. I swear he was dead. His skin was cold and he wasn't breathing. He sank his teeth into my hand before I realized what was happening."

"And the gunshot?" Chelsea asked. "It sounded like something happened and a gun went off when we lost your call earlier."

Dane shuttered, then pulled out another cigarette. He smoked it to the butt before anyone said anything. The sound of protesters beating outside at the front door hadn't let up at all. With no one listening, it seemed so much louder.

"When I called you, we had Kyle tied up and sitting on the floor in the corner. At first, I thought he was just sick, but he got out of his bonds and attacked me again. That's when the call got dropped."

"So you shot 'im?" The pilot asked.

Dane didn't say anything. He just nodded a silent confirmation. His gaze dropped to the floor. The room filled with silence again, reminding everyone of the ensuing danger right outside.

"The part that freaked me out wasn't even shooting him. Hell… I've known Kyle for three years. Even played tennis with his wife and kids a time or two. No, killing him came natural. Us or them, just kicked in I guess. The part that really fucked with my nerves was the fact that he got back up even after that."

"He *what…*" Chelsea covered her mouth with one hand.

"Yeah, lady. I shot him right between the eyes. He was done for a minute, but only a minute. When he started getting up again, I pushed him into that supply closet."

"I don't hear anybody in there." Benjamin said. "You're full of shit."

"You don't believe me? Feel free to *man up* and open that door." Dane said. "Just wait till I'm the hell out of the building first! Trust me. He's in there all right. And nowhere near as dead as he should be."

"Who the hell do you think you are talking back to like that? I'm Benjamin Watts! If it weren't for me this town would be dead!"

"Who the hell am I? Buddy… You've got a lot of nerve. This town *is* dead. Literally! Look around. And you want to know who I am?" Dane stepped up to Benjamin looking down at him, anger showing in his eyes. "I'm the motherfucker that got paid to come down here and clean up your mess. The whole thing is…"

"Exactly!" Benjamin shouted, cutting the big man off. "You work for me! And don't forget that." He bowed up, shoving a finger into the Dane's chest.

"Your job is to clean this up. That's what I'm paying you to do, right? Well quit pouting about it and do something!"

Dane cringed, his good hand balling up into a fist. He gritted his teeth. Chelsea saw veins bulging on his neck.

"You two need to just stop it!" Chelsea said, stepping between them. "This isn't helping anything."

"Hey, man. I don't reckon this conversation can pick up after we've all squeezed into the chopper? I don't know about ya'll, but I ain't all that comfortable with lingering around. What if those front doors give way or something?"

"Just shut up!" Benjamin yelled, turning his agitation to the pilot. "I pay you to fly... *Not* to have an opinion."

"You know, pal. I've only known you for a minute of two and I already don't like you!" Dane shouted. "The thing is... I..."

Dane's left hand met his mouth with another fit of coughing. When he was finally done hacking all over his hand, it came away with red mixed plasma and mucous. He strained his eyes for a second, and then went back to leaning against the desk.

"You said you shot your team leader." Benjamin said, walking over to Dane, a hard look on his face. "I want that gun."

"You can forget that, chump." Dane said between coughs.

The excitement of shouting had stirred up the undead man in the supply closet. The sudden pounding at the door startled Chelsea. June shrieked and clung tightly to the black man crouched down beside her.

Trying to ignore the jittering supply closet door, Chelsea said, "So, who are these people?"

"Who? June?" Dane looked over his shoulder at the big woman and the old black man. "She works here; does the dispatch calls. I thought we already established that."

Chelsea nodded at the obese woman trying to force out a smile. Her face only crunched up instead.

"And what's his story?" She asked, pointing to the old black man.

His eyes were wide, like he was taking in what was happening through a magnifying glass.

"His... his name is Teddy, but most people around town call him *Shorts*. He's homeless, mute and deaf." June said. Her voice wavered, clearly nervous. "Since, I'm generally the only one here at night taking calls during third shift, I let him come in and get out of the weather. I enjoy the company late at night. He tends to keep to himself. Most people try running him off, but he's really sweet."

The old black man looked scared curled up in the large woman's arms. His frame was so thin and frail that he looked like a mere twig in her thick arms. His clothes were ratty and dirt covered. There was no mistaking it. He was homeless. Being a native to the area, Chelsea could have sworn she had seen him around town a time or two. But like June had pointed out, the old man pretty much just kept to himself. You would think that someone his age would be set up in a retirement home. But that wasn't the case. Clarksburg was too small for things like that to matter.

"I hate to break it to you, *people*. But... I didn't get out of bed and fly all the way over here just to have a small chat." Benjamin sneered. "I came down here to make sure a job was getting done. Now if you please!"

"If I please, *what?*" Dane said. "What the hell do you expect us to do? My crew is possibly dead or even worse. We can't raise anyone on the radios and we are kind of out fucking numbered. Or did you miss that part?"

Benjamin started to go down that rabbit trail again. He was going to suggest that everyone do what he said, but before he could, everyone's attention was diverted. A car horn blared out with a long steady hum. It stopped, and then was followed by three short bursts.

"Someone's out there!" The pilot said.

"A lot of people are out there, idiot."

"Shut your pie hole, Mr. Watts. No one asked you."

The horn blasted again followed by what sounded like gun shots. Between the persistent banging at the police station entrance and the irritation of the lone ghoul held hostage in the supply closet, Chelsea was surprised they had heard any of it at all.

The attention that the dead had been giving to the double doors of the station slowly dissipated. They were being draw away from the entrance.

"We've got to do something!" Chelsea said.

"No we don't!" Benjamin threw his hands into the air. "Come on. We're going back to the factory. Then I'm going home. Forget this."

He grabbed the pilot by the shoulder and started toward the back of the station, but the pilot refused.

"Didn't you hear what I just said? Let's go!"

"She's right." The pilot said. "We need to see what's happenin' out there. Those people may need some help or somthin'."

"I can't believe I'm hearing this!"

"Nobody's telling you what to do, Benjamin!" Then Chelsea looked to Dane and asked, "You still got that gun?"

He nodded.

"Alright then…" She said. "Let's go to the roof and see if we can't figure out what's going on out there. If the people honking that horn, realize we have a chopper on the roof, it's likely they hope to get a ride."

"Hell, I don't blame 'em one bit." The pilot said, following Dane and Chelsea though the precinct.

Benjamin stayed behind with Ms. June and Shorty. Chelsea was thankful for that. The prick was driving her crazy. Who the hell did he think he was trying to control the situation? The entire thing was way over his head. For that matter, over her head. She was just thankful that this Dane character was actually being pretty level headed about the whole thing. He was right. The thing to do was call the National Guard or the military. Things were definitely out of hand. When she woke up tonight after getting all of the reports, the last thing she ever expected was all of this. Some sick people beating down the doors of the hospital, maybe, but this… this was just madness. People didn't get back up after you shot them in the head.

They just didn't.

TWELVE

"There's too many of them!" Noel gritted her teeth, while holding one hand against the roof for support. "We're going to die!"

Tom's red GMC truck turned sharp to the right, almost tipping over, as the truck sped through the police station parking lot. When Joe had first pulled into the parking lot, he did see a lot of the slow zombies working their way toward the station out in the streets, but that wasn't the issue. The two big vans that had blocked his view of the main entrance had become the problem. It wasn't until he'd passed the two vans that he saw *them*. There were loads of the dead already at the doors of the station trying to break in. That only lasted until the truck entered their view.

Joe stopped the truck in hopes that he could turn around and make a getaway before anyone of the monsters had a chance to come after them. In a way, he expected these creatures to be slow like the ones out in the street.

One of the dead that were shuffling nearby called out. The feeble little grunt had been enough to attract attention. His subtle moan drifted across the night and into the dead ears of the hungry horde. One of the dead at the door turned and spotted the truck. Two runners were the first to peel away from the precinct's doors. The rest followed. All were sprinters. Not a shuffler among the group.

Getting the truck back into gear, Joe fumbled with the shifter between Noel's legs. The lead ghouls collided with the truck before the truck started to move. With more than a dozen zombies piling onto the truck, Joe couldn't see where they were going. Countless bodies covered his view. Trusting his judgment, Joe pressed forward anyway. The truck began to move. That was when the driver side window shattered by a zombie's head being driven forward by more bodies behind it.

Noel screamed that they were going to die.

With the glass no longer a barrier between the dead and the living, the zombie lunged forward with both hands and reached in, wrestling with Joe, as he tried to maintain control of the vehicle. Its teeth gnashed as it pulled itself farther into the truck. Although its features were already badly maimed, having smashed through the window had done a number on the creature's face. Broken shards of glass protruded from its bleeding cheeks and forehead. Blood pooled from its animated mouth. A loose tooth dropped out and fell to the floorboard as the monster thrashed about on top of Joe. As it was pulling itself in, trying desperately to connect its teeth with flesh, slivers of glass that had imbedded into its arms, cut Joe in the face. Joe screamed.

Noel feared that the end had come.

With the sudden sharp pain in his face and the fresh cut leaking light droplets of warm, red blood, Joe took his foot off the gas and shoved the creature forward. The thing's head crashed into the steering wheel. The horn burst out, giving way to a few more short honks, as Joe repeatedly shoved the creature's head into the wheel.

The beating didn't slow the monster down. The zombie continued to thrash about. More arms began reaching into the busted window. Mangled hands reached past the ghoul and grasped at Joe's shoulder and hair.

"Fuck…" Joe muttered, trying to wiggle himself free.

Noel screamed bloody murder. She was so afraid that she didn't even realize that she had closed her eyes. Then a hand reached from her right side. She clenched tight, ready to feel the sudden sting of teeth biting down on her face. She hadn't heard the passenger side window shatter, but she assumed in the excitement that she didn't notice it. There were so many of *them* out there that the truck was violently rocking on its axles. But the sting of pain never came. She opened her eyes to see Tom reaching over her.

"Sit back," he shouted.

It was then that she realized he was reaching for Joe's gun. A sudden *thud* hit against the roof. Noel looked in the rearview mirror and noticed that a handful of ghouls had gotten into the bed and were trying to get in from the top.

She screamed again.

"Cover your ears!" Tom shouted.

The gun went off practically in Noel's lap. She watched as the creature attacking Joe took the bullet. At close range, its head erupted in a brutal display of confetti. For some reason or another, her mind flashed to her seventh birthday. They had a piñata to play with that day and she loved it. As much as she had hoped to be the one to make the candy spill out onto the ground, she didn't get the chance. One of her friends had sent the blow that did the job. Much like the toys and candy that cascaded out from the punctured piñata, the zombie's head exploded. Blood and matted tissue flew in all directions. The back of its head blew out with the deafening blast. It sent blood, pink meaty brain, and clumps of hair across the dash and all over Joe.

"Back up, Joe!" Tom shouted, pointing the gun out the window.

Noel's head was ringing and she realized that she couldn't hear anything when Tom shouted. With the gun pointed toward the burst window, she had an idea of what he had said and leaned as far back into her seat as she could. She covered her ears with both hands this time.

The gun went off in Tom's hand twice, then a third and fourth time. The dead that were trying to get into the truck fell away, but only for a moment. That moment was all that Joe needed.

"Drive!" Tom shouted, pulling the trigger again.

It clicked empty.

Just as another set of hands started to reach into the window, Joe kicked it into gear and gave it some gas. It was hard to maneuver the truck with a rancid body in his lap, but he made do. The truck buckled forward, pressing against the mob of bodies trying to get in. The truck easily moved the bodies aside as they picked up speed. Joe gunned it, almost colliding head-on with a parked car. He turned sharp, just in time to avoid total disaster. In under a minute, the truck was circling the parking lot and finally out of the mob's clutches. Although, they had run over a dozen undead ghouls, they weren't letting up. Those that could run did exactly that. They chased close behind as Joe worked his way to the back of the building.

With no more ghouls clawing to get in, Noel was reminded of the dead that were still in the bed of the truck when a loud *thud* on the roof got her attention. She looked over her shoulder to see two sets of legs standing in the back.

"We need to shake the ones in the back," she shouted, unable to hear herself.

Joe slammed the clutch and hit the brake as hard as he could. Along with sending Noel and Tom crashing against the dash, the zombies in the bed of the truck flew over the roof and onto the hood before sliding down to the gravel. Without hesitation, Joe popped it back into first and proceeded to run them over. The truck bounced as it ran over their putrid bodies.

Then suddenly, the dead ghoul that was still lying in Joe's lap started to come to life.

"Oh, shit!" Joe grunted. "Grab the wheel!"

Noel did and just like that, Joe shoved the creature out before it had fully come to. Its teeth nearly managed to connect.

"Fuck, that was close!"

"You're telling me!" Joe said, taking the wheel again.

With no more dead immediately endangering the truck, Joe drove around to the back of the precinct. The dead chased behind with eager anticipation. Many of the slower ghouls in the streets reached their arms out as if it would bring them closer to the truck. The night air filled with the agonizing moans of the dead. The action excited them.

"Where the hell are you going?" Noel asked.

"The back of the building!"

"Fuck that!" She insisted, looking over her shoulder at the runners still chasing the truck. "Way too many of them here. We need to go. We need to get the hell away from Clarksburg."

"That's the idea."

"How exactly is barricading ourselves in a police station getting out of town, Joe?" She said, still looking over her shoulder. "With the horn going off and the gun shots, this place is going to have twice as many of these fuckers scratching to get in within the hour. Last thing I want to do is get locked into a building with *them* trying to get in!"

The truck turned sharply to the right and jumped a curb sending the truck into the grass. The impact jarred the passengers about. The truck passed the back of the building and began to go around to the front parking lot once more.

"She's got a point, Joe." Tom grunted, bracing against the dash.

"Look guys. I agree. We need to get the hell out of here. What the hell do you think I'm doing?"

"Trying to kill us, that's what!"

"Come on, Noel. Look at the roof!" Joe pointed as they drove around the precinct for the second time. The dead were in full pursuit. "Don't tell me you can't see that helicopter. If it were up to me, we would be leaving by air and not on the ground. I don't know about you, but I am done fucking around. Let's get in the air where it's safe."

As much as she was done riding around in this little truck and almost getting eaten by a hungry mob of the living dead, Joe was right. Being in the air was a hell of a lot safer than being in the damn truck. She swallowed hard, knowing that it would mean that she would need to leave the safety of the truck in an attempt to get into the building. Her toes crunched tightly in her shoes as she hoped like hell that everything inside the station was safe, and that she would be guaranteed a spot on the helicopter once it did take off. She knew how that kind of thing worked. She'd seen enough movies to know. You had to be important or have something to offer in order to get at the front of the line in these kinds of situations. And if she had to, she would play her cards and be sure to be onboard when that bird decided to leave.

A loud *thump* jolted Noel from her thoughts. The truck collided headfirst with a female zombie. The woman's face slammed hard against the hood. A spray of blood and gore splashed across the windshield as she fell limp to the side. The truck popped up momentarily as the back wheels rolled over her tattered remains. It didn't stop her, and Noel didn't even have to look back to find out. She just knew. The dead woman would be getting up, even after a hit like that. Joe turned on the wipers trying to get a better look past the bloodied mess. It smeared the gore even worse.

"Ok, Joe. If we are going to do this… how the hell do you plan to get us into the building? There are too many people out here. We would be run down the minute we stepped foot out of the truck."

"They're not people, Noel." Tom hissed. "They're the damned. They're the soulless, Godless nation."

"No offense, Tom. But now's not the time." Noel scoffed. "When I want to hear Jesus tal…"

"There's people on the roof!" Tom interrupted.

"I see them!" Noel yelled.

Joe tried to look, but couldn't. He was too focused on the task at hand.

The truck circled the precinct for the third time. Joe was doing his best to keep the truck's speed moderate. He wanted to go fast enough that the runners were far enough behind, but slow enough that when he circled the building he wasn't right on top of them. It was easier said than done. For the most part, he was keeping their numbers at the rear in hot pursuit. But that wasn't the case with all of them. The truck collided with another zombie as it ran out hoping to reach the passengers inside. It seemed like each time they circled the building they were running into more creatures that were too slow to keep up with the pack.

"We can't do this forever!" Tom contended. "We're either going to run our luck, run out of gas or eventually be over run. More of them are joining in every minute we linger out here. If we're going to do something drastic, let's do it already."

"Yeah," Noel agreed, and looked over her shoulder again.

More than thirty flesh hungry ghouls sprinted close behind the truck reaching out in hope of catching hold.

"And my vote is we…" Tom braced himself. Another zombie collided with the side of the truck as they drove past, "get back on the road and find my wife!"

"I'm sorry, Tom. I do like you and all, but I'm siding with Joe on this one. The helicopter seems like the best bet. Assuming we can get in there and in the air, think how much easier would it be for us to go find her? It just comes down to how we're going to get inside." Noel ran her hand through her hair. "We just need to get their numbers down so that we can get inside!"

"That's it!" Joe said, rounding the police station for a fourth time.

"That's what?" Noel asked.

Joe didn't respond. Instead, he broke from circling the building. Taking a sharp left out of the parking lot and back into the adjacent street, Joe picked up speed driving away from the station.

"Where are we going now? What happened to the helicopter?"

"You were right, Noel. We need to draw them away from the building so that we have a better chance at getting in." Joe's grip let up some on the steering wheel as they broke away from the massive undead numbers. "It's obvious that they're going to follow us. They proved that by circling the building so many times."

"Brilliant." Tom said.

And sure enough. Noel looked over her shoulder and out the back window. Just like Joe had said, the dead, fast and slow, were working their way toward the truck and away from the building.

"Oh, my God! I love you, Joe!" Noel reached over with both hands giving Joe a big kiss on the cheek. "It's totally going to work, isn't it?"

"I sure as hell hope so," Joe said, his face beet red and still stinging from the cut.

"How far away are we going to draw them away before we turn back around?" Tom asked.

"At least a few blocks." Joe said. "I want to get far enough away that we give ourselves some time to get inside the building. But I don't want to get so far away that the people inside think we aren't coming back."

"Yeah, that would suck," Noel agreed. "I'd hate to get back and see that the helicopter has already left."

"If that happens," Joe assured, "we'll get in, get some more ammo and weapons, and be on our way before we have any problems."

With the roads ahead straight and narrow, the truck took no time to travel a few blocks. Joe stopped the truck in the middle of the road and waited.

"What the hell are we waiting for, man?"

"Just give it a second, Noel." Joe shifted into reverse and slowly started turning the truck around to face the opposite direction.

With the truck now facing the other way, they watched as countless zombies were running them down head on.

"Go!"

"No… Not yet. I'm going to wait till they're right on top of us before I gun it."

"That's just stupid, Joe. Last time that happened, one of them practically got hold of you after bursting through your window. Run those fuckers down now!"

Joe didn't say anything. He just shook his head and tightened his grip on the wheel with one hand while readying the other on the shifter between Noel's legs. The dead drew even closer. Their frantic steps as they dashed toward the truck were like a field of track runners plodding along on the pavement.

"Seriously, Joe… Don't let them get any closer!"

"Not till I see the whites of their eyes!"

"This ain't some fancy western, Joe. Drive already!"

"Joe!" Tom shouted.

The first zombie crashed into the hood running at full speed. Joe let up on the clutch and the truck took off. It collided into the countless bodies. As they forced themselves through the mob, Joe felt a few hands reach into the busted window. He wasn't going to let that happen this time and shifted gears. The truck picked up speed passing the eager cannibals. Unlike the slow pace they took to get away from the police station, Joe gunned it and had it into fourth gear in seconds. The tailpipe sputtered blackish gray fumes as he gave her all she had. The engine roared, leaving the dead fast behind.

"Alright! Now, that's what I'm talking about!" Noel celebrated, slapping Tom a high five.

The old holy man received the excitement awkwardly, but with gladness. The plan had worked, and although it wasn't a complete fix, it would definitely buy them some time to get into the precinct.

"Thank you, Lord!" Tom praised, as they made their way back to the building. "I'm coming, honey. Just hold tight. We're coming for you. I promise."

They rolled up to the building, not wasting any time. Joe insisted that they not even bother trying the front door and head to the back. There were still a lot of zombies lingering around, but they were all the slow ones that hadn't kept up with the truck when they left. They were going to make it. As they rounded the building toward the back, Joe insisted that Tom roll down his window to see if those people were still on the roof. If they were, Tom was to get their attention. If the back doors were locked, Joe wanted someone down there to let them in right away.

Tom did, and they were in luck. There were three people still standing on the roof looking down at the truck, two men and one woman.

"Hey…" Tom shouted upward, leaning slightly out the passenger window. "Hey… We need to get in! We are coming in through the back!"

Pointing to the back of the building while getting the attention of those on the roof Tom slid back into his seat. Pulling his arm back into the cab from the window, his eyes went wide looking at Noel and Joe.

"Well…" Joe said. "Did they hear you?"

"I think so." Tom said with a smile. "Soon as I yelled to them, they nodded."

"Good." Noel grinned, looking up trying to see them. "What are they doing now?"

"I don't see them now," Tom said, looking back out the window. "I think they're headed down to let us in!"

"Awesome," Joe said, slamming his palm into the steering wheel with delight. "Let's get going before we got too much company."

The truck stopped abruptly at the back of the building. From where they were parked, they could see a part of the helicopter blades peeking out over the roof's edge. The coast looked clear. There were what looked to be about a dozen shuffling zombies closing in, but they had a minute before they would reach the truck. As they looked out at the surrounding parking lot and the streets beyond, Joe reached out for his pistol. Tom still had hold of it.

"It's empty, I think." Tom frowned, handing it over.

"That's all right. There's plenty more where this came from." Joe suggested, nodding at the building. "Plenty of ammo in there."

He ejected the empty magazine, pulled the last magazine from his belt, and drove it home. The clip clicked. Joe checked to make sure the safety was off, then smiled.

"Okay, let's do this!"

The expression on Noel's face was both excited and horrified. She didn't want to go back out there. Not after all that had happened. The image of Jared's head spitting open on the cemetery gravel flashed in her mind. She choked up a little, whimpering at the idea that she had to leave the truck.

"Don't worry. Everything's going to be fine," Joe insisted, patting her on the shoulder. "I promise."

And as if to prove him right, the back door to the precinct swung open. The female from the roof and a really tall man wearing all white stepped out urging them to come inside.

"Look out!" The red headed woman shouted.

It wasn't her tone that startled Joe and Noel. It was the fear in her eyes and the direction she was looking. Noel turned to that direction to see what was so scary. She instantly wished she hadn't. The red headed woman at the door had been looking toward the passenger side of the truck. Before she or Joe had time to react, it was too late.

Tom screamed out in pain.

They could have sworn the coast was clear. A shambler had somehow walked up undetected while Joe was fidgeting with the gun.

The creature lunged even further into the cab. Tom's window was still down. It reared back with a mouth full of flesh, revealing why Tom had screamed. Thick chunks of cheek muscle and sinew peeled away on Tom's face as the creature drew back. Blood splashed onto the pale ghoul's face from Tom's torn skin. The zombie's throat bulged as it swallowed the meaty chunks. The zombie reached in with his dirt and blood covered hands. Its left thumb sank into Tom's right eye. Noel heard the socket pop in a squirting display of gore. Tom tried to scream again, fighting get free, but the zombie sank its teeth into him again. This time on the nose. The *crunch* it made almost made Noel throw up all over herself.

"Oh, my God!" Noel screamed, sliding as far away from Tom as possible.

She pressed hard into Joe, trying to force herself out the driver side. Joe struggled against her, trying to get a clear shot, but between her pressing against him and Tom flailing with the dead thing, he couldn't.

"Let me out!" Noel shouted, still fighting to climb over Joe.

He tried one more time to get off a clear shot and couldn't. With that, he opened the door and dashed out. Noel pushed him aside and clawed her way past him. Still screaming from the top of her lungs, Noel disappeared around the front of the truck the second she left the cab. Regaining his balance, Joe looked around. In the distance, there were dead everywhere, slowly meandering toward the truck. Frantic, Joe aimed the gun trying to make his shots count. None of the zombies in the street were of any real threat, yet. Dazed by the chaos, he saw a large figure in all white dash toward the truck. He gripped the gun tightly, aiming it toward the runner. But just as he was about to pull the trigger, he saw the man in white wielding a gun as well. The tall man aimed the gun into the street and fired.

Joe looked back.

The runners they had corralled away from the building were coming back. It was only a matter of moments before they would be on top of the truck.

"Oh shit," Joe said, trying to regain composure.

The tall man in white fired two more shots into the running crowd, and then reached up pulling the ghoul out of the passenger side of the truck and off of Tom. The creature fell to the ground and the man shot it in the face three times. With each shot, the head jittered and blood splashed out onto the pavement. It didn't stay down. The ghoul started to stumble to its feet again.

The tall man in white shoved the creature down again, then said, "Help me get your friend out of the truck!"

Joe nodded, aimed his handgun into the oncoming mob, and fired a single shot. There were too many. Making his way around the truck, he helped the man in white pull Tom from the truck. His white cloths were instantly smeared in red as they pulled Tom free and carried him inside.

Joe set Tom down on the cold tile floor. The old holy man started to say something, but his mouth pooled with blood and dripped down next to him.

There was one last thing all of them saw in the police station's back lot before the door slammed shut. Tom's red truck disappeared in a cacophony of bitter grunts and mangled bodies beating against it.

The persistent beating at the precinct's back doors began.

THIRTEEN

"Hold on there, Tom. You're going to make it." Noel said fighting back tears, and holding the old holy man's hand. If he was aware that she was there, she didn't know. She hoped he was beyond pain in his catatonic state. Lying with his back against the cold tile, his body started shaking beyond anything she had ever seen. Blood pooled around his head onto the floor. His white shirt that proudly displayed *John 3:16* was covered in blood making it almost unreadable. He coughed as he tried to speak. His head jerked to the side, sending even more crimson plasma smearing across the tile. His teeth showed dark red in between as he winced silent in pain.

The zombie that had attached him had nearly destroyed his face. His right eye had been punctured by a gnarly finger. Meaty white chunks and matted blood clung from the open socket. His other eye was bloodshot red from fighting through the pain. His upper lip on the right side of his face was torn away. The mangled tissue reminded Noel of Two-Face from old Batman cartoons she used to watch as a kid. It took her all of her willpower not to look away. The tip of Tom's nose was missing. The rest of it was crunched to distorted pulp.

His coughing fit finally stopped.

Noel squeezed his hand tighter.

"I... need... ible..." Tom groaned between jittering convulsions.

"What, Tom?" Noel leaned closer.

"My... my books." He winced in pain.

Noel looked over her shoulder at Joe. He shrugged, not knowing what to do.

"The Bible," she said. "He wants one. Get him one... now! He's dying for Christ's sake."

The red headed woman stepped over and handed Noel a book. Noel took the book and realized that she had been given a telephone book. It didn't matter. Big, yellow and bulky, Tom embraced it with a sigh of relief.

A sharp pain returned and distorted his bloody face further. Tom groaned in agony.

"The... Lo... is my streng... I shall not want..." He coughed up blood, holding tight to the book. "Joe... Joe... are yo... there?"

"Yeah, buddy." Joe said. "I'm here. We made it, Tom. We made it inside."

"I need... to promise me..." Tom said, splattering bloody between coughs. "My... my wife. My... ife... Joe."

"I hear you, Tom." Joe said soothingly. "I hear you man. She's here now, brother. Say hi, man. Your wife... She's here, man."

Noel looked up at Joe in surprise and shoved a knuckle into his leg. Joe shrugged his shoulders and pointed down at the mess that was Tom. Maybe he was right. *A little white lie wouldn't hurt, would it?* She thought.

Joe coughed again, then said, "I... I love you, honey. Be strong." He believed she was there with him. His words were clear as he forced back the spasms and jitters of pain. He reached out to grab her hand. "We will be together soon, dear. Let the Lord keep you." His hand fell limp to the floor before he was overcome by another fierce fit of coughing.

Noel had never seen someone die like this up close before. She didn't know what to make of it. Sure, she'd seen Jared get smashed into the gravel, and Trevor flip out on Kelly. She had witnessed Kelly's dad meet his end too. But this... this was different. Somehow this old holy man, despite the pain, had managed to put a smile on his face. It was hard to make out the smile among the mutilation, but it was there. He projected an aura of peace. She envied him in an odd way. He possessed something she'd been looking for all her life; hope. Noel had been an Atheist for as far back as she could remember. She didn't believe in anything after death. Why should she? A person didn't remember anything before being born, so why remember anything after… right? If that were the case, then even now in death, why did Tom seem so content? Was there something to it that she was missing?

Still holding tight to his hand, she thought back to all of the theological debates she and Jared had shared. That was one thing she had loved about him. He acted as if he had life all figured out. He was the type of person who would thoroughly research a subject before forming an opinion. She silently laughed at herself as she sat watching Tom die. Maybe she had it wrong all along. Tears ran down her face. There was something joyful about seeing him go. She originally had though she was going to hate Tom. All of those holy rollers were all the same. Blasphemy this and repent that. Maybe she wouldn't have liked him as much if she had been able to spend more time with him before all of this madness. She doubted that thought upon rethinking. Tom was real. Genuine. Jared probably would have disagreed.

She was so lost in her own thoughts that she didn't feel it when Tom's hand relaxed in her grip.

Stepping away from Noel, Joe decided to use the moment to introduce himself to the others.

"Hey, I'm Joe Montoya."

"Hi, I'm Dane." The tall man said, shaking Joe's hand awkwardly with his left.

"Are you one of the cops that was sent out with the cleanup crews?" Chelsea asked, not introducing herself.

"Cleanup crews?" Joe said in obvious confusion.

"No offense," Dane said. "But we can get to all of that later. We need to do something with your dead friend here… Before he. Well…"

"Yeah…" Joe sighed, looking down at Noel and Tom's battered body. "Before he wakes back up."

"Exactly!" Dane said, snapping his fingers sympathetically.

"Well, what are we going to do with him?" Noel asked, looking up while still on her knees beside Tom's unmoving body. "Sure as hell can't go sticking him outside, now can we?"

The back door to the station shook hard and rattled on its hinges. The dead outside weren't letting up. At least that meant the concentration of zombies in the front had moved to the back of the building. The back door would be much easier to reinforce than the ones in the station's lobby.

"Where do you suggest we put him?" Dane scanned the room for a solution.

"We could put him in one of the cells," Joe suggested.

"That's perfect."

Tom's clammy hand suddenly gripped tightly on Noel's palm. It startled her to attention. His one good eye looked as if it was rolled into the back of his head. She screamed, trying to pull away as he leaned forward. The book in his other hand dropped to the floor as he lashed out.

Just as his undead head lunged within mere inches of Noel's delicate arm, a single gunshot pierced the room. Tom's head kicked back. His body went limp as blood spurted from the back of his scalp.

"Oh, my God. That was so freaking close!" Noel said in a gasp.

"We need to move him, now!" Dane said, lowering the pistol.

It was still warm in his grip as he shoved it between his belt in the small of his back. Chelsea's stare froze on Tom's dead body. She clenched her stomach for a second and then turned away.

"Oh... I think I'm going to be..." She vomited uncontrollably in the corner of the room.

The warm splash of wet leftovers hit the cold tile floor at her feet. And when there was nothing left to puke, she continued to retch in painful dry heaves.

"Here, help me with him." Dane stepped forward, gently pushing Noel aside. "I take it you know where the holding cells are and you've got access to them, right?"

Joe nodded, grabbing Tom's lifeless body by the legs. The two men lifted the body in unison. Blood and gore stuck to the tile as it pulled from the floor. As they pulled him away, blood and brain fell from his head slopping to a small pile. Chelsea, looked at it for a second, wretched, and then turned away to puke some more. Noel watched as they dragged Tom off into another room that undoubtedly led to the holding cells.

God, I hope they're going to be okay. Last thing I need is for Joe to get bitten too. That was too freaking close, Noel thought, looking down at her arm, reflecting on how close Tom's bloody teeth had almost gotten.

There was no one else in the room, but the red head and her. Noel felt alone. She didn't like being away from Joe's side. She desperately wanted him to come back. She felt safer with someone she sensed she knew. The red head and that Dane character didn't know her. Joe was her friend and so had been Tom. But now Tom was gone. He was gone just like Jared and her friends. She wanted to cry. She wanted to give up. She was finished running. She was finished with freaking out like Kelly had done. She needed to be strong, if not for herself, then for Joe. He needed her just as much as she needed him. At least that was what she hoped.

She tried to compose herself and turn her attention to the red head in the corner, but she couldn't. Her emotions were getting the best of her.

The door that Joe and Dane carried Tom through closed. The noise pulled Noel from her thoughts and back into reality. The reality was that the dead were trying to get in and she needed to see about getting on that helicopter and get the hell out of Clarksburg. But before she could do that, she needed to feel better about being in the police station. The last thing she wanted was for the dead to spoil her chance before she caught that ride. The dead continued their persistence at the back door.

She eyed the door. She looked around the small room. She'd have felt better with something blocking the door.

The room didn't have much furniture in it. There were a few tall filing cabinets and a large number of cardboard boxes containing folders thick with documents. For a moment, Noel wondered if there was a file with Jared's name on it in one of those boxes. The amount of times he'd ridden in a cop car, there had to be.

She stood to her feet and eased her way around the gore-filled puddle of blood. She went to the first row of seven filing cabinets. She tried to pull it away from the others, but was only able to move it an inch or so. Putting all her strength into her effort, it began to tip rather than slide forward. This wasn't what she had intended. A little top heavy, the cabinet tipped too far forward and slammed hard as it fell to floor. The *crash* startled Chelsea away from her corner.

"What the hell are you doing?" Chelsea asked, wiping her mouth and then brushing her hair from around her ears.

"Moving this cabinet," Noel insisted. "We need to barricade the door!"

Noel nodded at the back door as it shook with each beating of a fist. Chelsea's eyes went wide. She froze for a moment.

"Well…" Noel said, leaning over the cabinet. "Are you going to help me move this or what? It's kind of fucking heavy."

Chelsea didn't respond. She just kept looking at Noel and then at the door as it continued to shake. Noel watched the woman's eyes scan the bloody mess in the middle of the floor a few times. Realizing the woman probably wasn't going to snap out of it, she tried pushing the cabinet herself. It slid a few inches and stopped. Her arms ached and she was breathing heavy even though she hadn't been at it long. The cabinet was either super heavy or she was really out of shape. Or both.

Leaning into the cabinet again, Noel pushed past her limit. Beads of sweat ran down her brow and stung her eyes. She closed them to avoid the burn and continued to push. The cabinet started to move. At first, only a little. Then, it started to move with ease. Noel opened her eyes to see the red head beside her helping push it across the floor. They exchanged a brief smile. The scrape of metal against linoleum cut through the air as the cabinet reached the door.

"Hi, I'm Chelsea." She said, breathing heavily.

"Hey." Noel said. "I'm Noel. Here… help me get another one. I want to make sure those fuckers can't get in. And if that means I have to move every one of these cabinets, then so be it."

Chelsea laughed. "Yeah, I know what you mean. Let's do it."

It took a lot of effort between the two little ladies, but they managed. It took some time to push an additional two cabinets to the door. Noel was surprised that Joe and Dane hadn't made it back yet. At the moment though, it didn't matter. She was freaking exhausted. Pleased with their efforts, the two leaned against the last cabinet they had laid in place.

"I like your hair," Chelsea said, trying to make small talk.

"Thanks," Noel said, rubbing the shaved side of her head. "Yeah, my parents hate it."

"Well, I think it's cute. Really."

"Thanks. I like it too and that's all that matters." Noel returned her gaze to the cell entrance door. "When do you think they're going to be coming back?"

Chelsea shrugged.

"So, what's the deal with... well, you know?" Noel said, looking up.

"I don't follow," Chelsea said.

"The helicopter. We getting the hell out of here or what?"

"Oh, that." Chelsea ran her fingers through her hair. "That belongs to my boss."

"No offense, but I could care less who it belongs to. I just want to know that we're getting the hell out of here sometime soon."

The instant her words came out her mouth, she wished she hadn't said them. If she was going to make sure she had a seat on the first ticket out, she needed to know who was in charge and who owned what.

Noel smiled, then continued. "Well, what I meant to say... is, Who do you work for?"

"I work... well. I *worked* for the G.A.C. south of here."

"Oh, that's so disgusting. You talking about the freaking golden arch factory place? That's so nasty!" Noel put her index finger in her mouth for emphasis. "Why the hell would anyone work there?"

"You mean to tell me you have never had a Golden Burger before?" Chelsea asked.

"Not no, but *hell no*!" Noel insisted. "You do realize that it's called *gac* for a reason right? Because that's all it is. If you eat it, it makes you gac. And besides, I'm a vegetarian. I don't eat meat anyway."

"Yeah, it is pretty lame." Chelsea agreed. "I guess I got sucked into the American dream. I think that's been the only thing keeping me from leaving."

"That lame, huh?"

"Yeah... It's that lame." Chelsea sighed, falling silent. Her eyes drifted to the floor then at her feet.

"What?" Noel asked, able to tell that something was on Chelsea's mind.

"It's just that my boss, Mr. Watts... He's just..."

"He's what?" Noel asked, sure to remember that name.

"Well, there's really no other way to put it other than he's a selfish *swine*!"

"Wow, been holding that in much, have we?" Noel grinned.

"I'm sorry. It's just that..."

"Don't worry about it. I don't need to know." Noel said, throwing up a hand. "Besides, what the hell is taking those two so long? I'd feel better if we went to check on them. Then get the hell out of here. We can pick this little conversation back up once we're airborne. How's that sound?"

"Deal," Chelsea said, smiling.

They both stood, making their way toward the door leading to the cells. As much as Noel liked Chelsea, she was mostly just glad to know that she had one person on her side. Now all she needed to do was get Watts to like her too. Maybe then she would be set in finding a front seat on the helicopter when it did decide to get the hell out of Dodge.

Neither one of them really knew where to find the men. Chelsea had more of an idea, because she'd walked through the precinct earlier. The only part of the police station that Noel really knew was the lobby. And she knew it well. She had probably spent more than a total of four hours, out of the dozen times that she had picked up Jared, when he was released. He was always getting into trouble for vandalizing, or breaking and entering. He had always just blamed his trouble on the way he dressed, or the fact that he was a skateboarder. Noel knew better. He was a troublemaker, not someone who just got profiled. That was why she liked him. He kept things exciting.

They walked through a narrow hall that had doors along both sides of the walls. She was glad that Chelsea was in the lead. It kept Chelsea from realizing that she was crying. She missed Jared, and still found herself not being able to accept that he was never coming back.

Ahead, one of the doors kicked open. Joe and Dane both stepped out into the hall engaged in a conversation.

"… and that's it. Just clean it up like that?"

"Yep, pretty much." Dane said. He looked rough. His complexion had grown pale and the bags under his eyes were getting darker. It also didn't help that he was sweating up a storm. Tom's corpse couldn't have been *that* heavy.

"So let me get this straight," Joe said, wiping his hands on his jeans. "This Watts guy expects you to clean all this up and you've already lost, how many employees?"

"I don't want to even get into it," Dane said, tossing his hands up in surrender. "Watts is a real piece of work. Let's just say that much."

"Definitely not wrong there," Chelsea said, butting in on the conversation.

"Hey girls. We were just headed your way to check on you," Joe said. "Sorry for the hold up. Dane here was filling me in on what's been going on."

"It's okay," Noel smiled, happy to have Joe in her sight. "We barricaded the back door. Could have used some help."

"Good," Joe grinned, returning the smile to Noel. "Let's go take a look at it. Make sure it's up to code."

"Oh... and us ladies aren't able to do it, is that it?" Noel put her fists to her hips.

"No, that's not it." Joe said, patting her on the back. "Just want to see how great of a job y'all did."

The four made their way back down the hall toward the back door to look things over. While they did, Dane continued to fill them in on what had happened so far. He also showed them his hand and what had happened to his friend and co-worker in the supply closet. Noel wanted to tell Dane that he was fucked, but couldn't bring herself to do it. In a way, she felt like he already knew. It was written all over his face. He seemed on edge. Scared. Not scared in the sense that they all were, but scared like he knew it was over for him. His time was up and it was just a matter of his body finally giving up on the fight that he would inevitably lose. Noel frowned, watching him walk along. He looked like crap. As sad as it was for him, she frowned because she didn't want to be anywhere near this dude when his body did finally call it quits. She didn't like the idea that he was here with them now. If it were up to her, this dude would be locked up in one if the cells already. Having him around was just endangering the rest of them.

"If you weren't one of the police sent out with the cleanup crews, then..." Chelsea asked.

"I was... well, I'm on duty. Me and my partner were on third shift this week. They rotate the officers every week."

"So, it was just you and one other cop to patrol the entire town?" Dane said, confused.

"It's a small town," Chelsea insisted, speaking up for Joe.

"Yeah, it's a pretty small place," Joe confirmed. "Even during the day we only have three units on patrol at a time. Aside from the kids snooping around at night, nothing really ever happens around here. At least not till now."

"Where's your partner now," Chelsea asked.

"Officer Barrett." Joe's head dropped low, his eyes scanning the floor. "He didn't make it."

"A lot of people didn't make it," Noel interjected.

"I'm sorry to hear that." Chelsea trying to sound sympathetic. She just sounded afraid.

Joe shrugged Chelsea off, looking at the barricade that Noel and she had made. It looked fine. Assuming the cabinets were full, which they were, it would hold. With the door locked, nothing was getting in.

"You move these on your own?" Joe asked, patting Noel on the shoulder.

"Yep." She said, he shoulders sore against his patting hand.

He rubbed his hand though her hair shoving her playfully.

"Awesome," he said. "Looks like it's going to hold."

"Hey, I helped too," Chelsea said.

"Well, it looks good." Joe smiled. "Now that we've got that out of the way, let's go up front and talk about getting the hell out of here."

"Finally!" Noel said.

"You mentioned the pilot is up front with a few other people?" Joe asked, looking at Dane.

Dane nodded, holding his balance against the wall. His hair was soaking wet and his skin was turning whiter by the minute. With his hand no longer in his pocket, everyone could see the bloody mess seeping through the bandages.

"Man, you look like shit," Noel said, saying what everyone else was thinking.

"I'll be fine." He wheezed. "I just need to lie down. I did lose a lot of blood, you know."

"No... it ain't that..." Noel started to say, but Joe nudged her to keep quiet.

"Well..." she shrugged. "What about Tom?"

"He woke up right after we set him in the cell." Joe said.

"Exactly my point." Noel said, staring at Dane.

The room fell silent. Sorrow and fear fell on the group like a thick fog. If they were going to do something to help or detain Dane, it needed to happen real soon. He was going to turn eventually and they all knew that. So did Dane. His eyes were glossed over showing his regret and frustration with this situation. He reached into his back pocket and pulled out his wallet. He struggled to open it, revealing a small strand of photos cased in plastic.

"That's my wife," He said, spitting up red plasma. "Been married a long time, you know. I'd like to call her if I can."

"She's pretty," Chelsea said, not actually getting close enough to Dane to take a look.

"And these are my two boys. They're all grown now. I need to tell them I'm proud of them. I haven't told them that enough, you know."

"You'll get that chance." Joe said. "Don't give up, man."

"Who the hell said I was giving up?" Dane stuffed the wallet away and stood up straight. Forcing back a fit of coughing, he said, "I'm fine. Seriously... like I said, I just need to lie down for a while."

"We know, Dane". Joe started to say.

The sudden scream from the front of the building cut him off before he began.

"What the hell was that?" Chelsea said.

"Sounded like June!" Joe insisted. "She still here?"

"Yeah."

Before any of them could reply or step into action, the door leading into the hall kicked open. It was the pilot. His face was flush with fear and his hair was a mess from running down the hall.

"Come quick!" he cried. "It's Mr. Watts. He's lost it!"

FOURTEEN

With the pilot in the lead, the five darted down the hall to the room where Benjamin Watts, June, and Shorts had been left.

"Where the hell did he get that gun?" Chelsea gasped.

"June keeps one in her desk drawer," Joe said. "You alright, June?"

She was being held in the corner of the room. She nodded her head with hands raised in the air in surrender to Watts.

"Oh, dear God. Joe, you're alive." June relaxed a little in relief. "Where's Officer Baily?"

"Shut the hell up!" Watts shouted, shoving the revolver in her face. "I'm running this show now, damn it."

"Benjamin, please calm down and lower the gun."

"Shut the hell up, Chelsea. I'm in charge. Not you, or you or you… and definitely not you, prick!" Watts spit toward Dane, while keeping the gun on June.

The room was the first beyond the lobby. It felt claustrophobic with everyone crammed in. June had her back against the wall behind her desk. Watts was standing beside her desk, close to the supply closet. Everyone else was standing shoulder to shoulder just inside the room. Joe stepped out in front of the group and put an arm up, pushing the others back, and suggesting that they keep their distance.

Chelsea looked around the room. Something was missing. The homeless old man, Shorts, she didn't see him anywhere.

"What the hell happened?" Joe whispered over his shoulder.

"Shortly after we came back down from the roof, Chelsea told me I should check down here. I did. And well…" The pilot paused, then continued, "He seemed cool at first. Mr. Watts was rantin' a little to himself, but then he just flipped out and pushed that big lady aside. He started diggin' through her desk. I didn't know what to do, so I came to get y'all."

"You did the right thing," Joe assured, reaching for his sidearm.

Watts puckered his lips and mimicked Joe, saying, "You did the right thing." His voice was high and feminine. "Shut the fuck up and don't even think about it cop. I own this town. I own you!"

"Okay, Mr… Mr. Watts is it? What do you want then?" Joe said calmly, while easing up on his gun.

"I'll tell you what the hell we're going to do!" Watts shouted, shoving the revolver even closer to June's face. "You're going to start by opening that supply closet."

"What the hell is that going to… p-prove?" Dane started coughing as he swayed.

"If that man in there is truly dead… then how the hell is he beating against the door to get out?" Watts protested. "Dead people don't come back to life! That's just crazy!"

The shouting of Watts' animated voice had only excited the zombie in the closet more. The door shook.

"Look… Mr. Watts…" Joe's voice remained call. "Even if that man in there isn't dead like you say. It's best we leave him be. It's obvious he's upset. We don't need to let him out. He might harm somebody."

"Come on!" Chelsea protested. "This is bullshit!"

"No one fucking asked you, woman!" Watts shouted, waving the revolver. "I tell you what else we're going to do… Not only are we going to let that man out of the closet, we are going upstairs, getting in the helicopter, and radioing for more cleanup crew members. We aren't leaving here until all of this is cleaned up. Is that fucking clear?"

"I like that idea," Noel grinned, raising her hand. Her black fingernail polished fingers poked out from behind Joe.

Chelsea nudged her.

"What?" Noel grimaced. "I wasn't kidding. The sooner we get in that helicopter, the better!"

"Noel…" Joe said disapprovingly.

"Thank you." Benjamin proclaimed. "Finally, someone on my side."

Noel smirked.

"Figures it would end up being the stupid mall rat." Mr. Watts groaned. "Forget thinking you're getting a ride with me, Goth-girl! Go back to Hot Topic or hell. Whichever you came from."

Noel's grin quickly faded.

"Not to contradict you, Mr. Watts." Joe disagreed. "But, although you're clearly in charge. I don't doubt you there… But who are you to say who gets a ride out of here and who doesn't?"

"Wow… goes to show they let anybody be a cop these days. Go back to Puerto Rico, you stupid Spic. I call the shots because it's my damn bird. That's how. There's only room for so many of us. There's the pilot and myself, of course. Then Chelsea, because we still need to go on that date… and hell, I might change my mind and actually bring the Halloween whore. She's kind of kinky looking. I could get into that."

"Screw you, pal!" Noel shouted.

"That's the point, sweetheart." Watts laughed. "But enough fooling around. You… yes, you. Hispanic boy. Take out that gun and drop it. Do it now! That's right. Take it out and drop it to the ground."

Joe slowly removed his pistol from its holster, and then set it lightly on the floor before him.

"What the hell are you doing, Joe?" Noel protested.

"That goes for you too, prick. I know you've got that gun. Yes, you Dane." Watts shouted looking to the back of the group. "Get rid of yours too."

"I can't believe this!" Chelsea scorned.

"Believe it, sister." Watts said, as the sound of Dane's gun *clinked* on the floor at his feet. "Now, both of you kick them over to me."

They did as they were told. Watts looked serious enough and Officer Joe Montoya didn't want to risk giving this scum any reason to pull the trigger on June. She was a nice lady. A little overweight, but nice.

"Talk about a rough first day on the job," Joe grumbled as both guns skittered across the tile.

Dane's gun landed under Benjamin's foot. Joe's slid past Watts, disappearing under the desk.

"Listen, Mr. Watts, I don't want any trouble." Joe insisted.

"Call me Benjamin. I feel like we're all well acquainted enough at this point."

"Okay, Benjamin," Joe said, trying to regain control of the situation. "What now… You have the guns. Now, let's talk this thing out."

"I'll tell you what we're going to do next." Watts waved the revolver at the group. "Dane over there is going to step away from the rest of you and open up this fucking closet. Then after this little walking dead charade is finally put to rest, we are all going to sit tight, while Dane calls more cleanup crews to come down and take care of everything. Is that clear?"

Chelsea frowned in disapproved.

"What's the matter, woman?" He continued. "You're the one that said I should come down here. Show some face time. Let the people know I cared. Well, I've had enough… and yeah, let's say I do care. I care alright. I'm not about to have anyone pulling my leg and messing up my future. I'm in control. This town needs me. When tonight's over, this town is going to worship me for cleaning all this up! For exposing this elaborate hoax. You guys might have each other fooled, but no… not me. I'm a C.E.O.!"

"Open your eyes, Benjamin. What's happening is real. Please see that and put the gun down!"

"No, Chelsea. Of all people, I couldn't see you getting in on this sick joke."

"She's telling the truth, man!" Noel shouted. "We all are. I've been out there. Almost got fucking killed. My boyfriend is dead! My best friend and her boyfriend are dead too! Joe's partner was eaten to death by his own fucking daughter, dude. This ain't no elaborate joke! You need to wake up!"

"Nobody asked you, kid!" Benjamin lunged forward with revolver at the ready. Aiming it at her, he said, "I'll let you talk when I'm good and ready… now, shut the hell up."

Man, we don't have time for this, Noel thought, watching Benjamin point the gun toward her. *Dane is sick as crap. The longer we linger around with this junk, the sooner he's going to turn and everybody's going to be screwed.*

Not comfortable looking down the barrel of a revolver, Noel turned away. Her gaze locked with Dane's only to reassure her thought process. He looked like hell. A light red line of drool ran down the side of his mouth as he leaned against the wall to keep from falling down. His focus kept wavering in and out. She watched as he strained to see just a few feet in front of himself. Noel thought back to Trevor on that dirt road and how fast he had turned on Kelly. Her skin crawled just thinking about it. She was starting to regret ever leaving the truck. At least then, Tom would still be alive and on his way to finding his wife.

Then Dane slumped forward suddenly. She knew he was going to crash to the ground dead beside her, but he didn't. He pushed himself away from the wall and through the huddled group. His steps were staggering as he tried to maintain his balance. With his bloody bandaged hand held close to his chest, he reached out for Watts and the revolver.

"Stand down!" Watts shouted.

The revolver kicked in his grip. The loud report made everyone in the room jump. As the bullet hit Dane in the chest, Watts' face went white with fear and disbelief. The Earth logo on his white shirt exploded, sending blood and fabric into the air. Dane winced in pain as the bullet tore through him, but he pressed forward anyway. Watts pulled the trigger again, but Dane didn't back down. The bullet hit him in the shoulder. Dane leaned hard to the right as the bullet ripped through. He regained his balance, landing on Watts before he had the opportunity to pull the trigger again. The revolver fell to the floor, sliding across the tile. Watts fell back off balance.

Watts pushed Dane's unmoving body off and tried franticly to reach the gun. He wasn't quick enough.

Joe lunged forward and scooped it off the floor. He aimed it at Watts' head.

Watts froze, still lying on the cold floor.

"Stop right there!" Joe warned as Watts was attempting to stand. "Don't make me pull the trigger!"

"What the hell is your problem, dude?"

"I'll tell you what his problem is, Noel." Chelsea said.

Watts glared at her with disgust. She ignored him.

"Benjamin Watts, the asinine pig that he is… is the one and only C.E.O of the Golden Arch factory that opened of a few years back."

"My husband works there." June said, still against the wall behind her desk.

"Yeah,… well." Chelsea continued. "Benjamin here, wrote off on a contract that allowed practically all of the contaminated waste from his factory to get dumped into the river. Dane here," she pointed at his unmoving body, "was paid to clean up his mess."

"You're talking about the Elk River?" Joe asked, still pointing the revolver at Watts' head.

"The one and only," she confirmed. "He's been dumping contaminated meat and God knows what else into that river for the last six months or more."

"Who cares!" Watts insisted. "It's not a part of the drinking water anyway!"

"No one asked you." Joe reached over and shoved the gun in Watts' face as hard as he could.

Blood ran down Benjamin's nose. He covered his nose with his hand while giving Joe a stern look.

"This might be true, but it's the cause of all of this."

"You don't know that, Chelsea." Watts said, still holding back the bleeding.

"It might not be the drinking water for Clarksburg, but it does connect to the cemetery." June insisted.

"What the hell are you talking about?" Watts instantly shut his mouth. Joe came forward like he was going to hit him with the gun again.

"Yeah… what are you talking about, June?" Joe raised a brow.

"You guys have never been to the welcome center?" She asked.

"Get to the point!" Noel argued.

"The river…" June continued. "It runs along the edge of Clarksburg. Everybody knows that. But what a lot of people don't know is that it also runs underground right through the Stonewall Cemetery."

"Okay, let me get this straight," Noel said. "You're telling me that whatever this prick has been dumping into the river also ran underground through the damn cemetery?"

"Yeah."

"You have got to be kidding me."

"Makes sense." Joe said. "The cemetery *is* where all of this started."

"What do you mean it started out there?" Chelsea asked.

"My partner and I had reason to go out there to check a few things out and the place was overrun with zombies. But those weren't like the ones outside right now. Those were dead. I mean really dead."

"Yeah," Noel interjected. "Me and my friends were out there tonight, and the dead people, the ones that were buried, came to fucking life and dug themselves out of the ground… if you can believe that."

"That's not possible." Chelsea said.

"Ha… now you're starting to sound like your boss," Noel grumbled.

"There's got to be over a thousand graves out at that cemetery. When we flew into town, I think I would have seen something like that. A mass of people that large walking around would be kind of hard to miss… don't you think?"

"Trust me, lady." Joe said. "When I say all… I mean *all* of the graves were over turned. And the bodies that were buried in there are outside somewhere walking around! I've seen it!"

"I think the big question now is, what the hell has this dude been dumping in the river? You work for him, Chelsea." Noel said. "What the hell has this creep been dumping in the fucking river?"

"I… I don't know. I've never actually been to the waste management area of the factory."

"She doesn't know." Watts hissed. "And I'm not saying shit; till you let me up and we get more cleanup crews in to take of…"

Joe stepped forward, shoving the revolver against Watts' temple.

"If you know something, buddy, you better speak up now, before I pull the trigger. Don't give me another reason to go with the other than the ten you've already given me! It'd make my day to drop you right here."

"You wouldn't do it," Watts challenged. "You're too weak. Weak just like the rest of this little town."

"You need to shut the hell up, Benjamin." Chelsea demanded. Her face was flush with rage.

Her demeanor only made Watts laugh. "Don't tell me you're siding with these lowlifes, Chelsea. You're better than them. You've worked too hard to stoop to their level of living."

"Look, dude." Noel argued. "I just lost a friend back there named Tom. And if there was anything I learned from him in the short time I knew him, it was that life is a lot more complex than any of us realize. That includes your stupid social status!"

"Has no one been hearing anything I have said since we got here?" The pilot insisted, with one hand in the air like he was at school. "Let's get the hell out of here. Standing around talkin' about all this can wait… can't it?"

Next to Watts on the floor, Dane began to move, spreading the pool of blood across the floor. At first it was just his hand, but then it was his entire body as he worked his way to his feet. As he forced himself to his knees, blood ran down his face and chest. A harsh *rasp* came forth from his lungs like an unnatural plea of agony. Ignoring the pain that should have existed in his bandaged hand, he pushed himself up. Breaking the flesh even more under his weight, the wound leaked anew. Red ran down his wrist quickly soaking through the bandages and dripped onto the floor. His eyes were milky white like that of an early morning fog.

"Shit…" Noel whispered, stepping back and pointing at Dane. "That dude's turned already!"

Watts' eyes went wide with terror as Dane's glossy gaze met with his. Dane's mouth opened, his head cocked awkwardly to the side.

"What the hell is wrong with him?" Watts said as he jumped to his feet to back away from Dane.

"Believe us now?" Joe said, aiming the revolver at Dane now. He hesitated with his shot to further prove something to Watts.

"Shoot him already!" Watts insisted.

Dane's dead corpse slowly looked around at everyone in the room. Rather than instantly charge everyone, it was as if he were reflecting on his surroundings. It was as if he remembered something from before death. His eyes scanned left and right at everyone in the room. No one moved, frozen in fear.

"What the hell are you waiting for?" Noel shouted, hiding behind the pilot.

Her shouts had startled Dane's reanimated body. He charged forward toward June. Luckily, she was still against the wall behind the desk. She screeched as

Dane collided with the desk. The desk slid across the floor and pinned her against the wall. She cried out.

As if it weren't hard enough to get off a close range shot without risking hitting June, everyone was screaming and shouting. Watts stepped forward trying to wrestle the revolver from Joe. Just as Watts rushed forward, Joe managed to push him down. Before he was able to aim again, Shorts appeared out of nowhere, blocking his shot. The old homeless man lunged at Dane. Dane fell away from the desk to the ground with Shorts on top of him.

Joe tried getting a clear shot once more, but couldn't. Shorts and Dane were shuffling every which way on the floor. Amid all of the action, Watts went for Joe's gun again, but before he got to Joe, he froze with both hands in the air. Joe looked up to see that Chelsea had run and snagged his pistol from the ground.

"Don't even think about it!"

"You wouldn't dare!" Watts said.

"Try me…" she replied, the gun shaking in her hands.

Despite her unsteady aim, Watts stood down. Something in her eyes showed she was definitely eager to pull that trigger.

Although Shorts was a mute, he sure as hell didn't sound like it now. Screaming out in pain, Shorts pulled his arm away from Dane's gnashing teeth. In the struggle, he managed to pin Dane under his legs. Sitting on top of his abdomen, Shorts slung a hard left hook to Dane's face. The *smack* sounded loud even over the shouts and screams around it. Had Dane been alive, that hit would have jarred him senseless if nothing else. But he wasn't alive. He was dead. The bacteria in his blood from the bite on his hand had finally caught up to his heart. And if you are dead, do you feel pain? Dane definitely didn't act like it. Rather than wince from the blow to the face, Dane only lashed out more.

Shorts didn't stop either. He swung another good left, but Dane was ready. He bit down hard on the homeless man's knuckles. Dane tore away the meaty skin. With a painful moan, Shorts watched as the skin peeled away revealing white, red, and pink. Blood spurted out amid the revealed bone splashing Dane in the face. With a satisfied swallow, his teeth sank down again. This time they latched onto the old black man's fingers. With a loud crunching groan, Shorts screamed. He tried pulling away, but couldn't. Dane's grip was too much. His teeth were locked down and not letting go. Something snapped in Shorts' hand as Dane continued to bite down. Blood pooled in his mouth, as he wiggled back and forth, jittering side to side like a dog playing with a toy.

Shorts pulled free from Dane's jaws. He whined as he fell back holding his wounded hand. Three fingers were missing, becoming nothing more than a mangled mess of dangling meat. Dane chewed in robust satisfaction.

Without hesitation, Joe stepped forward, aimed the revolver, and pulled the trigger. Dane's head slammed against the tile and his body went limp. The meaty, blood covered fingers in his mouth fell as his lips went slack. The loud report of the revolver sent everyone in the room in silence. Blood ran down Dane's head, the hole off center. Joe checked the cylinder. He had two shots left. Slamming it back into place, he aimed the gun at Shorts who leaned against the wall next to the supply closet.

His eyes went wide as he looked up at Joe.

"No, don't…" June was cut off as the gun kicked in Joe's hand.

Shorts fell limp against the wall. Blood ran down his head and into his right eye.

"Oh, my God. You shot Shorts!"

"I had to, June! I'm sorry!" Joe shouted.

The room fell silent for a moment. Then Joe grabbed Watts by the throat, shoved the revolver in his mouth and spit on him.

"I'm done fucking around. If you know something, you better speak up now." Joe demanded.

Watts stood silent.

"So be it," Joe said shoving him away. "There's one bullet left in this gun and it has your name on it. And yes… this mess is all your fault. So guess who's going to help drag these bodies to the cells in the back?" Joe shoved the revolver into Benjamin's chest. "Now move!"

Watts proceeded to do as he was told, although he did hesitate and groaned about it as he started to pick up Dane's lifeless body. Joe motioned for the pilot to help Watts with the bodies. After picking up Dane's gun from the floor, he handed it to the pilot.

"If Mr. Watts tries anything, shoot him!"

The pilot nodded, taking the gun. Watts tried to sneak a smile at the pilot, but the pilot shook his head.

"Sorry, Mr. Watts, but I'm with these people. Whatever's goin' on here, I ain't playin' around. If that factory of yours is really behind this, then I recon we ain't friends no more."

"What are you doing with the bodies?" June asked, still pinned behind the desk.

Helping her get unstuck, Joe said, "We've got to lock them up. If we don't, we're all still in danger."

"They're still going to wake back up!" Noel butted in.

"What are we going to do after we put them in the cells?" June asked, stepping out past the desk and rubbing her legs.

"I don't honestly know." Joe sighed.

"I'll tell you what the hell we're going to do," Noel insisted. "Get the hell out of here."

"As much as I'm ready to go, where are we going to go?" Joe asked. "And to be honest, if that Watts guy really does know something we don't, then I want to find out."

"Agreed," Chelsea said, the gun gripped tightly in her hand.

"We don't have time for this…"

"I'm sorry, Noel, but we need to find out what's behind all of this. We can't just let him go."

"Then lock him the hell up in one of the cells. Let someone else deal with him after we've gotten to safety!" Noel protested.

"That's a great idea." Chelsea said. "Lock him up and interrogate him."

Joe mulled over it for a second, and then looked to Chelsea. "You're the one that worked for him. You tell me. You really think this guy could be capable of causing all of this? Do you really think he's withholding something?"

"This is Benjamin Watts we're talking about here, right?" Chelsea said. "He's the scum of the earth. I can tell you that much, and no I wouldn't be at all surprised if he knew something we didn't."

"Well, could they have been manufacturing something other than food at that factory?" Joe reiterated.

"It's possible," Chelsea said. "I wouldn't put it past him. Benjamin is only interested in what would make him more money."

Realizing that Joe was pretty set on getting to the bottom of all of this, Noel gave in. As much as she was ready to get the hell out of town, she wasn't going to leave without Joe. And besides, it wasn't like the pilot was going to leave without everyone else. Or would he? He seemed even more ready to get the hell out of Dodge than the others. She smiled, realizing she didn't need to force her spot onto the helicopter once it did leave. She just had to sweet talk the pilot. Hell, maybe she could even talk him into rushing everyone to leave. As much as Joe felt secure in the station, she sure as hell didn't. Look at what had happened so far, and all within the first thirty minutes of getting inside, at that.

"Look…" Noel said, locking gazes with Joe. Her words were soft and regretful. "Let's just get this over with, please. I'm ready to go. As much as you think we're safe here, we aren't… okay? We're just not. Look at what's happened. Tom's dead and we've already added two more to that list in the back. Please… let's just get him to talk and get going."

Joe stepped forward taking Noel into his arms. "We're going to get out of here. I promise."

Yeah, I feel like I've heard that before, she thought thinking back on the cemetery and all that had happened so far tonight.

"Let's just go…" She said, looking up at him.

She didn't know why, but although she didn't feel safe in the police station knowing they had a quick way out on the roof, she did feel safe still wrapped in Joe's arms. Her body went limp in his embrace. The weight of the night's horrifying events had tied the muscles in her shoulders into knots.

FIFTEEN

Noel sat staring at the blood on the floor. It was a smeared mirror image of Shorts' and Dane's recent struggle. The room was quiet and one overhead light flickered in an eerie glow of synchronized blinks. The effect was faint. In fact, so faint that she had only noticed it after being left alone in the room. She'd been sitting in the silence for more than ten minutes before she'd noticed it herself. Had it always been there? It didn't matter. Nothing really mattered anymore. Joe would disagree though. She guessed that was why he was in one of the other rooms with Chelsea, interrogating Watts.

Sure, like anyone else she wanted to know what was going on aside from the obvious. A part of her wanted to get down to the bottom of the question on everyone's mind; Why? But like that flickering light, it didn't matter. If it were up to her they'd leave Watts locked up in one of the cells and be on their way before anything else happened. The silence ushered in terrible images from earlier of the biting and the gnashing and the spitting and the pulling. The visceral images just wouldn't leave. She tried pushing them back, but like everything else, it was pointless.

That was part of the reason why she found herself alone at the front of the station. She needed to collect her thoughts. She was tired of the cascading emotions. One minute, she was freaking out of control, the next a mini-Rambo pushing her friends to keep moving. Then after that, she returned to freaking out again. She favored the warrior in her most and yearned for it to resurface. This emotional roller coaster was tearing her up inside more than the carnage ensuing all around her.

She rubbed her eyes, taking a deep breath. Her heartbeat slowed more to normal. She found herself regaining control. She focused on how she felt when pushing those cabinets into place at the back of the precinct. That was the person she needed to be. Not a frail little girl who desperately wanted her father to rush in and save the day. Noel didn't really know her dad, because he was so busy with his own life. That was beside the point. For some reason, she just felt like dear old Dad showing up, would fix it all.

He wasn't going to show up tonight and she knew better than to hope for it. He never showed up when it mattered, and now when nothing mattered, why would he?

She let out a deep breath. Just before Joe and Chelsea disappeared to hassle Watts, Joe sent the pilot to the roof. He had been sent up to make sure the helicopter was ready to make flight. Noel could tell the pilot liked that. Hell, he was even more ready to skip town than she was.

She had tried to talk Joe into giving her one of the guns, but he had brushed her off in his impatience to start the interrogation. She wondered how it was going. But more than anything she felt tired and was curious as to what time it was. She loved guessing games, like headcounts at a show, or what time it might be. If she had to guess, it was probably close to four in the morning, by now. And if that was right, then the sun would be up before too long.

She looked around the room, but the clock on the wall looked like it hadn't been working for quite some time. For no real reason, she picked up an empty shell from the ground and tossed it at the broken clock. She had watched Joe dispense them from the revolver earlier. The shell missed the clock, ricocheting off the wall to the tile. The hollow metal *tinked* as it bounced and settled on the floor. She picked up another one to throw, but before she could lob it at the broken device, the storage closet rattled. The creature on the other side moaned out in protest. The sound of the shell must have stirred the ghoul that was locked away inside.

She jumped, dropping the shell from her hand. It wasn't until then that she even remembered that *thing* was in there. Her heart raced for a moment from the adrenaline and then began to calm. No longer comfortable with sitting alone in that room, Noel walked down the hall toward the back of the precinct. The further she got, the louder the banging at the back doors became. For some reason, although louder, it was a lot less eerie and stressful.

She walked through a set of doors, and just when she could have sworn she heard Joe yelling off in the distance at Watts, June walked up.

"Hey there." June tried to smile. She still looked pretty shaken up. "How are you?"

"All right," Noel said. "You?"

Honestly, Noel didn't care. She was too tired to care. Her mascara was running down all over her face. She had to be covered in blood more than she realized. She imagined she looked about like Dane did right before he died.

"You look like you could use a bathroom to clean up in."

"You read my mind, June. I look that bad, huh?"

"I hate to admit it, but yes, child. You look like you could use some cleaning up," June said, showing Noel the way to the bathrooms.

"Your name is, June, right?"

"Yes, dear. That's right."

"Cool," Noel said, thankful to be getting a chance to clean up a little. "I'm not the best at remembering names and I can't honestly say my mind has been all here tonight."

"Can't say that I blame you." June patted her on the back after walking her through a few doors to the restrooms. "Here you go. I'll be right outside if you need something."

"Thanks a lot," Noel said, glad to have June come to her aid.

Noel sized up the large woman, like a guessing game, and started to wonder how much she really weighed. She couldn't really see how someone could let themselves go like that, but June was really nice. Although the heavy set woman didn't look anything like Mr. Rogers from the TV show, she kind of reminded her of him. June just had that quiet innocence that screamed *won't you be my neighbor.* Noel flashed back to her childhood and how much she used to love the Mr. Rogers show. The times had changed since then. Her views on life had too. Mr. Rogers just seemed like a creepy old man that liked little kids. She laughed at herself as she made her way to the sink. Maybe June liked little kids too.

She did call me 'child,' Noel thought, looking at herself in the mirror.

Noel's hair was a mess. Had anyone seen her on the street, they probably would have thought it was how she wanted it to look. But it wasn't. She looked like a disheveled mess. The ungodly amounts of hairspray, she'd put in her hair earlier that night, had only helped create the tangled mess. Looking in the mirror, she had guessed right. Her mascara was smeared down her cheeks in thick black streaks. Her eyes had swollen bags under them from being both tired and emotionally overwhelmed. She had done a good bit of crying tonight. Pushing her thick black hair back, Noel ran the water until it warmed and she started scrubbing her face with her hands. It took some effort, because she was one to overkill the eye liner. She used a few napkins to dry. The runny mess of her makeup wasn't fully cleaned off, but Noel thought it was good enough. It looked a lot better than before. It felt a lot better too. Like the weight of a thousand horrifying nightmares, the dreams were washed away, as she watched the water and black makeup swirl down the drain. She wiped the dried blood from her arms and neck. With her skin no longer sticky, her clothes felt all the more grungy and stiff from the matted gore and grime. Her shirt felt heavy on her shoulders

She sighed heavily, looking at herself in the mirror for a while.

Maybe that's all this was. A stupid nightmare. And tomorrow, when the sun came up, it would all be gone. Just a distant memory that she would never have to relish in again. She thought of Jared and what he would think of the dream. He would probably laugh at her and say the dream sounded awesome. What a jerk. She was starting to question what she had ever seen in him.

"You doing all right in there, sweetheart?" June's voice was muffled between the door as she called out from the hall.

"I'm fine," Noel replied. "Just need a minute."

"Take you time, dear."

"If you're letting me take my time, then what's the rush…," Noel mumbled softly.

She tossed the damp napkins into the trash and used the bathroom. It felt good to finally release her bladder. She hadn't even realized she had to go that bad. It was as if she'd just sat through three movies back to back without taking a pee break.

After cleaning up, Noel stepped back out into the hall to greet June, feeling a little fresher, and a lot lighter.

"See… Now isn't that better?" June asked.

"Yes… lots." Noel grinned. "On our way to the bathroom, I thought I heard Joe's voice. Are the cells close to here?"

"Yes, honey. Just through those doors there. We don't need to bother them though." June fidgeted against the idea.

As much as Noel didn't want to be anywhere near the walking dead or seeing Tom no longer dead, she wanted to know what the hell was going on. And more importantly, how much longer all of this was going to take.

"You don't have to come," Noel suggested.

"And you don't have to go. Let's just wait here till they're done, dear."

"As much as I don't want to go in there…" Noel said. "If you don't mind, I'm going to go see if we can't speed this thing up. I don't know about you, but I'm ready to go."

"Amen to that, child."

Noel smiled, not because June was so nice, but because the obese woman just reminded her of Tom. She nodded, leaving June in the hall. Stepping through the door that they had come through to get to the restrooms, Noel could hear Joe and Chelsea having it out with Watts. She followed the voices as they grew louder. With only two turns down a narrow corridor, she found Joe and Chelsea standing in the hall. She was surprised at how many doors and hallways this place had for such a small police station.

"That's not good enough, Mr. Watts!" Joe slammed his palm into the holding cell door. "I'm not letting you out until you tell me what's been really going on at that factory of yours!"

The hallway to the holding cell was wide. The walls were white cinder block and there were at least five doors on each side of the hall all the way down. Noel assumed that each door led to a cell. The doors were white with dollar-sized windows at near eye level. Below that, at waist height were round metal screens that allowed communication. Noel noticed that, because Joe seemed to focus on the metal screen, when yelling into the door at Watts. Below the screen was what looked like a six inch slit just big enough to pass a food tray. The door Joe was standing at was the third on the left. Noel's heart fluttered just seeing him as she silently walked up. The feeling reminded her of a middle school crush. She brushed the idea off and walked up behind him and Chelsea. She didn't consciously think of him that way. She wasn't even attracted to him. And even if she were, she would beat herself senseless for dropping Jared so easily. Sure, he was dead now… but their relationship had meant a lot and had been her longest one yet. Chelsea was standing beside Joe, still holding tight to one of the three guns. She didn't realize it, but she was blushing when she called out to them from behind.

"Hey, Joe." She interrupted his rant at the cell door. "Any luck?"

Before Joe could turn to address her, the door behind her jolted with a simultaneous bone crushing *thud*. Her heart sank, and then leaped into her throat as she swallowed hard. She spun around to meet the door behind her. Goose bumps ran up her arms, making her body flash from hot to cold.

"Oh shit…," she said.

Dane's snarling face and blood covered fingers pressed against the small dollar sized window in the cell door. Blood smeared across the glass as he beat against it in protest. Noel stepped back, bumping into Joe. Her eyes scanned the other doors to see Tom in one and the old black man in another.

"Oh, my God. They're all dead." Noel gripped the chest of her shirt, her muscles tightened in fear.

"Well… yeah." Chelsea said. "I thought you had already figured that one out."

"I did," Noel scorned, stiffening to her full height and turning to face her friends. "Still… they startled the shit out of me!"

"Sorry about that," Joe said over the noise of their fists pounding against the cell doors. "Should have warned you."

Noel smiled and then pulled it back the moment she realized Chelsea had seen it.

"So… Any luck with the Mr. Watts dude? If not, let's go already," Noel groaned.

"I'm working on it!" Joe insisted.

"What the hell do you plan to pull out of this dude anyway?" Noel asked. "Even if he did tell us something, what the hell would you even do with the information, once you had it, huh?"

"Well… I…"

Noel cut him off. "Like seriously, Joe. Let's say just for shits and giggles that this dude talks. You get what you want out of him and boom! We have someone to point the blame at. Awesome. Well… guess what. As soon as we get out of all this and people get sent in to clean this shit up, not only is it getting cleaned up, it's getting covered up. This is America. That's just how it works."

From within the cell, Watts started laughing. "Thanks… at least one of you realizes this is a big waste of time. Now let me out!"

"No!" Chelsea shouted, slamming the barrel of her gun into the cell door. "I don't care. I'm tired of people like him getting away with this type of crap. This is my hometown for crying out loud. He's not going to get away with what he's done. You hear me! You are going down for this, Benjamin."

"Wow… Hold a grudge much?" Noel lifted her hands at Chelsea. "Look… I've got just as much right to go all hell fire and brimstone. This is my hometown too. Hell, I've lost some people tonight. But pointing the blame right now's not going to solve anything. We need to be focused on getting out of here alive. Not slapping somebody on the hand."

"Amen, sister." Watts chanted from behind the door.

"Hey, fuck you, pal. Nobody asked you." Noel said. "And cut the holy crap!"

Unlike when June had said it, he made her blood boil just hearing that word.

"Look," Joe said resting his hand on Noel's shoulder. "We just need some time with him. I know you're ready to go. You're not the only one that's made that very apparent, okay. You want to know why I am doing this? I'm doing this, because you're right. This kind of stuff always gets pushed under the rug. And my first day on the job or not, I don't aim to let that happen. Somebody needs to tell the world, and if that somebody is going to be us, then please… just give me some time so that I can figure out what the hell it is we need to tell. All right?"

Noel nodded, shrugged, and sighed all in one. No matter how convincing Joe made it sound, it was a waste of time in her eyes. The dude in that cell probably had enough money to clear his name and any other person's name he wanted to when this was all over. Yes, Watts was a complete ass for letting his factory dump countless amounts of waste into the river; a river that apparently had underground streams that happened to somehow infect an entire cemetery. He might be a prick, but it wasn't as if he knew something like that was going to happen. He sure as hell seemed clueless from what she could tell. Hell, this guy thought that the man in the supply closet was still alive.

"Yeah. It's whatever," Noel said.

"Okay, good!" Joe said. "We're going to figure this out."

Chelsea smirked. It looked sarcastic in a way. Noel didn't know it for sure, but it looked like Chelsea was a major part of the driving force behind the idea to interrogate Watts. Noel didn't like that one bit. Didn't like her being alone with him. She brushed it off and left them to what they were doing.

In the hallway by the restrooms, Noel was surprised to find that June was no longer there. She wondered where she could have gone. Maybe, she was back in the office right outside the lobby at her desk. But what for?

She made her way back to that part of the police station, blood still all over the cold tile floor and a deader than dead zombie agitated in the supply closet. She looked up at the broken clock, still wondering what time it was. The curiosity getting the best of her, Noel opened the lobby doors and walked inside. June was nowhere in sight. Ahead was a double door with one large desk leaning against it. There was blood on the floor. It looked as if someone had been dragged through the room, smearing the blood in a straight line, through the door she had just opened. Unlike the rest of the precinct, the lobby floor was carpeted and the blood had soaked into the fabric.

Chairs and a few tables, covered with magazines, lined the walls. On the wall to the left was a poster of missing people. She scanned the black and white photos, but didn't recognize anyone. On each side of the double doors, there was a window as tall as the door. The glass was about as wide as her body from shoulder to shoulder and reached from the top of the doors to the bottom. She stepped around the desk barricade to look outside. A light breeze filtered through giving her chills. With it came the stench of the dead. The rotting putrid odor reminded her of the cemetery. She glanced over to see that the door was opened just a crack letting the air in. She was instantly glad that they had corralled the dead to the back of the building. There was no telling how much longer this barricade would have held. The desk didn't even look that heavy.

Noel looked out the window to see a few cop cars lining the parking lot. Two large yellow vans, the ones they had seen when they drove in, still sat there. In the distance, the night sky looked as if it was starting to break into lighter grays. The sun was getting ready to break for sure. Man, she wished she knew what time it was. There were ghouls still lingering out in the streets and even a few in the parking lot. Aside from that, everything seemed pretty quiet.

Suddenly, a man with green hair popped out from behind one of the vans. He was there one second and gone the next. That couldn't have been Jared. It just couldn't. That would be ridiculous. Then again, everything about tonight had been really messed up. And to confirm her initial thoughts, the man appeared again.

Oh, thank God. It is Jared, she thought tapping on the glass with her knuckles.

Instant regret.

The thing that was Jared jerked hard to the right facing the precinct entrance. Its neck was twisted. Bone jutted out from the side. Red and black dried blood soaked the area around the wound running down the shirt. It was Jared all right. Noel grimaced upon reading the band name on the shirt. *August Burns Red* was clear as day across the front, even with the bloody mess. Had Jared's favorite band not given it away, the beard would have. No one else in Clarksburg had a beard and green Mohawk. Jared's reanimated corpse jittered and jerked with excitement as it examined the double doors across the parking lot. The side of his head looked like it was smashed in, making the memory of his attacker tackling him to the ground flash in Noel's mind.

Noel swallowed hard and felt something crack inside her throat. Her eyes went wide with fear. Her feet felt like they were welded to the floor. Her knees buckled. Although she had already gone to the bathroom, Noel felt something warm and wet begin to run between her legs and down onto her steel-toed boots. The smell lingered for a moment, before she realized she had just pissed herself. And rightfully so. It wasn't the sight of Jared that had her shaking in her boots. It was all of *them* that had her frozen in fear.

The stench of rancid decay grew strong as the breeze from the door reached her nose. Jared slushed toward the door at full speed. She wasn't worried about him and the fact that she was looking at him now as a reanimated ghoul. It didn't bother her nearly as much as she figured it would. It was the hundreds of ghouls shuffling behind that made her panic.

Jared slammed into the doors at full speed. The door rattled, jarring Noel from her catatonic stupor. As Jared pressed against the doors, calling out like a ravenous banshee, the desk shook against the blood covered carpet. That didn't stop her from looking out at the dead as they shambled toward the doors in enumerable droves. These dead were different and Noel instantly recognized them. They were the dead from the cemetery. All of them. Their skin was sucked tight to their boney bodies. As they meandered across the lot and the streets breaking the shadows, dust and dirt still fell from their bodies. Jared beat against the door to get in to feast on Noel. It was attracting the others.

Eyeless and mangled, they made their way toward Jared's irritated attempts to get inside. Festering with worms and unimaginable bugs, even in the dusk of night, Noel could see things crawling in and out of their sores and holes.

In disbelief, she looked on as the dead continued to stumble across the lot, a sea of bodies coming from all directions. She could only guess that they had spent the entire night working their way toward town finally making it to the police station.

It wasn't until the first rancid bone-dry zombie stumbled into view past the parked vans that Noel screamed. Her throat felt hot and the sound bellowed out from deep within. Filling the back of her throat with blood, the screaming didn't seem to end.

SIXTEEN

"Did you hear that?" Chelsea said, turning her attention down the hall.

"That sounded like Noel!" Joe grimaced at the thought.

They stood silent for a moment, listening intently. The high-pitched scream stopped only to continue again. Joe swallowed hard, his stomach twisting in knots.

"Yeah, that was definitely, Noel," He confirmed.

Stepping away from the cell holding Watts, Chelsea leaned in close to Joe and whispered. "Why don't you go see what's going on. I'll stay here and make sure this loser doesn't try anything stupid. I'll see if I can get him to tell me something. He's a *pig* if you catch my drift. Maybe he'll talk if I let him think I'm on his team," she winked.

"All right," Joe said. "I'll be back in a minute. Hopefully, it's nothing serious."

He retrieved his handgun from its holster, checked the safety, and began to walk down the hall. Just before reaching the door, he looked back to see Chelsea smiling back at him. She waved the revolver to let him know that she was in control of the situation. The hall was silent as he stepped out. He disappeared, closing the door and headed to find Noel.

Chelsea cringed as she turned her attention back to the cell.

"Smart move, getting that guy out of here." Watts said, leaning against the cell door. Unlike before, when he'd shot Dane, his voice was calm and assertive. "Now, let me out. Let's get out of here before he comes back."

He reached between the slit in the door softly touching Chelsea's arm. She let him feel her for a second and then slapped his hand away with the butt of the revolver. His hand retracted back into the cell. He hissed out in pain.

"You bitch."

Maybe for once, Watts was right. She was a bitch. She was a bitch for letting him get away with so much for so long. In the time she had spent as his personal assistant, she had watched him sign off on more than just that damn contamination contract. She should have stopped him well before the factory waste started being dumped into the river. Well before all of the sexual harassment and name calling. She wasn't his babe, his woman or a whore. That's right. She hadn't heard him call her that to her face, but she had heard him refer to her as such to others. Men mostly. She had let it all slide and for what? Better pay? Better living and a nice house away from Clarksburg. She had spent her entire adult life running away from this small town. Now that she'd finally succeeded, she felt ashamed. What would her parents think if they knew what she had sacrificed to gain her successes? Sure, her parents had made the drive a time or two to her new home outside of town and her dad on many occasions expressed his feelings. He was proud. She had done so well for herself in such a short time. But at what cost? She had helped Watts cut so many corners to make that extra buck, and had even turned her eye from the waste management contracts, although she knew better. Thinking about it made her feel sick. She made herself sick. Did she even know herself anymore?

She turned to the window looking in at Watts. He was still rubbing his hand. She glared at him. Silently, she lifted the revolver and pointed into the cell through the six-inch slot. She coughed to get his attention.

"Hey, now…" He looked up. "What's the deal here?"

She cocked the hammer to the safety position. It clicked as she slowly pulled it back.

"Hey, now!" Watts protested. "What the hell are you doing? Put that away!"

"Give me just one reason why I shouldn't."

"How about for starters we get you a new office." His voice wavered. "A… a few m-more digits on the paycheck. Is that it? Is that what you want? Just let me out of here and we'll make it happen. I swear!"

"Not good enough!" She insisted, pulling the hammer back even more. It clicked home ready to slam the cylinder if she pulled the trigger.

"Stop this right now, Chelsea. You've made your damn point, all right?"

"Oh, have I, Benjamin? I don't think I have. But oh… you better believe I'm going to."

"What's that supposed to mean?" Watts looked to the wall as if he could see through it to the hall. "Help me!" He shouted. "Get this stupid bitch away from me! You've lost it, woman."

"That's the last time you're going to call me *woman*. I have a name, you sexist pig."

She shoved the gun forward, but it slammed against the hole not going any further into Watts' cell. The metal clank echoed down the hall as the two solids restricted one another. Had she turned the gun to its side it would fit through the opening, but she didn't. Instead, she pulled the gun back again leaving just the barrel peeking through the opening.

"You think I don't know what's going on here?"

"What the hell are you talking about, wo…" Watts coughed, both hands over his head. "I mean… Chelsea."

"Don't play dumb, Benjamin. Earlier, back with all the others… you said I didn't know what's going on. Well I do."

His eyes rolled around in his head, trying to decipher what she was talking about. Chelsea laughed, able to tell that he was in deep thought and had no clue what she was getting at.

"Oh, come on now… You mean to tell you me you think I'm just some dumb blonde you hired to play cute? Well I'm not. Number one, I'm a redhead. That was your first mistake. Your second was to think that I don't read everything that comes across my desk. It's my job. *Remember*?"

"What…" Watts pleaded.

"Does *Jewel Venom* ring any bells, Benjamin?"

"W-what the hell a-are you talking… about?" Watts stumbled over his words.

"That's right, Benjamin. I read over the files. What the hell have you done? What the hell have you gotten into? More importantly, what the hell have you gotten Clarksburg into?"

"I don't know, all right!" Watts yelled, his voice unconvincing.

The cell fell silent. She sighed, tired of beating around the bush. She glared through the glass in the door with vengeful eyes. Watts stared back, but only for a moment. His gaze broke, falling to the floor. His eyes glossed over with shame and disgust. Chelsea imagined that what he was feeling had nothing to do with what he had done and everything to do with getting caught. He hated not being in control. His sorrowful expression was probably nothing more than the remorseful feeling of realizing he had messed up down the line. Messed up by letting Chelsea have full access to his files or not hiring someone with less brains and more breasts.

Chelsea slammed the barrel of the revolver into the door, jarring her boss from his silent daze. He looked up wide eyed and tense.

"I am only going to ask one more time. What is *Jewel Venom*?" Her words were firm.

"What the hell are you asking me for? You read the damn files!"

She didn't respond, but only glared harder.

"Okay, look…" he said, then coughed, clearing his throat. "Nationwide sales have plummeted over the last…"

"It always comes back to money with you, doesn't it?" She shouted, cutting him off.

"You want me to talk or not? This whole thing wasn't my fucking idea, all right? Corporate put me up to it."

Chelsea nodded, suggesting he continue.

"Like I said… Nationwide sales have plummeted in the last few years for the fast food industry. Golden Arch isn't the only company feeling these effects, okay. With the economic slump and the push for everyone to become environmentally friendly, things are changing. The world's going in a new direction. You can't tell me you haven't noticed."

"What does any of this have to do with what's going on out there?" Chelsea demanded, waving her hands toward the invisible parking lot and beyond outside.

"Just give me a second. Damn."

She sighed, letting him continue.

"With the push for everyone and everything to go green. More fuel efficient cars. Global warming. The war in Iraq. People are becoming more aware. Not only of what's going on around them and about the cause and effect of their choices, but they are paying more attention to themselves as well."

"What the hell are you getting at, Benjamin?"

"People are opposing the fast food industry. More and more people are not eating meat for health reasons and it's hitting the corporation hard. If we…"

As Watts was rambling on, Chelsea's minded drifted off. More people not eating meat? Vegetarians? Although Chelsea had no freaking clue where Watts was going with all of this, her mind drifted to a certain young Gothic girl. Noel's face flashed in her mind. She thought back to the conversation they had at the back of the building. Noel had been pretty disgusted when Chelsea had mentioned who she worked for. Even laughed at the company acronym. Chelsea silently laughed to herself not ever noticing it before now.

G.A.C.… Because it makes you want to gac, she thought, looking back up at Watts who was still talking.

"… and that's when Corporate stepped in. It was their idea. Not mine."

"What the fuck, does sales and health have to do with any of this shit?" Chelsea said.

"Have you not been listening to a word I've said, woman?" His eyes went wide, regretting the word.

She didn't notice.

He swallowed hard and he continued before she had the chance to pick up on the demeaning remark. "With the decline in sales and people becoming more aware of what they eat, things for us had become drastic. Do you know what the obesity rate is in America? More than a third, Chelsea. And that's just the adults. Hell, look at that June lady that works here at the station. It's out of control. And you know who they're pointing the blame at? Us… Not just the fast food industry, but corporate America in general. That's why something drastic had to happen you see."

"You still haven't answered me, Benjamin. What is Jewel Venom?"

"Seriously, Chelsea. Why do I have to go over this? You've read the files."

"I only skimmed them, all right. And a lot of it went over my head. Like Octopimia-something. What the hell is that?"

"Octopamine," Watts laughed. "The corporation. The boys at the top. About three years ago, right before we opened the factory south of here, they teamed up with company involved in Neurogenesis or some shit. I really don't know what they're about. Something to do with the brain. Chemicals and stuff."

"As if you weren't already pumping stuff into the food as it is, Benjamin. What is it?"

"Well, I don't know exactly, to be honest. All I know is that the Jewel Venom is actually from some wasp overseas. The new factory was set up, not only to take care of product demand, but to also test out this new chemical."

"Venom, Benjamin? You didn't think this might kill some people? What the hell where you thinking? Or where you thinking at all?"

"That's the thing, Chelsea. This wasp venom isn't like that. It's from some wasp called the Jewel wasp and the chemical that it affects in its victims is something called Octopamine. That's what really caught our attention. That's why they've been testing it out at our factory. In bugs, this octo-thing is related to the chemicals in the brain and causes temporary paralysis."

"So this wasp that you're talking about puts its victims in a catatonic state? How would putting people in comas increase sales? Why the fuck would you even think about associating that with the food industry. That's just idiotic, Benjamin."

Watts shrugged, and then continued. "It wasn't my call. I just run the plant. You know that. And besides, the effect that this venom is supposed to have on humans is totally different. Octopamine in bugs is different in humans. In bugs, it dealt with motor function and in humans it regulated fat in the body or some shit. I don't know. The venom attacks the same chemical in both bugs and humans."

"Oh, yeah, Benjamin?" Chelsea shouted. "And what effect were you going for exactly? Cannibalistic crazies? Cause that's what you ended up with!"

"I don't know what went wrong, okay? I didn't plan this. Any of it. Corporate had it in their heads that this Octopamaine chemical in humans had something to do with the fat cells in the body. I said that. The goal was to create a burger that had all the great attributes of fast food, while offering a unique way to lose weight. The wasp venom, under the right conditions, was supposed to trick the neurons in the brain into attacking fat cells. The venom manipulates Octopamine somehow. I don't know how it works."

"And you weren't worried about long-term side effects or anything?"

"That's not my job!"

"It never was, was it?" Chelsea felt sick to her stomach. "Well, I'd say your little science experiment worked, Benjamin."

"This wasn't planned!"

"Just like you didn't plan on dumping it all into the damn river?"

"That was another one of corporates ideas. We had to hide the fact they we were testing various venoms. Dumping the failed test subjects was the best way to get rid of the evidence."

"Test? Subjects… really?"

"Just dumb chimps mostly. Like anyone cares about…"

"Shut the hell up!" She insisted, slamming the heel of her shoe into the door. It shook, startling Watts.

He squirmed against the wall. His arms fidgeted at his sides. He was clearly afraid of what she might do, or what might happen in general. Chelsea grinned, watching through the glass in the door. Seeing him on edge pleased her. Her heart filled with pride knowing that this chauvinist pig wouldn't be getting away with any of this. Or would he? Noel had made a pretty valid point earlier. Guys like Benjamin Watts were loaded with money and had pull in every branch of government. They were above the system. If he got out, he'd just pull some strings and clean his hands of all this in a heartbeat. That wasn't fair. Life wasn't fair. Not to the dead outside trying to get in and not to her. She didn't disserve to get caught up in all of this. And she sure as hell wasn't getting dragged down with him either. Watching him wiggle awkwardly made her fell bigger. Feel in control. She liked it. Maybe this was why Watts was the way he was. Addicted to the rush. She felt the blood coursing through her veins and each enthralling beat of her heart as it pounded against her chest. A chill ran up her spine as she smiled at him looking frail and defenseless.

"You think you're going to get away with this. Don't you?"

As much as he tried to hide it, the smile showed through. "Come on, Chelsea. You know as well as I do that we try helping…"

"Don't even pretend!" She shouted, cutting him off once more. "Just answer this; have you already introduced this Jewel nonsense into the market?"

Watts fell silent. His eyes scanned the floor around him. She couldn't tell, but it looked like he was holding his breath. Watts ran his fingers through his hair, stalling to answer her. He shuffled his feet and coughed.

"Well…" She insisted. "Is it in the open market or not, Benjamin? God help us all if it is!"

"It's not, all right?" Benjamin stomped. "They were in the testing phase still. How the hell was I supposed to know that any of this would happen? Underground rivers that go through the fucking cemetery?" He threw his hands in the air. "Underground rivers… give me break. That *June* lady doesn't know what she's talking about. Stupid fat bitch. And even still, so what if the underground rivers are there? Like I was supposed to know about them or that the shit we were pumping into the river would end up under the damn cemetery."

"Actually, Benjamin." Chelsea scratched the scalp of her head with the revolver. "That type of information *is* something you should have checked on."

"You're absolutely right, Chelsea. I'm sorry!"

Chelsea gritted her teeth against those words. "Do you really mean that, Benjamin?"

"Truly… I do!" Watts insisted. "I've realized the error of my ways."

"Well… in that case," she said, unlocking the cell door. "Let's see about reversing this mess."

"That's what I've been trying to get at the entire time. Finally… you see it my way." Watts smiled, stepping toward the door, eager to leave the cell and get to the helicopter.

She stepped aside letting the door swing open to the groans of the hinges. Watts stepped out. Smiling ear to ear, he nodded at Chelsea as she let him pass.

"I'm glad you're finally seeing things my way, Chelsea. We need to get some more cleanup crews in here to take care of this. Then, when this has all blown over, we can start anew. Bigger. Better. More."

"Yep... we sure can." Chelsea sighed as Watts started walking down the hall. "We sure can."

"What's that?" He asked and turned around to face her.

Chelsea blacked out when the gun went off. The loud report of the revolver rocketed through the room as she squeezed down on the trigger. The gun kicked in her hand exciting the three dead prisoners in their cells. Dane, Tom, and Shots all moaned in harmonious agitation. The doors jolted and jittered against the persistent beating of excited undead fists. Her knees buckled and her vision began to blur. She felt faint. The last thing she saw before total darkness overwhelmed her was blood and meaty tissue exiting from Watts' throat. His eyes went wide with terror and disbelief. Both hands became covered in crimson as he grabbed at the bloody mangled wound.

SEVENTEEN

With pistol at the ready, Joe Montoya ran through the precinct toward Noel's screams. Had he known the job would have been this demanding, he would have gone to college to become a lawyer. This was just outlandish. The dead returning to life. His partner dying in front of him. He had even shot someone. He'd never even fired his gun before, other than at the range. All of this happening on the first night on patrol.

With each foot in front of the other, he darted through a set of doors and down the hall toward the lobby. Joe's heart raced with thoughts of the inevitable. He had seen too much tonight. Had let too much happen to those around him and he wasn't going to let that be the case with Noel. He came to the front office after turning the corner. He couldn't help, but think that the lone ghoul in the supply closet had finally broken free, and was only moments away from devouring Noel's helpless body.

Joe leaped into the room, while panning the gun back and forth, ready to fire. The room was empty, the supply closet still closed. The door leading to the lobby was partially open. Hammering fist against the doors and ravenous howls of eager entry reached his ears.

"Noel?"

"Oh, dear God. Joe!"

Joe raced into the lobby. The doors leading out into the parking were buckling inward. The desk holding it closed was sliding across the carpet. A dozen bloodied and mangled skeletal hands reached in from outside.

"We need to go!" Joe shouted.

He grabbed Noel by the shoulder and tried to pull her away. She didn't budge.

"J-Jared's out there?"

"Who? What?"

Before she could answer, the door behind them kicked open. June crashed into the room.

"I heard some screaming. What happe… Oh my God!" June's mouth dropped open as her gaze fell upon the massive horde pressing against the entrance to get inside.

The double doors swung wide open from the mass of bodies. The desk tipped back, and forced Noel to the ground. She screeched out in pain as it pinned her leg beneath.

Joe dropped to her aid, but before he could pull her free, Jared's mutilated body climbed over the desk and crashed into him. Joe lost grip on the gun and held the creature's head at bay to avoid the gnashing teeth. It fought desperately, but Joe's hold was solid. He fell back into a row of chairs as Jared's reanimated body wrestled him to the ground. June and Noel both screamed as the horde of undead, rotting bodies slowly shambled into the lobby, trying to climb the large desk in their way. The stench of rancid decay filled the air as they piled in.

Joe's eyes watered against the odor as he pushed Jared away. Jared crashed into the wall on the other side of the lobby, but unlike his mangled brethren, he was a runner. He quickly regained his undead footing. Joe took the opportunity to retrieve his pistol, but he hadn't seen where it had landed.

Finally, he located the gun under a chair and snatched it up. Before he could aim it at his attacker, the green haired zombie changed course.

June turned to run, but it was too late. Her attacker was too fast. Jared leaped onto her back in full sprint.

June flew forward, and slammed face first to the tile, splashing blood across the floor as her face collided with the cold linoleum. Her nose erupted, filling with blood as cartilage and tissue folded upon impact. Straddling her back, Jared fell on her with gnashing teeth.

Joe stood, aimed the gun and fired. Jared fell limp onto the obese woman. Meat and torn fabric from June's back fell loose from his lips. The hole in the back of his head bled out from the bullet entry. Joe turned to help Noel, but she was already at his side, pushing past him to run. Joe looked past her at the double doors. More than five zombies had already made it over the desk and had risen to their feet. The doorway was so thick with bodies that Joe couldn't see past them. He only saw one dry skin-tight corpse after another. Riddled with worms and festering things, not a single undead ghoul had eyeballs. The years of rotting under the earth had turned them to dust. Joe didn't know what was worse. Dealing with fresh runners or having to look at the rot festering puss buckets of decay. His throat felt dry as he breathed in the awful aroma that permeated the lobby.

Noel didn't stop running. She jumped over Jared's unmoving body and disappeared around the corner. Joe looked up to see her sprint away in fear. Even though Joe's shot hit home, blowing out the undead punk's brains, it didn't matter. Jared would be up and moving around in minutes.

Joe ran out of the lobby, closed the door behind him and pushed Jared's lifeless corpse off June. June's back had been bitten. Joe sighed at the disheartening sight. She was a good woman. She wasn't moving, but he could see that she was still breathing. Kneeling closer to check her vital signs, the door behind him rattled. Joe jumped, looking back.

Joe grimaced, not wanting to leave June behind. But she was out cold and there was no way he could carry her. And besides, it was too late. She was a goner. He looked down and examined the peeled meat and blood on her back.

"I'm sorry, June." He said, and stepped away from the shaking door.

As Joe reached the corner to leave, the bursting wood and shattering framework of the door exploded behind him.

Over a dozen rot decomposed ghouls fell to the floor on top of June. Joe gasped in horror as he watched them begin to feast. More of them fumbled through the opening to join in on the cannibalistic madness. With rotting boney fingers, they tore through her clothing. As if it were just as easy to peel away, the ghouls tore into her skin pulling at the meaty flesh. June suddenly woke up screaming as the dead feasted on her. Joe watched, as she tried standing to her feet, but the dead were too many. She was overwhelmed. A female zombie reared her head and bit down on June's thick arm. Blood splashed around the wound as the undead creature thrashed about with her arm in her mouth. Even with her loud screamed, Joe could hear the crunch of meat as the ghoul's teeth sank deeper into the arm peeling flesh away like dried Play-Doh. June's skin tore with a wet smack splashing the female thing in the face like red paint from a bursting water balloon. June's cries started to fade as more than two dozen sets of teeth sank into her body on all sides.

Joe pushed back the urge to vomit as he looked on. He aimed the pistol into the horde feasting on his co-worker. Dust and black ash erupted from splintering ribs and skulls with each pull of the trigger. With the plume of dust came the pungent odor of death. Joe coughed against the stink. Just when he though the gagging was going to get the best of him, more zombies piled into the front office from the lobby. June's body disappeared beneath a wave of eager, hungry bodies. With the dead hovering over her, those still spilling into the room kept moving. They were more interested in Joe as he stood frozen with shock as the blood feast continued.

Joe broke from his stupor and aimed at the lead zombie as it shuffled across the room toward him. He fired. The bullet landed home. The zombie's head kicked back in a spray of dust and fragile bones. The jolt must have been too much for its old feeble skeleton. The dead thing's head fell to the floor. As the head collided with the hard surface, the skull split open. Black sludge poured out. The foul acidic stench was too much. Joe vomited. He looked back up to see the headless body slumped lifeless to the floor. The head still continued to move. Its teeth gnashed at the air. Then… Then it happened and that was when Joe had enough. The headless thing started to move.

Joe freaked. Stealing one last look into the room, before he turned to run, more than twenty of the dead filed into the workspace. More followed. It seemed never ending.

He was done hesitating. He turned and ran.

Before he even advanced two steps he collided with someone. Expecting maybe Noel, or Chelsea, he was surprised to look up into the pilot's face.

"Where the hell is everybody at?" The pilot said. "We've got to get goin' and now!"

"I know. I know." Joe took a breath and looked over his shoulder.

"The parkin' lot. It's…" The pilot started to say, but his words were cut short when the first of a massive horde rounded the corner.

Excited to sense their prey, the dead raised their arms in pursuit. A guttural moan of hunger followed.

"I know!" Joe shouted again, pushing the pilot the other direction. "They broke through the barricade!"

"Oh, shit!" The pilot said, turning to follow Joe back the way he'd come. "Where the hell is everybody?"

"Noel's not with you?" Joe said in panic, still running.

"The scary looking girl? No, I didn't see her when I came down. I dozed off in the helicopter waitin' on y'all. And then I hears some stuff. And shit man… They're everywhere. The parking lot is loaded with the fuckers. And I got a say, they looked pretty pissed!"

"Where else could she have gone? There's only one way to the roof!" Joe said. "We've got to find her and get Chelsea and Mr. Watts."

"You can't be serious? This right here is why we should a left already!"

"Now's not the time to argue about it. Let's just to find the others!" Joe shouted as he rounded the corner and crashed open a set of doors that led farther into the precinct.

The dead weren't far behind. Although, they had quickly left them in the dust so to speak, Joe could still hear them. Hear them getting closer. The sounds of their rasping moans filled the station. He could also hear the persistent beating at the back of the precinct. He hoped like hell that the rear door wouldn't end up giving way like the ones at the front. Although his worries of escape were low with the helicopter on the roof and the pilot at his side, his heart raced with the need to find the girls and the decision of what to do with Watts.

"Let's check on Chelsea. Maybe Noel went there?" Joe said.

Joe stopped for a moment and mulled over the situation. He couldn't risk what happened to June, happening to the pilot. He looked back the way they had come, listening to their pursuers shuffling through the station. He could hear their countless steps like one large muffled rumbling low to the ground. His brain fired to life with the *'what if'* of the pilot's demise. He imagined the pilot's face ripped into by a dozen gray clammy hands. His thoughts flashed red. Where would they go if that happened? How would they escape? That would be the worse event of the night for sure. More devastating than losing his partner or watching Tom's eye gwtting squished by undead fingers.

"What?" The pilot asked.

"Do this for me, will you?"

"What?"

"I can't risk losing you. You're our ticket out of here." Joe said. "Go to the roof and wait for us."

"No argument there!"

"Listen…" Joe grabbed him by the sleeve of his shirt. His stare stern, his grip firm. "Get the chopper running and ready to take flight the second we hit the roof. I don't want any reason for those things to run us down once we get up there."

"Already a head of you, pal." The pilot said, trying to pull away.

"And I swear to God above." If Joe's eyes were made of fire, they would have burned straight through the pilot. "If you leave us down here... I promise you. Don't even try me, because I'm serious. If you leave us for anything, I'm going to come after you. Chances are we wouldn't make it out of here. But mark my word. Dead, alive or undead... so help me, God, I will hunt you down and kill you."

The pilot swallowed, clearly getting the point.

"Now get up there and get things ready." He shoved the pilot away. "Now go! I'm goanna get the girls and Watts and we're out of here."

The pilot didn't turn back. He took off, eager to get to the roof. He rounded the corner, and then seconds later disappear.

Joe heard the door leading to the roof swing open and then slam shut. Satisfied with the decision to send the pilot topside, he stepped back into action. Time was running short. If he took too long to find Noel and get Chelsea and Watts, the dead that were lingering in from the entrance would end up blocking their path to the roof. He couldn't afford for that to happen. He needed to act fast.

Backtracking a few paces to the cells, Joe kicked the door open.

"What the hell happened?" He whispered.

Chelsea was on the floor with the revolver still in hand. Watts lay closer to Joe on the floor, facing her. He had a large puddle of blood still growing around him on the floor. The dead in their cells were more eager than ever to be let out. Did they realize somehow what was happening outside? Did they realize the station was slowly being overrun?

Something staggered and then fell to the ground behind Joe. Frantic, he turned and saw nothing. Then, *they* appeared. Not the rotting undead, but two runners. Unlike the rotting putrid creatures making their way in, these ghouls were fresh with newly acquired wounds. Each one held its individual scars of afterlife. Torn throats and punctured stomachs told Joe more than he wanted to know about how they had died. At first, he feared that the dead at the back of the station had gotten in. That couldn't be possible. He could still hear them pounding to get in, though. The two mangled figures were probably a part of the horde coming in from the front. And since they were faster and more coordinated, they managed to work their way through the crowd to the front of the pack. That had to be it.

The lead zombie spotted Joe. It snarled and hissed, pressing toward him. It collided with a desk, but didn't slow. Papers and a stack of pens and pencils flew across the air momentarily, only to fall to the floor unnoticed. Joe stole a glance back into the cell hall to see Chelsea still lying on the floor by Watts' bleeding body.

He turned back to the two aggressors, aimed and fired. The gun jumped in his hand with each rapid squeeze. The bullets tore through the dead with ease. Small pin size holes ripped through the lead ghoul's chest and shoulders. The closer it got, the tighter he gripped the pistol in his hands. His palms burned and his skin went cold as he watched blood spurt from the zombies as they ran at him.

"Focus…" He told himself. He had to concentrate. The shots needed to count. He needed to aim higher.

Adjusting his aim, Joe tried again. He bit down on his lip. Something warm filled his mouth. The lead ghoul was almost on him, the other just behind. The gun kicked. The 9mm's loud report rang in his ears. The lead ghoul's head jarred in a violent backwards motion. The dime-sized hole in his head right above the left eye confirmed the shot. Still in full sprint as it took the shot, the body stumbled forward landing inches from Joe's feet. As it felt to the floor motionless, the second creature came into view. Its mouth was wide and blood and spittle dripped down its chin as it snarled. Joe fired. The shot hit the zombie in the cheek. Blood splashed out, flying across one of the many desks, but the monster still raced forward. He fired again, two sporadic shots. The thing slumped to the ground as the bullets punctured the brain. It might not be dead, but at least it would buy him some time.

He waited for more runners to suddenly dart around the corner. Nothing happened. Nothing jumped out. The only thing he noticed was the rapid pace of his beating heart. Joe ducked back into the cell hallway to figure out what the hell had happened with Chelsea and Watts.

"Chelsea…" He whispered, slowly working his way toward her. "Chelsea. Are you okay?"

She didn't respond. Joe stopped and leaned down by Watts' body. Ignoring the fact that he stepped in the puddle of blood, Joe checked for a pulse. Nothing. The back of Watts' throat was blown out. Bits of cartilage and spinal cord protruded from the back of his neck out of the small bullet hole.

Shot must have been close range to do that type damage, Joe thought, stepping away from the corpse.

"Chelsea. Wake up." He said, shaking her.

She wasn't moving. He quickly examined here for cuts, shots, or bites. He didn't see anything. He shook her again and then looked down the hall, half expecting it to flood with the undead. It didn't and he was thankful. That didn't mean he couldn't hear them. They were getting closer. Their grunts and agitated parade grew louder with each moment he lingered.

"Fuck," he said, and then looked at Chelsea. "Wake up!"

He didn't have time for any more delay. He picked her up and heaved her over his shoulder. Thankfully, she was much smaller than June. Making a mental note to find out what had happened with Watts, Joe raced down the hall. Her weight pressing him down made it hard to breath. Forcing a deep breath, he repositioned her body so that he could still handle his firearm if necessary. Stepping over the two lifeless zombies that he had just immobilized, Joe made his way across the precinct to the roof. He would have to drop her off at the helicopter and come back for Noel. He didn't like the idea. Time was running short. But he had no other options.

Climbing the steps to the roof was no easy task. The stairwell was uncomfortably dark and narrow. Joe knew where the light switch was, but didn't take the time to turn it on. He just climbed instead. Once he was on the roof he hurriedly took Chelsea inside the helicopter. The rooftop was windy, the propeller blades in full swing. Setting her down inside, he tried telling the pilot that he was going back for Noel, but couldn't even hear his own voice over the choppers blades. He shrugged, giving the pilot a concerned look, and then turned making his way back downstairs.

Running as fast as he could down the steps and back into the building, Joe did the only thing he knew to do. He started shouting. It wasn't like he needed to be quiet. The dead already knew he was inside and were working their way toward him now.

"Noel!" He shouted, kicking the door open at the bottom of the steps. "Noel… Where are you? We need to go!"

Not sure why, but he darted back into the cell hallway. She wasn't there.

"Shit. Where the hell are you? Noel… Noel!"

Trusting logic, she definitely wasn't toward the front of the building. At least, he hoped like hell she wasn't. Otherwise, she was minced meat for the hungry mob. And if he didn't hurry, he'd be in that boat too. He ran to the back of the building. The back door was still closed and the cabinets still were in place. Thankful that the barricade had held, he scanned the room.

"Noel!"

Something shifted in his periphery. It was Noel. She jumped up and into his arms.

"Oh, dear God. I thought you'd left me!" Noel said, holding tight to the Hispanic policeman. "I got lost. I tried finding the roof, but I got turned around. I didn't know where to go, Joe. I'm so scared."

"Me too, Noel. But we don't have time for this. We need to go!"

He grabbed her by the wrist, yanking her away from the door and back the way he'd come. Just as he started to round the corner leading to the door that would send them to the roof, the first of an endless horde crashed in. Joe's heart stopped. As they poured into the room, the lead zombies collided with the desks, as the zombies behind pushed them forward. Their bones broke and shattered under the pressure. Dust bellowed out in a thick cloud of rotting decay. Joe covered his nose and looked around for something, anything to use as a weapon. His pistol wasn't going to be enough. There were too many of them. He could easily take down the lead creatures, but they would just as quickly be replaced by those behind. Rustling protest filled the room as the zombies shuffled in with outstretched arms.

Going against his better judgment, Joe fired into the crowd as they started blocking the path leading to the stairs. The sound of crackling bones filled his ears as each shot enveloped the room. The gun *clicked* empty.

"Shit." He said, throwing the gun at them.

The bullets had done nothing to slow them down or lower their numbers. Neither did throwing the pistol. The heavy gun smashed into the face of one of the zombies. A loud *thump* and the crunching of bone echoed out as the thing's face caved in. If fell to the ground, worms spilling out all over the floor. But that didn't matter, because before it came to full rest on the floor, another ghoul had already taken its place.

"We're going to die here!" Noel gasped, watching the dead fill the room.

"Don't say that." Joe pushed her back and scanned the room for something, anything. "We're going to make it. Have faith."

"Like Tom?"

"Yes… like Tom."

Noel trembled in his arms. Between the chaos and the sound of stuff being knocked about, Noel started praying. Her words were faint. Joe tried to ignore her. He frantically scanned the room for anything that would help their situation. The path they needed to take to the stairs was blocked. There were only three or four zombies on that side of the room, but not for long. Joe looked around, scanning for something to use as a weapon, while pushing Noel back. With each slow step backward, he caught a few of her mumbled words.

"Please… God. Tom… anyone up there. If you really are there. If you really are listening. Please help us." Noel's eyes were shut tight.

Joe felt something come over him as he heard those words. Then he spotted a tall aluminum lamp to his left. Letting go of Noel, he reached over, taking it in both hands. He held it like a spear and yanked the cord from the wall. The light in the room diminished as the bulb blanked out, no longer surging with electricity.

Joe charged forward.

"What are you doing?" Noel shouted, reaching out for Joe to pull him back.

"What I have to," he shouted, holding the long lamp horizontally. With it out in front, he screamed. "Ahhhh…" and collided with the rancid mob.

Expecting their resistance to be much greater, Joe almost lost his footing as the zombies buckled under his weight. The lamp was just wide enough to pin a line of more than six of the undead ghouls. Their brittle bones folded under the pressure as he shoved them back. His lungs filled with the dust and decomposed particles. He pushed back the thought of bone clouds entering his lungs and pushed forward more

"Move!" Joe shouted, trying to get Noel to run down the hall, as he pushed the mob back. "Move, I said!"

That's all it took. Noel bolted forward. The space that Joe had provided with the makeshift weapon wasn't much. As she ran past, she felt undead hands pull at her hair. She screamed, not looking back.

"Keep going," Joe groaned, still trying to hold the dead at bay.

As she stepped past the dead opening the door to the stairwell, one lone zombie's hand pulled free a lock of her jet black hair. She grimaced, feeling her neck pull forward, as the hair came loose.

Luckily for Joe, the undead, as rotting as they were, were uncoordinated. Despite their many attempts to lash out at him with their teeth, he prevailed at keeping them at a safe distance. If he was going to make it to the door, he needed make more space. He pushed forward even harder. Sending the horde against one of the desks behind them, bones broke and separation occurred. Snapping at the waist, hips broke and spines split as they collided with the desk. As more of the undead spilled into the room, they started reaching around his makeshift handheld barricade. He was becoming overrun.

Noel screamed down for him from the stairs. He tried to look back, but couldn't. A zombie fell on him from the left. He tried to shoo it away, he couldn't let his guard down from the horde he was holding back. It clawed at him. Its boney skinless fingers tore through his police uniform. He winced against the pain as it tore into skin.

"Go to the roof, Noel!" Joe shouted, trying to keep the dead from falling on him.

If he were to turn for the door, the dead would be on him before he'd get to the stairs.

"Go, I said." He shouted, trying to look over his shoulder.

The stolen moment came at a cost. The ghoul at his left dug into his shoulder trying to sink its teeth into him. Joe jumped back, trying to kick it while keeping the others at a safe distance. It took shouting at her again, but Joe finally heard the sound of Noel's steel-toed boots tromping up the stairs. He didn't hear the door close behind her as her footsteps faded. Joe cringed.

Why didn't she close the damn door?

He had no choice. If he was going to make for the stairs, the longer he waited, the less chance he would have of making it out alive. He couldn't hold them back much longer. He closed his eyes and took a deep breath.

Giving the lamp one last heavy push forward, he let go and turned toward the door to the stairs. As he saw them come into view, the fleeting hope that he'd actually make it passed through his mind. First days on the job were a bitch. Hands grabbed at him from behind. He clenched his fists, biting down hard on his lip. Blood pooled in his mouth as he reached the first step.

Then… then the sharp burning heat coursed through his legs. Warm and wet, his calf burned with the sensation of what at first seemed like an overworked muscle. Surprised, Joe watched himself fall forward, the steps slamming toward him. It wasn't until the teeth that were sunken into his leg let go that he realized what was happening. Countless arms and gnashing teeth fell on him within moments. Had he been screaming when they started to feast, he couldn't tell. A surge of bodies and the sounds of their satisfied groans filled his ears like the hum of an active hornets nest. What he found more shocking than the darkness engulfing him by the aggressively piling bodies was that he felt no pain. Only warmth and the burn. It was all over his body like sunburned skin. He looked up momentarily, able to see past the darkness. His intestines and visceral insides stretched out before his eyes in undead hands. Joe felt fear. Not of death, but of himself. He heard laughter and fear gripped him when he realized it was his own.

EIGHTEEN

Noel and the pilot waited for Joe as long as they could. But even that wasn't very long. Not even half a minute after Noel jumped into the helicopter, Joe's painful cries reached the roof through the beat of the chopper's propellers. His scream faded. A horde of hungry undead shambled out onto the roof. Freshly covered in blood, some carried visceral gore and intestinal muck. Instead of the brave policeman, the pilot could wait no longer.

Before the first zombie had time to touch the helicopter's landing skids, it lifted into the air. Amidst the chaos, Chelsea woke from her blackout. The three watched in horror as the roof filled with animated corpses. As they lifted higher into the air, the scene in the parking lot became more apparent. Droves of the dead were still working their way toward the station from the street. At least, four dozen were clustered at the front doors, still slowly pushing into the building. A group of ten ghouls, not nearly as rotting or grotesque, were still at the back doors banging endlessly to be let in.

With the rising sun at their backs, the helicopter drifted through the air away from the small town. They had enough fuel to get far away from Clarksburg. And that is what the pilot intended to do.

All of that had happened more than three months ago.

Not long after that horrifying night, Chelsea showed up on the scene, determined to blow the lid off everything that had happened. It didn't work. No one listened, and like most things in life, money fixed everything. Chelsea was incarcerated and admitted to the Bloomington Mental Health Association against her will. She was never heard from again.

Speaking of not being heard from ever again, the pilot disappeared shortly after. Last Noel heard, he gathered up his family and disappeared to some secluded island or something. She couldn't blame him. As for her, she was happier than she had ever been, despite the constant night terrors. She hardly ever slept these days. But who needed to sleep when you were as busy as she found herself. Sadly, it had taken the death of her friends and family to find her true calling, but she was thankful that in the end she had found God. The monastery needed her now, and that was where she intended to stay. On the nights when she could sleep, she dreamt of Joe and how she longed to one day be just like him. She felt like Tom would have approved.

Across America, the Virginia Power Plant explosion was devastating news. An entire town left in devastation. The presidential speech regarding America's great loss ended on a positive note. At least, the population of Clarksburg was much smaller than a city like Atlanta or New York. Cleanup crews had been sent in to deal with the 'so called' hazards and damages left by the tragic plant explosion.

That's when Beth Lena Mae found herself clapping happily at the news. She and her husband of over forty years lived in Weston, which wasn't that far south of Clarksburg. News of the plant explosion was a big scare for her. She was always keeping up with the catastrophes of the world. Her husband, Mark, had told her time and time again not to watch *CNN*. That crap only stressed her out, which in turned, stressed him out. They were getting too old to worry about that type of thing.

But this… this was different. This was close to home. Too close. With nearly three months of constant updates about the cleanup and potential radiation, Beth was so grateful to not have any power plants like that around Weston. With the news switching from the Clarksburg explosion to some high school shooting in Florida, Beth changed the channel.

A month after that tragic night, Golden Arch Co. had come out with chicken nuggets that were guaranteed to be a healthy weight loss substitute to their already famous greasy nuggets. Beth laughed at the idea as she watched the commercial advertising the new food. Those nuggets probably tasted like cardboard. The new food options quickly caught on and all of the other fast food chains shortly followed suit.

Nothing happened. No one got sick. No one died. More importantly, no one turned into crazed, zombified cannibals. In fact, the opposite happened. The new food did exactly what was said it would. People were happier and they were losing weight. The fast food industry regained its financial momentum and plunged into a new future of heavily processed food. But that was nothing new. Chemically altered food was a thing of the past and all G.A.C. managed to do was prove that it would also be a thing of the future.

Just as the commercial ended giving way to one of Beth's favorite talk shows, Mark sauntered in the living room door. With rod in hand and boots dripping wet, Beth grimaced.

"That's new carpet, Mark. Take it outside!"

"This ain't new carpet, Beth. This carpet came out of Margret's old house."

"Well, it's new to me and you're soaking wet. Take it outside," she said, looking away from the television toward the door.

"Oh, all right, honey." He said, smiling ear to ear.

"What are you so happy about this time, Mark? Where have you been all day anyway?"

"Turn off the TV, honey and get the kitchen ready for dinner. We're eatin' good tonight."

"Oh, is that right?" Beth rolled her eyes. "That new fishing spot that you and Buck been raving about all week?"

"Yes!" He said with excitement.

For only a moment, he stepped outside the door and returned with more than two dozen fish hooked to his catcher's net.

"Wow, Mark. Looks like you had a hell of a time."

"You can say that again," he agreed, still lingering in the doorway.

"Well…," she insisted. "What are you doing still standing there? You're soaking fish water into my new carpet!"

His smile turned to a frown, as he stepped off the carpet, and he went back outside. Before the door closed, Beth heard him say that he was going to Buck's house to help him clean up his share of the catch.

"There's more?" she asked.

"Sure is." Mark peeked his head back into the door. "Buck caught twice as many as this. And we weren't even out there more than an hour!"

"That's amazing, dear." Beth boasted. "So… where is this new fishing spot anyway?"

"I'm not tellin'. It's a secret."

"Oh, come on, Mark. Like I'm going to tell anyone."

"The *Elk River*!" He said, closing the door as he went on his way to Buck's with the days catch.

THE END

OTHER PUBLISHED WORKS BY
P. A. DOUGLAS

WATCHERS
EPIDEMIC OF THE UNDEAD
THE END: A ZOMBIE NOVEL
HORROR STORIES AND TERRIFYING TALES

NECROPHOBIA
Jack Hamlyn

An ordinary summer's day.
The grass is green, the flowers are blooming. All is right
with the world. Then the dead start rising. From
cemetery and mortuary, funeral home and morgue,
they flood into the streets until every town and city is
infested with walking corpses, blank-eyed eating
machines that exist to take down the living.

The world is a graveyard.

And when you have a family to protect, it's more than
survival.

It's war!

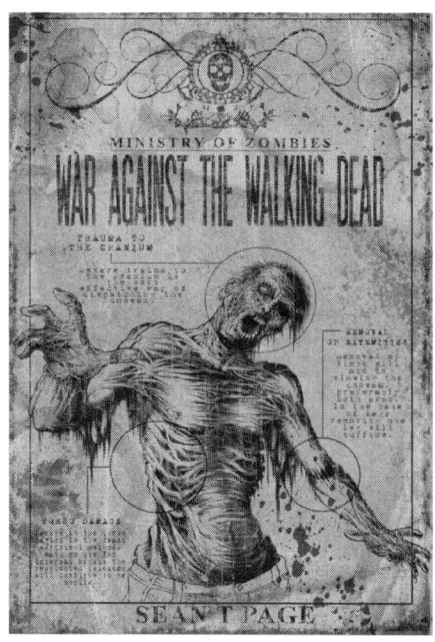

More than 63% of people now believe that there will be a global zombie apocalypse before 2050...

Employing real science and pioneering field work, War against the Walking Dead provides a complete blueprint for taking back your country from the rotting clutches of the dead after a zombie apocalypse.

* A glimpse inside the mind of the zombie using a team of top psychics - what do the walking dead think about? What lessons can we learn to help us defeat this pervading menace?
* Detailed guidelines on how to galvanise a band of scared survivors into a fighting force capable of defeating the zombies and dealing with emerging groups such as end of the world cults, raiders and even cannibals!
* Features insights from real zombie fighting organisations across the world, from America to the Philippines, Australia to China - the experts offer advice in every aspect of fighting the walking dead.

Packed with crucial zombie war information and advice, from how to build a city of the living in a land of the dead to tactics on how to use a survivor army to liberate your country from the zombies - War against the Walking Dead may be humanity's last chance.

Remember, dying is not an option!

WHITE FLAG OF THE DEAD
Joseph Talluto

Book 1
Surrender of the Living.

Millions died when the Enillo Virus swept the earth. Millions more were lost when the victims of the plague refused to stay dead, instead rising to slay and feed on those left alive. For survivors like John Talon and his son Jake, they are faced with a choice: Do they submit to the dead, raising the white flag of surrender? Or do they find the will to fight, to try and hang on to the last shreds or humanity?

Surrender of the Living is the first high octane installment in the White Flag of the Dead series.

RESURRECTION
By Tim Curran

The rain is falling and the dead are rising. It began at an ultra-secret government laboratory. Experiments in limb regeneration-an unspeakable union of Medieval alchemy and cutting edge genetics result in the very germ of horror itself: a gene trigger that will reanimate dead tissue...any dead tissue. Now it's loose. It's gone viral. It's in the rain. And the rain has not stopped falling for weeks. As the country floods and corpses float in the streets, as cities are submerged, the evil dead are rising. And they are hungry.

"I REALLY love this book...Curran is a wonderful storyteller who really should be unleashed upon the general horror reading public sooner rather than later." – *DREAD CENTRAL*

Dead Bait

**"If you don't already suffer from bathophobia and/or
ichthyophobia, you probably will after reading this amazingly
wonderful horrific collection of short stories about what lurks
beneath the waters of the world"** – *DREAD CENTRAL*

A husband hell-bent on revenge hunts a Wereshark...A Russian
mail order bride with a fishy secret...Crabs with a collective
consciousness...A vampire who transforms into a
Candiru...Zombie piranha...Bait that will have you crawling out
of your skin and more. Drawing on horror, humor with a helping
of dark fantasy and a touch of deviance, these 19 contemporary
stories pay homage to the monsters that lurk in the murky waters
of our imaginations. *If you thought it was safe to go back in the
water...Think Again!*

**"Severed Press has the cojones to publish THE most
outrageous, nasty and downright wonderfully disgusting
horror that I've seen in quite a while."** – *DREAD CENTRAL*

ZOMBIE ZOOLOGY
Unnatural History:

Severed Press has assembled a truly original anthology of never
before published stories of living dead beasts. Inside you will
find tales of prehistoric creatures rising from the Bog, a
survivalist taking on a troop of rotting baboons, a NASA
experiment going Ape, A hunter going a Moose too far and many
more undead creatures from Hell. The crawling, buzzing, flying
abominations of mother nature have risen and they are hungry.

"Clever and engaging a reanimated rarity"
FANGORIA

**"I loved this very unique anthology and highly recommend
it"**
Monster Librarian

BIOHAZARD
Tim Curran

The day after tomorrow: Nuclear fallout. Mutations. Deadly
pandemics. Corpse wagons. Body pits. Empty cities. The human
race trembling on the edge of extinction. Only the desperate
survive. One of them is Rick Nash. But there is a price for
survival: communion with a ravenous evil born from the furnace
of radioactive waste. It demands sacrifice. Only it can keep Nash
one step ahead of the nightmare that stalks him-a sentient,
seething plague-entity that stalks its chosen prey: the last of the
human race. To accept it is a living death. To defy it, a hell
beyond imagining

**"kick back and enjoy some the most violent and genuinely
scary apocalyptic horror written by one of the finest dark
fiction authors plying his trade today" HORRORWORLD**

2221999R00132

Printed in Great Britain
by Amazon.co.uk, Ltd.,
Marston Gate.